Spirals of Time

A Paul Marzeky Mystery

Stefan J. Malecek, Ph. D

DEDICATION

This book is especially dedicated to all of the wonderful women who have graced me with their love.

And with love and gratitude to all those amazing souls who have assisted me along the sometimes arduous path I have walked. You know who you are.

ACKNOWLEDGEMENTS

I want to acknowledge all of the amazing individuals who have passed through my life and the few who have managed to stick with me through what has not been an easy lifetime driven by my personal travails and the ever-present lodestar of my art, my ability to write saving my life over and over.

I want to give fervent thanks and acknowledge the great value that my dear friend and editorial assistant Andrea Scholz has brought to my work. She has assisted me in many ways to help make my work more visible and available beyond the limited realm of my laptop. Bless you.

"We write to taste life twice, in the moment, and in retrospection. We write, like Proust, to render all of it eternal, and to persuade ourselves that it is eternal. We write to be able to transcend our life, to reach beyond it. We write to teach ourselves to speak with others, to record the journey into the labyrinth. We write to expand our world when we feel strangled, or constricted, or lonely. We write as the birds sing, as the primitives dance their rituals. If you do not breathe through writing, if you do not cry out in writing, or sing in writing, then don't write, because our culture has no use for it. When I don't write, I feel my world shrinking. I feel I am in a prison. I feel I lose my fire and my color. It should be a necessity, as the sea needs to heave, and I call it breathing."

— Anaïs Nin

EPILOGUE

January 1968

Camp Evans, Republic of Vietnam

"INCOMING!"

The shit comes in like a freight train slamming full speed into the earth, even your intestines shake—and the Fucking New Guy shits his pants. "INCOMING!" You can always hear a round coming long before it hits, telegraphing menace as you just didi for the nearest bunker. "INCOMING!" Even in deepest sleep, you're awake and running even before you have your eyes open—only making the cherry mistake of taking off your clothes once, lessons learned. "INCOMING!" The call shatters the night or busts up a card game. If you get moving, you likely won't die—though I once saw a bunker that took a direct hit from a 122 mike-mike rocket that killed everyone inside. "INCOMING!" The whole world turns into a giant cocktail shaker. California dudes always say it's the same same as a major quake, but they're lying. It's far more terrifying, far more devastating. "INCOMING!" Sometimes Charlie would just drop in a single harassment round at 0-dark-thirty. Other times the shit would rain down night and day, like living a nightmare with your eyes open. Luke the Gook was usually long gone by the time we reacted. "INCOMING!" You ignore the noise and the shock, the smells and shit, all part of the daily reality to be endured—better ignored than too deeply explored on your journey through hell. "INCOMING!"

CHAPTER ONE
The War Continues
St. Louis, May 1969

The desire to be free of his father's influence reached a peak the morning Paul finally decided to kill him.

He'd arrived at his parents' home, site of countless hours of his childhood torture. He was exhausted, dragging his suitcase up the short flight of concrete stairs. Although he had smoked a joint to take the edge off his anxiety, he could not help but feel uneasy. The doors were all tightly closed, blinds drawn, and air conditioning blasting away full bore.

He approached the front door, trepidation warring with too many old memories, and almost decided just to walk away, take a cab to the airport, and head back to San Francisco. He'd only come here after extensive conversations with The Toad, his friend and mentor at the 14th General Dispensary in Qui Nhon, where they had co-authored a massive pile of communiques that they called a "manuscript," that filled a large manila folder they had talked about turning into the definitive book on Viet Nam and The Universe beyond.

Toad had argued that he needed to "go back there and take care of some unfinished business," most especially getting grounded with women. Toad knew he was far too raggedy to handle Northern California in his current condition—fresh from I Corp and five months with the 101st Airborne doing what he called "combat psychiatry" flying around to fire bases, and fire support bases, even occasional calls to battalion aid, and once having to let somebody out of a metal Conex container to interview him.

If that had been the whole of it, he might have made a relatively easy transition of it. But he had decided not to return to duty after a rowdy R&R in Taiwan, that ultimately resulted in his getting strung out on smoking opium while awaiting a Court Martial from which he skated only because of some top-flight testimony from his supervisor at the time, Dr. Magnus Browne, a world-renowned expert on combat stress who bamboozled the judges with his impeccable credentials and unassailable testimony.

He had returned with pinpointed, bloodshot eyes, sallow skin with just a hint of jaundice, and weighing fifty pounds less than when he had last been seen. He was also sporting the scraggly beginnings of a moustache and beard, and wearing battered blue jeans, well-worn combat boots and a fatigue jacket. He also was guarding his eyes behind the darkest sunglasses he could find.

He rang the doorbell and his father parted the blinds with a finger, and harshly inquired, "Yes? May I help you?"

Tears formed at the edges of my eyes as I answered, "Pop! It's me!"

Before he could make a further move, his mother had grabbed his father around the waist and pulled him away, then practically tore the locks off the door and threw it wide open. Before he could move another inch, she grabbed him in a crushing hug that almost emptied the oxygen from his lungs.

By this point, she was sobbing uncontrollably, and just wouldn't let go of him. His father stood by like a bewildered spectator, not even pretending to want to say hello, much less participate in Paul's joyous homecoming.

Paul was as tall as his father, an even six feet. He'd arrived back in the world weighing only one hundred fifty pounds, completely jaundiced as a result of kicking a serious opium addiction.

Paul felt totally strange and alienated. Flashbacks of the horrible days of his childhood kept trying to creep in around the edges of his stoned awareness, as his mother intermittently flitted in and out of view, sobbing or chirruping, bringing him a soda, a sandwich, an ashtray, and asking if he wanted anything else. His father uncomfortably shook his hand and resumed watching the baseball game on the television.

Within minutes, he felt like he had already had enough. As an alternative to just immediately skying up back to the Bay Area, he went to the kitchen telephone and made some phone calls. The first was busy and on the second he connected with an old friend from high school.

"Bolar! Hey man, just got home from the 'Nam and out of his Army!"

His old friend immediately invited him to come spend a few days. He told him he would be leaving immediately (about an hour's drive) to come get him. His mother had been hovering and immediately started crying when she heard what his plans were.

"But, you just got here! You can't leave already! Your sisters will want to see you!"

His sisters were both married and had children. Paul knew it might be days until they might get free. Besides that, he was aching to be in the wind, and certainly did not want to sit around and answer shallow, insipid, uncomfortable questions about the last year of his life. Within the hour, Bolar appeared, made nice with his parents (after all, the parental pairs had known each other his whole life)

Paul loaded a change of clothes and a large bag of flowertops into a small canvas carrier. They stopped at a 9-0-5 Liquor Store and picked up several bottles of Johnny Walker Black, and three packs of cigarettes—and they proceeded across the Eads Bridge in Edwardsville, Illinois. There was a party already in motion. Apparently it was Bolar's girlfriend's birthday as well as a pre-graduation celebration for several people they knew at the Southern Illinois University campus there, so his call had been propitious and eminently timely.

Paul felt completely overwhelmed to be in the presence of so many stoned and crazy people—especially when he didn't have a weapon! Plus, there were all these wild and crazy women whirling, swirling, dancing, jumping, even doing cartwheels in skirts! Jesus! What had he been missing hanging out in the fucking jungle with a bunch of guts with little yellow men trying to kill him?

He kept his hat on, covering his crew cut, and pulled low over his brow, chose a spot in a fare corner of one of the rear rooms, and rolled a couple of 'Nam style party bombers. In very short order, he found himself surrounded by a small part of his own as the word got out about the superior weed being smoked in his little corner. He moved very little during the next twenty-four-hour period except to piss. He was drinking his own Scotch, an occasional ice-cold beer, three or four kinds of weed (none as good as his own), and Drambuie. He'd been offered LSD, but it was too crowded with too people he didn't know. He slept for brief snatches, there in his little corner, and then sat up when a beautiful co-ed offered him a cup of thick, strong, freshly brewed coffee. And asked if he'd like "something a little stronger for a wake up?"

"Wow! My fantasies run wild! What did you have in mind?" he replied, Raising his eyebrows Groucho Marx style.

"Not that! Want some of these?" she said and opened her palm to a handful of green and white Dexedrine.

He started to reach for them, and she interposed. "Trade you for a joint of that weed of yours."

Paul laughed and dutifully rolled a regular-sized joint, and they traded, both with big smiles.

Paul considered for just a moment, then took two of the capsules with a swig of Scotch, and waited. It was not too long before he felt the stirrings of a bristling, sparkling energy in his ankles and belly; and almost immediately on the heels of it, found himself up and dancing madly without any reference to partners, simply frenetically enjoying the energy and just kickin' out the jams (as per the MC5).

Time from that point forward simply spun out of control like a mentally ill centrifuge—until it finally disappeared somewhere in the wee hours of the second morning. He began being fueled by all kinds of weed and hash, Benzedrine, and a little bit of crystal meth—of course, on top of more Scotch, vodka, and an offer to smoke some opium.

So, when Bolar approached him as to whether he wanted to stay or find his own way back, he elected, somewhat reluctantly, to take a ride with him, as his childhood friend had to report for the early shift at Monsanto. By the time he stumbled in the front door of his childhood home at five o'clock in the morning, rank with grunge and not having slept for over fifty hours, he was ripe for the confrontation with his father that had been brewing all of his life.

It all began innocently enough.

His father was no longer the mighty and fearsome figure who could almost make him shit in his pants simply by scowling at him. He was now just a frail old man recovering from a stroke, but it didn't prevent him from grandiosely believing he could still terrorize Paul.

"Where have you been?" the older man harshly demanded, as if he had been locked in a time warp, awaiting Paul's return—and still believed he could demand Paul's immediate subservience.

Paul fought down the raging sixty-foot wave of revulsion that rose in his belly, and struggled as best he could in his unhinged and disinhibited state, to not free his violent clenching muscles that were responding to thousands of years of conditioning to pummel the shit out of the old man.

"I told you. I went to a party in Edwardsville."

"That was two nights ago!" Again, the intrusive, corrosive edge ate at him like sulfuric acid on raw skin.

"So?"

"Your mother and I were worried about you!"

Paul's scalp prickled, a fiery itch spreading down his face to his neck, and threatening to burst all his blood vessels.

"Why?"

"We worry you might get hurt!"

"I just survived fourteen months in fucking Viet Nam! I can certainly manage two nights in South St. Louis!"

"That's not the point!"

"Then what the fuck exactly is the point?"

"Don't use language like that with me, young man!"

His father's voice lashed his tender nerve endings as if they had been flayed open, rage exploding in barrage bursts in his solar plexus.

The rage exploded in his belly, sending white-hot streaking tendrils that burst in his solar plexus, as Paul took another step toward him, and amped his voice to a roar.

"I'LL FUCKING TALK TO YOU ANY FUCKING WAY I FUCKING WANT TO, OLD MAN!"

"I'll be damned if you'll take that tone with me!"

His words ignited a Zippo raid in Paul's head, setting fire to what small restraint Paul had left.

"THAT'S IT!" he shouted into the older man's face, and swiftly closed the space between them.

A picture of throwing his father down the concrete steps and stomping on him until he stopped moving came full blown into his head like Athena from the skull of Zeus.

"I'VE HAD A LIFETIME OF YOUR FUCKING SHIT, OLD MAN! I'M NOT GOINGTO TAKE ANY MORE!"

Paul, fulminating like a rabid dog, eyes bulging, vision burning like a red veil, saliva splashing down the front of his shirt as an orgasmic thunder pounded through him like a breached hydroelectric dam, and all the built-up shame and hatred of decades released in a gush of pure violent emotion.

There was no thought, no planning. It felt as if he had become part of the fractured cinema in his head, unreeling like a fugue, only one in which he was so totally immersed in his role that there was no separation.

He slapped his father hard across the face. Before the stunned old man could react, he grabbed his father by the collar and started dragging him across the hard wood floor, the old man's legs kicking and bumping spasmodically, as he cursed Paul repeatedly, attempting to lay hands on him. Such was the power and force of Paul's intention that the lava flow of invective only emboldened his higher purpose. He realized in that moment that the man in his hands was the lifelong source of all those who had abused and misused him—most especially and most recently Command Sergeant Major Hoxley of the 101st Airborne Division.

Paul felt as if he had been anointed by the Universe, an Avenging Angel empowered to rectify past judgments and ill-delivered punishment and harm. There was power crackling all around him as he muscles smoothly performed the task of dragging his father to the door as if preordained in the antediluvian history of time. It felt so good, so natural.

Paul felt possessed, fully in thrall to the otherworldly energies as he allowed his executive functions to fully embrace the redemption of this lifetime, his entire timeline, scraping together the crumbs and debris of his tattered self-esteem, to be redeemed it in a few moments of purest violence. His father had quit struggling. He seemed in shock and had gone from struggling and sputtering to limp and catatonic. He felt illuminated on his bright and shining path, redeeming and championing that innocent child that still lived within him, who was urging him on to wreak revenge for all of the hits and slaps and insults he had been unable to thwart. He was invincible, unreachable.

As Paul paused to unlock the locked, bolted, and chained front door, he felt a whirlwind at his back, a force not unlike a small hurricane.

Then suddenly, his mother appeared wraith-like, an apparition from the ethers, wearing the slip she invariably wore for sleep, hair electric, eyes wide, red and freaked; her once voluptuous gymnast's body jiggling with excess fat as she flung herself headlong at Paul like a missile, completely smashing the hold he had on his father and throwing herself between them as a strident shriek cut through his reverie like a plasma cutter through titanium.

"PLEASE DON'T KILL YOUR FATHER!"

Her intervention had allowed him to stumble back out of Paul's immediate reach. The rage was overflowing from his every corpuscle, but the flavor and intensity of it was for his father alone. He had a whole other channel that was hers, but not in that moment, though he did momentarily consider smashing her in the face as hard as he could. The older man, still stunned, tried to get his footing while Paul's mother staunchly stood between them like the meat in their ancient emotional sandwich. It was a familiar kind of schizophrenia.

It wasn't her words or even he manner in which they were expressed so much as that they acted as a pattern interrupter that shattered the particular trance he had entered.

First a ragged bark, then wave after wave of raucous unexpurgated glee poured out of Paul as he laughed, then stumbled back, grasping his chest, unable to get his breath. It was so fucking hilarious! It was perfect!

His parents turned toward him simultaneously, hands still on each other's arms, frozen, wide-eyed, like a benumbed pieta.

Paul coughed violently, as tears ran down his cheeks. Then he wiped his eyes on the sleeve of his chambray shirt, and smiled, an eerie, twisted gesture that was almost a rictus.

The old man, the tyrannical bastard who had long used him as his personal punching bag, physically and emotionally, cringed under the scathing glare.

Then, as if the incipient violence in his belly was still craving release, he stepped forward and projectile vomited what seemed like gallons of vile bile onto the concupiscent pair.

"NEVER. AGAIN!" he spit at them.

And left to find a diner, to have coffee and breakfast before looking for a place to stay for a few days. He needed some alone time alone where he wouldn't be disturbed; where he could examine the contents of his drug-addled brain; and where he could get his feet on the ground in this brave new world to which he had returned, with none of the influences or questions, demands or problems, of others to bother him. Little did he know then that it was the beginning of a pattern that would inform the rest of his life.

Paul would tell this story many times down through the years, always accompanied by hearty laughter. But he would always remember that excruciatingly beautiful moment, filled with the emancipating fragrance of exultation and liberation.

CHAPTER TWO
The Very Next Day
St. Louis   May 1969

Paul went to visit a childhood friend, Nadine, who had been holding all of his packages of contraband shipped from Southeast Asia. They had shared a bottle of red wine and several joints before they shared the night together. She gave him the names of some hip spots in the Central West End (CWE), the hippest neighborhood in St. Louis, bordered by both St. Louis University and Washington University that provided a bastion for bright minds and non-traditional thinkers from around the globe. He gifted Nadine one of the kilos and promised to stay in touch.

Paul was a relative stranger to the CWE, but he knew he would be bored shitless if he had to spend even another minute in the South St. Louis neighborhood in which he had grown up. As he wandered Euclid Boulevard, he kept meeting hip people and finding hip establishments like the Pseudonym, Left Bank Books, and The Gypsy Cowboy. He found great eateries like Balaban's, Europa 390 and the Fatted Calf.

Magical things were happening in the city of his birth, relative miracles really, in comparison to the desolation of his early years. He found a new comfort and welcome in being able to participate in this very special slice of space and time.

Paul remembered when he had visited Gaslight Square when he was still in high school, but had been a relative outsider to the bohemian renaissance that was happening on the north side in those nascent days of the early-1960s—when marijuana was still called "tea" or "boo," and those who used kept very tight circles and a great deal of confidentiality amongst themselves. He knew something was happening, and went there when he was drinking on weekend, but his fake ID wouldn't stand scrutiny for him to get in the clubs. He was aware of future luminaries—like Barbara Streisand, Phyllis Diller, and the Smothers Brothers—who were appearing in clubs and cabarets along the multi-block area centered on Boyle and Olive. It was a perfect complimented to the Central West End, just a few miles west.

With his short hair, and lacking awareness of the "coming revolution," Paul looked like a very conspicuous outlander, even though he had experienced firsthand the belly of the beast created by the existing order, and quickly slotted himself in amongst those who were anti-war. He regularly encountered so many unique individuals—the strident "politicals" quoting "The Little Red Book" of Chairman Mao; straight up peace and love advocates, sometimes quoting Guru Nanak or Chogyam Trungpa; and the speed shooters, the heroin addicts, and the straight up psychedelic freaks. Everyone appreciated good weed, and that had been Paul's passport to the inner sanctums of hip society—he readily shared his killer weed, and developed a bit of a reputation because of it, though he adamantly refused to sell any of it.

Many of the hip folks lived so much more underground lives than he. Marijuana was still somewhat of an underground phenomenon—after all, it was the Middle West and the entrenched conservative attitudes of many generations still held sway. Paul on the other hand rarely left the house without a pocket full of rolled joints, ready to smoke at a moment's notice. He was still in 'Nam mindset, and didn't care who knew.

It was that same kind of insouciance that had led him to ship home multiple packages of double-wrapped thick surgical tubing stuffed with red and lime-green tops, tightly taped, and then surrounded in aluminum foil heavily larded with cinnamon, and encased in olive-drab socks. The G-2 had it that it was the best way to defeat the drug-sniffing dogs, though rumor also had it that loads had been stolen at the Cypress Street Mail Terminal in Oakland by hip entrepreneurial thieves. On a whim, he had thrown a 100-gram block of black tar opium into one of the packages—though he had had no intention of using any. This latter had provided enough cash to readily rent an apartment from which he could plot what he hoped would be his rather immediate, and permanent, liberation to the West Coast. It became a necessary move when it finally dawned on him that he would be there more than the two weeks he had originally intended.

So, with Nadine's guidance, it was to the CWE that he went to seek refuge, and had the good fortune of finding a small, one-bedroom apartment for rent by a landlady who was sympathetic to his pleas and a handful of ready cash. Despite his having told her he was looking for a job, he really wasn't. But the more he had seen of the burgeoning hip culture there, the more he decided he might stick around, at least until winter started to show up with its blustery finery. He wanted to participate in "cultural renaissance" that was happening then and there. On one of his walks through the neighborhood, he had seen flocks of beautiful young nursing students pouring in and out of the building at the Barnes Hospital complex called the Steinberg Pavilion. Since Five Steinberg was the psychiatric unit, he decided that his background might be an entrée to finding a job there to enhance his income and save the necessary dollars to move West. It never occurred to him that he would be there more than a couple of months.

As he stepped into Left Bank Books on the corner of McPherson, Paul went to the back racks to peruse the metaphysical materials, looking for something mystical. He literally ran into a young Black man, with a short Afro and horn-rimmed glasses. They each stepped back. and watched a series of reactions flash across each other's' faces, before they both grinned and started laughing. The other man had a copy of *Man and his Bodies* by Annie Besant in his left hand when they shook hands, and then dapped.

"Paul Marzeky."

"Bobby Short."

"You a vet?"

"Yeah. You?"

"Yeah. 101st."

"1st Cav."

"Cool! Welcome home!"

"Yeah! You too!"

"When'd you get back?"

"I been home about a year and a half. You?"

"Let me see. Three o'clock this afternoon will be 408 hours!"

They slapped palms again, both cracking up.

"No shit!? That's what, like two weeks?"

"Seventeen days, and every one of them precious!"

"Damn straight, brother!"

"Hey! I notice you've got Annie Besant there."

"Yeah? Any good?"

"One of my favorites! I love the Theosophers!"

"This is my first encounter. I was just looking for something unusual."

"Well you found it!" Paul said, and did a quick scan of the immediate environment.

"Hey! When was the last time you smoked any weed from the 'Nam?"

Bobby immediately stepped closer, and whispered.

"This ain't the 'Nam, man! There's lots of narcs around!"

Paul whispered back.

"OK. When was the last time you smoked any weed from the 'Nam?" and cracked up.

Bobby looked at him very seriously for a moment, then laughed too.

"Too long ago. You got some?"

"Does the Pope shit in the woods?"

"Well let's go!"

"Where?" he said as the exited the building.

"Well, my wife's home, so..."

"Let's go to my place!"

"Cool! Where's that?"

"You know where Lake Street dead ends right off Waterman?" It was about a ten-minute ride.

"Sure do."

"424. Second floor front." That's my car, he said, pointing to a 1964 Austin Healy Sprite that he had bought on impulse and for which he had paid cash.

"Nice wheels. I'm right there," he said pointing to a brand-new Toyota.

"Well, follow me!"

Sitting on the couch with coffee, Paul broke out a large red hand of marijuana.

Bobby did a double take.

"Jesus! Haven't seen anything like that in a long time!"

"Beautiful huh?"

"Any for sale?"

"Naw. Personal stash only. But I'll gift you some!"

"Cool!"

They wandered through a very stoned dialogue for the next hour and a half. They had both been born in St. Louis; entered the Army in 1966 (Bobby went to Vietnam in 1967, Paul in 1968); and enjoyed music, chess, reading, and psychology. Bobby told him in passing that he was working as an Adult Psychiatric Worker (APW) at Jewish Hospital, and that they had an opening on the afternoon shift. Bobby said he would put in a good word. Then they hugged and dapped as Bobby left, agreeing to stay in touch.

CHAPTER THREE

Encounters of another Kind

St. Louis   late May, 1969

Paul allowed the relative quiet of the staff room to wrap itself around him like a proverbial blanket. He was burning with energy and had not had a moment to himself the entire shift. His exposure to in-patient psychiatry was an on-going learning experience. Outside in the far distance, the former speed freak woman in the seclusion room continued to scream curses at him. He lit a cigarette, poured a cup of strong home-brewed coffee from his thermos, and took out his journal to jot down the first two stanzas of a new poem that he had managed to memorize while sorting through the frenzied activities of the shift so far.

After he hurriedly wrote them down in his journal, scratched out a change here, and added a word there, he closed the black-pebbled, plain paged book, and closed his eyes for a moment.

He had arrived ten minutes early, in order to have the time to walk through the unit and assess the emotional acuity of the patients before shift change. He'd entered the unit and re-locked the all-steel door, that contained a wire-mesh Plexiglas window, behind him. No sooner had he entered the unit than the imprisoned clientele had deluged him with questions, requests for meds, and other things less appropriate, if not outright psychotic. He had simultaneously been sorting through a montage of sense impressions that were clamoring for his attention, while his intuition worked overtime. He always trusted that it was feeding him proper information, and almost always acted upon it without restraint. One of the new female patients flashed by and looked at him seductively—until he reminded her to pull up the top of her hospital gown. Then she snarled at him, showing blackened stumps of teeth, and called him an "asshole!"

He laughed and walked further onto the unit, pulling the sleeves of his corduroy shirt down, and then tugging on the sleeves of his Levi's jean jacket. He nodded to Reverend Dave, (as he vehemently demanded to be called), an occasional methamphetamine shooter, currently getting stabilized on Lithium Carbonate after his latest run-in with the police and a brand-new diagnosis of Manic Depressive, Depressed. He'd been on the unit a little over two weeks, and had settled in nicely this time.

He was one of their "frequent flyers" Paul knew from a previous admission. He was like a weather vane for the collective mood of the unit, and occasionally mumbled his assessments to Paul about who he thought might act out. Today he seemed preoccupied, made only brief eye contact, and grunted—and then continued with an art project with which he seemed engrossed.

Moving on toward the Nurses' Station, three other patients approached him, beseeching him as if he were a recalcitrant Pope hearing petitions for release from Hell. One woman wanted an immediate Valium, another was Herve, a floridly psychotic man who babbled at him in a rapid-fire burst of speech filled with disconnected information, non-sequiturs, and neologisms. Paul kept walking and failed to acknowledge the appropriateness, or lack thereof, of either of their requests. The third was Reginald Spokes.

"Hey brother, what's happening?" Spokes was a tall, spindly, dark-skinned Black man, who sidled up to him, and offered an open palm to slap.

He was one of the few people of color Paul had ever seen on a unit that was almost exclusively populated by members of the more uptown White enclaves and suburbs, especially given that this was the quite prestigious and well-endowed "Jewish Hospital of St. Louis," perhaps the most exclusive medical center in the city proper.

Reginald called himself "Slick Spade," and liked to think that his adopted moniker was a *nom de guerre*, and himself a revolutionary. His father was a fully tenured professor of economics at Washington University (WU), and his mother a neurologist at Barnes. Reginald had grown up in a very upper-class home in University City. WU Medical School used the Barnes Hospital complex as a teaching facility. Five Steinberg was the psychiatric in-patient unit.

There had been a certain amount of hubbub when Reginald was admitted. Jewish Hospital rarely admitted people of color, except via the Employees' Entrance through which daily flowed a retinue of housekeepers, cooks, and maintenance personnel.

Reginald had been admitted for "depression and suicidal ideation" after his mother found an enormous stash of both Black Panthers' literature and a bottle of nameless white pills in his bedroom. She considered them both to be dangerous, and her son a potential victim of a conspiracy to corrupt "her little boy" (even though he was twenty-three years old). Much political wrangling had ensued before Professor Doctor Spokes got involved, and insisted that his son be admitted "for observation," rather than being arrested and put in jail. The Board of Trustees immediately agreed, and sent down the Olympian mandate to admit him.

There were very few clinical staff of color, with the exception of Lois Miller, the caramel-shaded Psychiatric Social Worker for the unit, who swiftly approached as Paul answered the young man's question and slapped his palm.

"Ain't nothing shakin' but the bacon, my man!"

"Mr. Marzeky! How many times have I reminded you to not use street language with the patients?" queried Ms. Miller. Reginald gave her the once over with plenty of eyeball lust.

"Hey pretty girl!"

Lois swiftly turned her angst and anger on the young man. She would have said that she was merely being "clinically appropriate," even though most of the staff knew she eschewed her ethnic background and played it down as much as possible with skin creams and straightened hair. It was rumored that she was dating a White guy.

"Mr. Spokes! I will ask you again to keep your comments to yourself!" she huffed, and then made her way to the shift report.

"Later, man" said Paul as he followed in her footsteps, on the way to shift change report. "I'll be here all night."

Margaret Combs was the Day Charge Nurse. She had beautiful eyes—and she also had a very sharp tongue, with which she lashed anyone daring to come late to shift report when she was in charge. She wanted to get out as quickly as possible, and go home. She shifted her considerable bulk, pulled down the edges of her rather voluminous blouse, harrumphed once, and spoke.

"It's been a quiet day overall, though the energy seems to be building. The new admit, Maryanne, one word, Butler. 27, Caucasian, brown and brown. Five foot seven, but only weighs one thirteen. Her UA was clean, but long history of LSD, marijuana, and methamphetamine. Picked up at Gaslight Square last night, exposing her breasts, being hypersexual and inappropriate."

Paul felt himself growing sleepy—most of the staff preferred it overly warm for his taste—and he sensed that Margaret had been waiting to rebuke him. She had waited until she was caught him nodding.

"Welcome back, Mr. Marzeky!"

"Just didn't sleep really well last night.

Paul had smoked a joint and wrote for three hours before coming in. It was far more invigorating than anything he knew he would encounter there.

Margaret ran through the roster of the other clients, none of her information carrying any portent of impending disaster. Jessica, the PM Charge Nurse, polled the staff about which patients with whom they wanted to work. Paul asked for Reginald and three others with whom he had previously worked.

He did a quick census count of the patients, determining where each of them was and what each of them were doing. He shared a few words here and there, keeping a running track in his head. We should be sixteen, he thought, and all I've got is fourteen.

"Where the hell is Motorcycle Mike?" The young man's treatment plan included his being allowed to rebuild his Harley-Davidson engine in his room as Occupational Therapy.

Paul had checked all of the patient rooms after a re-count. The laundry room should be locked, but still...

John John, another of the Adult Psychiatric Workers, seemed to have had the same idea as he, and arrived at the laundry room door at the same moment.

They heard loud voices before they even looked inside.

"Oh yeah, baby! Fuck me good! Oh God, that's SO good!"

He and John shared a quick glance. Paul stepped to the left, and grasped the door handle. They both nodded again, and he jerked the door open.

At that moment, "Motorcycle Mike" was standing between Maryanne's wide-spread legs as she sat atop the dryer with her pajama top askew, right breast exposed. His penis was deeply inside her and he was pumping furiously—so much so that he didn't stop even when they wrenched the door open. She however, immediately started shrieking, not even trying to cover herself. She screeched in his ear when he came closer, and then started frantically crabbing away from him. Mike's penis quickly shriveled and he lurched, wildly attempting to grab John, who stepped aside and swung the door into the man's charging body. Mike howled as the door handle slammed into his crotch, but, being strong and fifteen, he simply bounced off the dryer and came charging out. He made a wild, one-handed grab that missed, but then connected solidly with a left that knocked John out cold, and he crumpled to floor. Paul pushed the Panic Button before he shouted.

"I NEED HELP HERE! RIGHT NOW!!"

Paul stepped back and set his feet, preparing for the next crazed charge he knew was coming. Paul heard the approaching footsteps of staff pounding down the linoleum floor of the hallway. He figured Mike would explode through the door before help got there, and reminded himself that he couldn't just kill the guy, but only use as much force as necessary to protect himself and the patient. Predictably, "Motorcycle" came straight at him. As Paul stepped aside, the young man's momentum carried him into the opposite wall where he crashed with great force. Paul stepped back, believing the worst was over. When he bent to check his pulse, Maryanne jumped on Paul's back and made a swipe at his eyes with her long, chipped, red-painted fingernails.

In Paul's head, he was suddenly fighting for his life, and reacted with war-honed skills. He grabbed the woman's left hand in both of his, and bent her wrist back toward her body with great force while spinning around and keeping her arm extended and immobilized. Just as the troops arrived, he was preparing to land either a knife-strike to her throat or an open palm wedge to drive the bridge of her nose into her brain.

At length, Margaret finally arrived, having not gotten off the unit at all quickly.

"Let her go!"

"Get off her!" screamed Lois, beating at his arms.

The female patient was sobbing, great gouts of mucous running out of her nose as a cascade of tears welled from her eyes.

"He hurt me! He was gonna kill me!" she shrieked, pointing with her right forefinger.

As they were checking her vital signs, John John stood up, and shook his head.

Lois offered to get him some support, but he mumbled his demurral.

"I can get to the ER on my own!"

Margaret by then had checked both patients' vital signs, and had assured herself that neither of them was in immediate danger—though for insurance purposes she knew they both needed to go to the Emergency Room.

Lois sniffed haughtily and said "I called the Nursing Supervisor."

"Why'd you do that? Instead of comin' down here to help us?"

"I think you used excessive force on both these patients!"

"You don't know shit, lady! You weren't even here!"

"I'm filing a complaint!"

"And I'm filing a counter-complaint—because you don't know shit! You. Weren't. Even. Here!" he said emphasizing each word.

"I don't care! You're a violent young man!"

"And you're a fucking prissy princess!"

"How dare you!"

"You prance around the unit like you're surveying your realm! And then you don't show up when we need help! You're wasting your expensive education, lady!"

Margaret finally stepped in and displayed some authority.

"Both of you stop! Right now! The Nursing Supervisor wants to talk to both of you as soon as you've both filled out an Incident Report!"

"She doesn't need to! She wasn't there! Ask John John what happened! He was there with me! We got attacked!"

"NOW!"

When he had washed his face and hands, he sat down and wrote out in excruciating detail exactly what had happened. It took him a few minutes, and then he re-read it before signing it. It would still require a supervisor's signature before it was official, but she was on her way. He was expecting a grilling from the Nursing Supervisor, a tall, large-boned woman in her late 50's named Theresa Tompkins—and he resented it. She had obviously gotten an earful from the other two women before he arrived, as they all seemed to be giving him the "stink eye" when he walked in. He knew that John John's version of what had happened would support his, but in the meantime, he had to work on his desire to simply kill the fuck out of both Margaret and Lois. Theresa took his IR, and simply laid it aside on the table before she started in on him.

"It was not excessive! I was protecting my eyes! How would you like to explain an employee going to the ER who got blinded because he didn't protect himself?"

"There's no need for that kind of language!"

"It seems pretty obvious to me that you've convinced yourself of my guilt, and taken the side of Lois and Margaret before you even talked to me!" He took a deep breath to quell his rising rage and continued, "And neither of them was even there!" Pointing, he said, "They were sitting on their asses in the Nurses' Station when John John and I got attacked!" He took another deep breath, and continued.

"By the way," he said now in a slightly cooler tone, "have you even bothered to talk to him about what <u>actually</u> happened?"

"Well...uh...he's still...in the ER."

"So, the answer is 'No!' and I stand accused!"

"That's not true! I'm simply asking questions as part of the investigation into an Incident Report!"

"And clearly already decided that I was wrong and guilty! And you haven't even read my IR!"

The woman blanched, and then turned beet-red from the collar of her blouse to the edges of her hairline.

"I just haven't had time yet!"

"But you had enough time to talk to two women who weren't there! And accuse me without any evidence!"

Paul was seething. He felt a flashback building on the verges. Memories of the many times he had been accused of lying by his self-inflated asshole father who had preordained him guilty clamored in his head. He had had to "own up" for his "own good," to "tell the truth, you'll feel better" after he had sat in a chair in the middle of the kitchen being interrogated as if by a Gestapo interrogator. The accusations were both completely false and concocted by him, or groundlessly rooted in other peoples' accusations. His father had always felt somehow duty-bound to punish Paul for crimes known and unknown, many created by the hatred in his own head. Paul always eventually "confessed" that he was "guilty," so he could get out of the chair and go to the bathroom before he peed on himself—and to get away from his fascist father. Such situations were one of the biggest triggers for his rage—though he was usually not aware of it until after he had "acted out" his anger, usually verbally. But there was a time when he threw a guy through his apartment window...

This kind of unfounded accusation, based on incomplete evidence, was prejudice, pure and simple. Not like racial or gender prejudice, but equally damaging. And it wasn't like they were going to apologize when the figured out they were wrong. They would just blame him anyway, just so they didn't have to admit that they had chosen the wrong path!

After all of the hullaballoo with the Nursing Supervisor, he'd been allowed (quite reluctantly, it seemed) to go back to the unit again. By then, the patients' dinner had come and gone, and small clusters of patients had gathered to play cards or board games, while some continued working on art projects they had started during OT. The arrival back on the unit, within minutes of each other, of Motorcycle Mike and Maryanne signaled small exclamations from the female clients and brief eye contact from the males. The Nursing Supervisor had apparently spoken to them both in the ER.

By all accounts, they had offered up self-serving stories of Paul's brutality and abuse, while not getting anywhere near the truth about what they'd been doing in the laundry room. John John had been adjudged to be sufficiently recovered from his mild concussion to be allowed to go home with his girlfriend, but had first insisted on giving a much broader account of what actually happened when he wrote his IR. Motorcycle Mike considered himself to be a hero, even bragging to the other clients about his inappropriate behavior. A meeting had been scheduled for the next morning with both his parents and the Hospital Attorney to discuss the ramifications of his assault on a staff member and his sexual misconduct. (The results of a pelvic exam would eventually prove the presence of sperm in Maryanne's vagina that matched Mike's blood type. Maryanne would eventually break down and tell the truth when threatened with being charged with having sex with a minor).

The only one who did not seem upset or otherwise involved was "Slick." He was sitting in one of the overstuffed chairs that weighed approximately 400 pounds—theoretically so that none of the patients could pick it up and use it as a weapon.

Paul approached him and said, "You're one of my patients tonight, so let's get together and talk after I get my break. With all of the bullshit going on around here, I haven't even had time to eat."

"Works for me."

"You doin' OK?"

"Nothing to me, man. When you crazy white folks do some stupid shit, I just watch!"

"Man, I got that!"

"Just between you and me, brother man, the people in charge on this unit couldn't supervise their way out of a paper bag!"

Paul laughed, almost choking as a wave of psychedelic energy streaked through him, causing his field of vision to turn dark and fill with small purple dots. (A neurologist friend had once told him that it was the final stage before blacking out completely). Paul decided for the billionth time that he had to cut back on smoking everything!

Paul identified with "Slick" more than he did with Lois and her stuffy, pretentious, and always-oh-so-correct ideas and behaviors. He'd been working the unit for three weeks now and was constantly planning his escape to San Francisco, where he fantasized planning to live the uninhibited life of a libertine, basking in the golden light of all that "free love" about which he had heard so much. St. Louis had treated him well in that department, very well indeed. But his long-time dream always had been and still was to move to San Francisco. It had been one of the sustaining features of his fantasies in Viet Nam, of living a life filled with exciting women and the best drugs in the world when he got home.

His brain was throbbing as he took out his journal to continue working on the phone he had started earlier. He decided to tentatively call it "Life Prayer," part of it admittedly stolen from the song sung famously by Jeannette McDonald in the 1936 film "San Francisco."

> I feel so stuck in the ordinariness of everyday,
> while driven, haunted by dreams and visions of greatness
> I am impotent to fulfill, as my precious life force
> slips away more and more, day by day by day,
> enmired in the usual while valor and honor await.
> In the silence of the night torturous screams pursue me
> into what I thought was to be a new life.
>
> Yet my past is still a preoccupation,
> clinging to me like an invisible wrapper,
> obscuring my efforts, coloring my every action
> with shades of deeds undone,
> life unlived, achievements frustrated
> rotting like the dead, moldering.
>
> New life! New life! I cry!
>
> San Francisco! San Francisco!
> Pearl of the Golden West!
>
> City of my dreams!
> Please bring me home, your lost son!
>
> I want you like no other.
> I love you like no other.
> Please bring me home again to go roamin' no more.

CHAPTER FOUR
The Plan, Moving Forward
St. Louis   Early-June 1969

Paul took upon himself the authority to confront raging, delusional, aggressive, or bullying patients. Sometimes a gruff tone of voice was enough; other times it took his "laser beam look" to settle down an escalating psyche. Other times a show of force was sufficient. Having three or four people standing by his side as he delivered a request to a patient to quit talking too loudly, for example, really enforced compliance. After all, it was the patients' temporary home. He and the staff were entrusted with the welfare of all on the unit during the eight hours they were there. They were tasked with being "Big Mom and Dad." Paul sometimes thought of himself as "The Sheriff" when he waded into a fractious fray.

He seemed to have an almost natural ability in taking patients down. It turned him on in a mano-a-mano gunfight challenge way. It became an almost daily experience too—someone either attacked him, or he had to intervene to prevent an assault on another. It gave him the best adrenaline rushes he'd had since Viet Nam, the intense connection he had there with his brothers. Now he lived for those moments of heightened consciousness (notwithstanding his occasional use of amphetamines).

He needed almost constant stimulation to chase away his boredom, depression, and ennui. Being in the city of his birth, he was in a holding pattern that threatened to get deeper the longer he stayed, and swallow him up like an enormous quicksand pond. He was definitely not living the life he had imagined! He deserved better. He felt like he had paid enormous dues, not just the 'Nam, but his entire life had felt like penance. He had envisioned living loose and free, smoking weed, going to concerts, and having enormous amounts of gratuitous sex with amazing and awesome women; a life rich in adventure and brimming with meaningful encounters with incredibly gifted people.

Yet here he was working a job simply to afford the privacy he craved, and the time he needed to sort out his head. He still felt confused sometimes, as if his mind were moving at a different speed than his body, as if they had been separated at the waist. He needed quiet and lack of distraction as an antidote to the deeply engrained and unforgettably implanted memories that haunted him, that flashed into his mind at odd and unaccountable moments; that sometimes took control of his body before he could even think; took his mind hostage and seemed to force him to act in violent, instinctual ways, as if he had no other option.

He had felt so greatly liberated from the ordeal of war, and developed so powerful a sense of redemption at having returned—that he thought himself exempt, that he had paid his dues; and owed no more to the daily *sturm und drang* of "normal" life. He was pissed off at having to work at all. He wanted to be, felt he should be, unbound by time's strategies and schedules. It just burned as if he were filled with molten lava that flowed out of every orifice, and erupted in a burst of rage, or a momentarily overwhelming desire to just viciously slaughter anyone who had fucked with him at any time in any way. Other times, all he could do was sit and cry, body wracked with spasms, seeking the blessed relief that came afterward. He knew he had greatness within him, and feared mightily that it might slip away from him forever in the pursuit of surviving the ordinariness of regular life.

He had been granted his wish—to be awakened in the crucible of war. Coming down from that tremendous high, it had been almost impossible for his neurohormones and opioid peptides to adjust. He had been jacked to the max and beyond—and he still could not adjust to the difference, or to the idea that maybe, just maybe, it had been a doorway, and now he was really having to do the work that it had embodied as a vision. Now maybe it was time for the hard work entailed in becoming a real writer. His experiences had been thrilling, exciting, scary, mind-blowing, excruciating, awesome, horrible, shitty, amazing, exhilarating, joyous, even transcendental—never to be repeated or recreated, never to be erased. His euphoric recall of the high times, the good times, the great times was tremendous—and he wanted to deny the absolutely shitty, gritty, totally fucked up times, of which there had also been plenty.

He was like a junkie who kept trying to re-create after the first high, the imprinting high, the memory of which never leaves, just kept driving him on and on and on, hoping against hope to have that primal experience just once more. When smoking heroin on aluminum foil, it ran all over and you had to "chase the dragon" with an aluminum foil straw to keep taking it in. The metaphor of chasing the dragon seemed so very apt for many areas of his life. Sometimes too he felt as if he had been released from prison, had come out filled with dreams of glory and greatness, of redemption, maybe even revenge, though the latter, as Machiavelli had observed, was a dish best eaten cold.

He was young and alive, and home from the war—though the latter was something of a mixed blessing to own. The longer he was home, the harder it seemed to integrate what he had experienced overseas; and the more glaring were the disparities he witnessed all around him in daily life, especially between young people and the so-called "Establishment" with its increasingly virulent and draconian methods and goals. He found himself becoming more and more oppositional to the way the world was being run, and the increasing ocean of bullshit, lies, and disinformation that were broadcast as "truth" through the "mainstream media."

When he spoke of his revelations with his friends in the "underground," they spoke of the "revolution" in reverential, or strident tones, they seemed more like firebrand preachers, promoting a new ideology—while he, having seen "the belly of the beast," found it easy to criticize their rhetoric too. He had seen both sides of the ostensible "debate" of ideologies, and found it well-nigh impossible to put much truck into either right or left wing. He was angry and disillusioned enough to empathize with those who favored extreme action, but after what he seen and heard, a witness to history, he was hard put to agree with the fantasied socialist regimes the "politicals" dreamed up, with their, of course, occupying places of prominence in their version of the New World Order (a term long associated with global Empire building). He agreed with the intended outcomes of change and overthrowing the government, but he had heard no one really speak to a solution that contained a better, brighter future than the execrable one in which they were now immersed.

He had implemented his original vision of having greater contact with student nurses as added value of working at the hospital. They had proven to be a sexual cornucopia beyond anything he'd ever imagined, especially as they too were feeling the awakening waves of liberation from ages old suppression. The young women were excited and exciting, hungry to experience as much more life as was he. Many were away from home for the first time, willing to really spread their wings (and their legs), and fly.

As he sat there and reflected, he was shaken from his reverie by a woman's shriek, followed by a gruff, rough male voice bellowing. It shattered the delicate crystal palace of his daydreams as the walls of the outside hallway reverberated like an echo chamber. He bounded to his feet, and ran immediately toward the danger—primed, mobilized, all senses alert, ready for action.

As he turned the corner, he was struck by an odd tableau. It was the new patient—Walter something or other, Browden, that was it—all six feet four, two hundred fifty pounds of him, standing with his head down and hands at his sides. He looked like he might be blushing, even though his long blonde hair partially obscured his face. Anne, a female APW, was standing in front of him with a scowl on her face, and her right index finger pointing at him. It looked like she might be scolding him. Paul mis-read the body language, and immediately assumed that she was having a confrontation. He rushed up like a misguided knight errant.

"What's going on?" he asked, rather more gruffly than he had intended, anger leaking out of him like radioactive isotopes from a corrupted container.

He knew the new guy carried a diagnosis of Manic-Depressive Disorder, Mixed. He experienced both high and low, mania and depression, vacillating in extreme ways. Paul looked at the man and watched a living demonstration of "rapid cycling," as the man's eyes were mirrored his inner states, as they shifted from forlorn and despondent to filled with raging fire, and back again in the proverbial blink of the eye. Paul knew immediately that he'd a mistake. He tried to ameliorate the situation by backing away as quickly as possible, but it was already too late. As Admiral Yamamoto said after the bombing of Pearl Harbor, "I fear that we have but awakened the sleeping giant."

"I'm sorry. I made a mistake. Looks like you're doing just fine here, Anne."

Paul started backing away, arms at his sides, palms turned outward toward the man, voice soft, words calm, his formerly hyper-alert nerve endings calming as the electrical impulses from his amygdala stopped zipping like pulses along an icy telegraph line. His intuition was screaming at him not to shut down the power supply quite yet, and he was right. With a huge roar the new patient turned toward him, arms spread wide as if to simply engulf Paul in his meaty paws and extinguish his breath.

Paul responded in all the ways in which his combat-readiness and his facility training had taught him. He stepped back, and spread his legs shoulder-width apart while simultaneously shouting at the top of his lungs "I NEED SOME HELP HERE! RIGHT NOW!!"

The enraged man-beast lunged at Paul, who ducked under the outstretched arms and placed himself between the man and his fellow staff member. But the patient was very fast. He reached behind himself and grabbed the sleeve of Paul's shirt, and started dragging him closer. Instead of resisting—in part not to rip one of his favorite shirts—he allowed himself to go with the energy, and started to fall forward which seemed to surprise the patient.

The large enraged patient growled again as four staff members rounded the corner headed for the melee. Paul meanwhile moved forward on his toes, and then, abruptly, planted his feet, and the man kept going. As he did, Paul pivoted and pinned his arms at his sides, locking his fingers together, as the large man bellowed like a wounded water buffalo. Paul's strength was fading as the staff backup arrived.

"Get an arm! I'm losing my grip!"

As others stepped up to secure the man's limbs, the man began thrashing and fighting.

"Take him down! Take him down!"

It was a great idea in principle, but two of the staff were new and relatively untrained. Anne had secured an arm, and was gripping it tightly to her chest as the man tried to whirl and twist. Paul addressed himself to the other APWs.

"Get his legs! Goddamn it!"

Both of the newer staff members finally managed to get the man's legs in their arms, but not yet secured.

"OK! On three," he said, making eye contact around the gathered group, "take him down! One, two..."and used his own leg to help kick out the raging patient's left leg as he shifted his center of balance and pulled the struggling man to the floor. The other team members more or less coordinated with his rhythm. The Charge Nurse came running up with four sets of leather restraints. The cuffs were swiftly wrapped around his flailing appendages, the bracket pushed up through the closest hole, and the strap pulled tight.

"Everybody ready?" Paul quickly surveyed their work, and they took him to the seclusion room, where they restrained him face down so that he wouldn't aspirate. Then they gathered in the Nurses' Station for a re-hash of the event.

Anne slipped into the room, and closed the door behind her, glaring at Paul. She refused to speak to him, even though he looked at her and raised an eyebrow. Paul grimaced, sighed, and then blew out his breath.

Christie Jenkins looked pissed. And she was even more pissed than she looked. She never cursed or used any form of vulgarity, so today her use of language spoke volumes.

"So, is somebody gonna' tell me what the fuck happened?"

Everyone in the room looked around with varying degrees of incredulity before Anne finally spoke directly to Christie.

"Can we clear everybody else out of here, Christie? Paul and I were the only ones who know what happened."

After the rest of the staff left, Anne spoke, again directly to Christie, spitting and sputtering with unsuppressed rage.

"This man," she screeched, pointing her right index finger at Paul, "agitated the crap out of the new patient Walter Browden!"

"That's bullshit, Christie! I heard her scream!"

Anne jumped up, and said "When this...this idiot came charging down the hall, the patient, the goddamn patient who hasn't spoken a word since he got here three days ago, spoke to me. I was so shocked, I must have made a noise. But I definitely did not scream!"

"Bullshit! I heard you in the break room!"

"I did not scream!"

"OK! Shriek then!"

Seeing the unbelieving look on his supervisor's face, he tried again.

"Christie, I swear! Loud and clear! She screamed!"

Looking at Paul for the first time, Anne said "This man is impaired! He needs professional help! I swear he's either hallucinating, or..."

"Or what, bitch?"

"Mr. Marzeky, that's enough of the language! I will not warn you again!"

"Yes, ma'am. And again, I ask, 'Or' what?"

Now Anne looked sheepish for the first time. She would neither speak nor meet his eyes.

"'Or' what, Anne?!"

She just stood there, with her eyes downcast.

"'Or' what, damn it!?"

"Anne, perhaps you should let Paul and I talk privately."

Anne nodded her head, and walked out the door.

"What?" queried Paul, fear and rage flushing through him like two streams of tracers pouring from dual .50s into a distant tree line.

"What?" he asked again, looking more perplexed the longer he was forced to wait, and no answer was forthcoming. Christie looked distraught and uncomfortable. At length she looked up and said "Paul, please sit down. I'm...very concerned about some of the reports I have been getting."

Paul jumped out of his chair, and started to raise his voice, rage radiating off him like sunshine off asphalt. Christie held up her hand, palm out, toward him.

"Please sit down. I know you just got back from Viet Nam."

Paul sighed. Here we go again, he thought.

He flushed with suppressed rage and shame, and the planes of his face twisted like a medieval gargoyle's.

"Please don't get me wrong, but it seems that you have been...overreacting a bit."

"'Overreacting?'"

"Some staff have mentioned that you seem...edgy sometimes, with the patients, too quick to react. Angry even sometimes. Too forceful."

"How confidential is this conversation?"

"I need to talk with you about what I have been hearing."

"That doesn't answer my question! Are you looking for an excuse to fire me?"

"No! But we have to talk. Unless you have done anything truly egregious, the details of this conversation will stay between us."

"I thought I was doing a good job here!"

"I appreciate your presence here. You seem to really relate well with the patients."

"And?"

"I know you just got back, so I've been reluctant to bring this up, but...well, what do you think? Do you think you sometimes act too quickly, or too forcefully?"

Paul shut down and turned inward. He was immediately flooded with thousands of pictures, not only from the 'Nam and its frequent iniquities, but of the many other indignities he had endured in his life rolled through his head like a runaway bobsled down an icy chute.

He looked up with tears in his eyes, voice sodden with suppressed emotion, to try to keep his shame hidden from his supervisor, who held such an inordinate amount of power over this portion of his life.

"Ma'am, I may have overreacted. I swear I thought I heard her scream. And when I rounded the corner and saw the patient towering over her...I thought she was in danger. She's totally minimizing her reaction. I swear I heard her! I was in the break room!"

"I will question her more closely later. But right now, I have to determine what to do. I am responsible for every single person, staff and patients, on this unit. And when I have long-time staff members, people who have worked here for years, expressing concerns about you, I have to listen."

"'Concerns?'"

She took a deep breath, looking into the far distance, then released it and looked directly into his eyes. She took in the shaggy hair (obviously growing out), and the Zapata-style moustache, not at all unusual for the younger generation. He wore faded corduroys, and a dark green T-shirt under a chambray work shirt with a pen in the pocket hole. She noted that the jaundice he had had when he first started, had all but faded. He seemed to have gained maybe twenty pounds, and she could no longer see his rib cage through his shirt.

"I have been told, well actually seen, you...patrolling the unit like you were in the jungle!"

"Ma'am, as I made clear to you when I started. I was a Social Work/Clinical Psychology Specialist in the 'Nam. 91G20 versus those who worked the in-patient units, 91F20, Neuropsychiatric Specialist. So, again as I told you, I never worked with in-patients before, though I have a lot of experience with a variety of psychiatric conditions."

"I understand that. But how does that apply to your...actions here?"

Paul took a deep breath, and looked directly into Christie's eyes. His internal dams were bursting. He wanted desperately to keep the depth of his human misery from overflowing. He congratulated himself for having smoked half a bomber before he'd come in. It had given him a little edge—some might call it dissociative—that allowed him what he perceived as the illusion of a degree of separation from his otherwise tumultuous emotions. Christie seemed to be compassionate, a trait in women that always excited a desire for emotional, even sexual, connection. He had longed for a solid intimate relationship his whole life, and in that moment, he felt a deeper level of relatedness to Christie.

"It may seem that I 'patrol' the unit, but I'm concerned for the well-being of every person on this unit too; though," he said, contrition dripping from his face and eyes like a penitent, "I admit, mostly for the staff. I...feel like we back each other up. Most of the staff reminds me of the guys I served with."

"But this isn't a war zone!"

Paul's ephemeral restraint collapsed in that heated instant. He jumped out of his chair, face straining to not release the volcanic emotions roiling in his belly. Christie shrank back into her leather executive office chair, face showing that she had felt almost physically assaulted.

"This is a dangerous place! I do my best to keep everyone safe!"

Christie sat back, perspiration pouring out from her beautifully coiffed hairline, considering where next to go with this truly unusual conversation.

"That's...I guess I have never heard an APW express an opinion quite so forcefully before."

"An 'APW?' Why is it unusual that I have concerns for the well-being of the staff?"

"Because usually it's someone with far more education that expresses such...compassion!"

"I have a tremendous amount of life experience, and a strong clinical background."

"I admit we don't normally get anyone working in your position who has so much experience."

"I don't understand. Does that negate my concerns, or invalidate my actions?"

"No, but I must express my concern that you react in...potentially dangerous situations...quite forcefully."

"And?"

"Are you agreeing with me?"

"No. I am asking what's next. What does that mean?"

Christie took a deep breath, and refocused on Paul.

"I don't want you or anyone else to get hurt out there! No one!"

"You're worried about liability issues!"

"That too! But...more, actually, for your well-being."

"What's that mean?"

"I'm concerned that maybe you've started working too soon after coming back."

"I've done a damn good job here! No one has ever been hurt on my shift! No one!"

"I really do appreciate that, but...I don't know how to ask this without upsetting you."

"What? Come on, spit it out. I promise you I will be OK."

"Have you...are you in therapy?"

Paul sighed deeply and hung his head. Then he sighed before meeting her eyes. A tear rolled slowly down his right cheek.

"Christie, sometimes I feel...boo-coo fucked up. I'm sorry about the language. I know how sensitive you are. Sometimes I act like everybody was in the 'Nam."

"No, go on please."

"I'm different...than before I went. To tell the truth, I'd rather not be working. I came home...with this fantasy, and I'm pretty pissed off that I'm not living that life. The world just isn't living up to my expectations."

"You didn't answer my question."

"No. I'm not in therapy. I'm not service-connected, so I don't have the VA. They don't really give a shit anyway. I did talk to the Vet Center, but...they didn't seem terribly therapeutic. I...could probably use some help, but I don't need anybody chattering at me, telling me I'm wrong about Viet Nam!"

"And you don't have insurance benefits here yet either."

Paul took a deep breath, and contemplated how honest he could be to be with this woman, who just happened to be his supervisor.

"Look, I never promised that I was going to be a "career employee." He sighed. "My intention is to move to San Francisco as soon as possible, always has been."

"Oh. I thought it might be something like that."

"Why?"

"I have heard you talking about San Francisco, listening to rock music."

"Didn't think I was being that obvious."

"So. Here we are."

"Yes, indeed."

"I have been ignoring most of what I have been hearing about you being too assertive, even aggressive and challenging some of the patients. But I think I'm going to have to write you up officially this time."

"I did not do a goddamn thing wrong! I responded to her shrieking!"

A phosphorescent flare of utter white rage shot through him as if he had touched an ungrounded mega-watt electrical line. He jumped up out of his chair, knocking it over as he sputtered to find a more coherent reply. A Technicolor montage of images assaulted him, an insane psychedelic collage of disparate parts and discarded objects bisected by the sharp lightening blast of excruciating pain that sliced through his sternum that stopped his confused stammering. His face turned ashen and he slumped back down into his chair.

Christie looked stricken as she made to move toward him, but he stopped her with an open-palmed hand, and took a deep breath that returned the color to his face.

"I'm...OK. Just gimme a minute."

"Are you sure?"

"Look, you just do what you have to do, and so will I. I'm just going to tell you up front: I'm not letting anybody get hurt on my watch."

CHAPTER FIVE
A Brave New World
St. Louis   June 1969

A well-deserved day off tomorrow! Thank fucking God! He really needed it. It had been extremely hectic at work. He absolutely needed some time to unwind his mind.

What time was it?

11:50 PM.

He'd made good time getting home. Hard to believe that just twenty minutes ago he had been at the bin surrounded by the loonies! He lit the bedside lamp and allowed his gratitude to flow as he broke an orange flower top into the lid of a small metal box, and rolled a medium sized joint. With this weed, he didn't need anything bigger. Just one hit. Unless he felt greedy. Like tonight. He decided to smoke half right now, and then refresh his head in another couple of hours. The glorious feeling of freedom pulsed through him as he sat on the edge of his bed, and contemplated what LP to put on the turntable.

Sailor. The Steve Miller Band with Boz Skaggs on bass. The sound of the fog horns that opened the "A" side of the album always reminded him of San Francisco. The tune set up such a longing in his chest that he thought his sternum would crack open and all of his internal organs would pour out. And *Quicksilver Girl!* Jesus! How could anybody listen to it and not crave some loving? A woman who would give him everything he needed and still be herself. His fantasy was a warrior woman standing back-to-back with him, holding off a roomful of thugs with her foot-long, razor-edged knives. He fervently hoped she would one day come to him in all her radiance.

He pulled a few other records from the stack that sat against the wall across from his bed, right next to the low table that held his stereo equipment. *The Jimi Hendrix Experience*; Country Joe and the Fish (what Joe called the "first anti-war band"); Joni Mitchell; Buffalo Springfield; and then, almost as an afterthought, *Quicksilver Messenger Service* (all Virgos!)

He frequently thought of the collection of dispatches he and Toad had put together. He couldn't really call it a manuscript—it was a mish-mash of thoughts, ideas, poems, and scribblings that characterized the times they had shared in the 'Nam. Looking through them, he felt a re-kindled sense of connection and brotherhood. And longed for it, longed to not feel so isolated, locked within himself seeking a way out.

In that moment, he felt supremely aware of all the amazing energy, all the incredible events, people, and experiences that were happening all around him, all around the world simultaneously—but, he just knew, in San Francisco. He was so afraid to miss out on the many such extraordinary events, once-in-a-lifetime events that he would never get another chance to experience, really experience, and treasure forever because he was in St. Louis, not there. He was concerned that he might not be adequate to the task, might not have enough power or will or strength to liberate himself and join the joyous throng in The City by the Bay. He knew it would be the highest of highs, just living there, doing whatever passed for ordinary life there, higher than any high he had ever experienced.

He wanted so much to make progress, to go forward, feared he might fall short of achieving a perceived hip status for which or by which he would be well and truly loved and really feel like he belonged in the world, to continue the rebirth that he had started; that demanded that he completely embody and inhabit it. He wanted so much to be a part of the intelligencia. His oldest fears always attempted to surface like a submarine in the Arctic. He wanted so terribly to be whole enough to be the new man he was declaring himself to be, shorn of his raggedy past and all of the hindrances that had so plagued him.

And he had to ask: Was it all true? Was he really new?

He feared looking back from the future and having missed opportunities NOW, especially when he might meet people in the future who had actually been there and contributed to the making of the historic events currently unfolding. There was no specific reason for him to be feeling it right now, just a general sense of emotional malaise generated by his depression and isolation. He knew he had created his fears, had used them to keep others at a distance because he was too afraid to let anyone in, to let anyone catch a glimpse of that quivering, shivering soul that still lurked in his deepest shadow—the one he worked so assiduously to hide from all and sundry.

In that moment, Paul felt as fragile as a butterfly that had not yet pumped sufficient blood into its wings to fly. He had fought mightily to create and manage a fierce and truculent façade—gruff and untrusting, maybe even paranoid, but he was acutely aware of being a true stranger in a strange land. He both longed for and feared encounters with hip people with their long hair and beads, with their greater cultural awareness and significant knowledge of events and people, about whom or which he knew little or nothing. He felt as if the first two decades of his life had been lived in a vacuum with no input or contact with anyone or anything other than the extremely constricted information that his parents funneled to him, despite his superior intellect.

For the hundredth time that day, he fervently wished that his hair would grow faster. He viewed it as a magic carpet;

as if longer hair would be, or could be, or even should be, a passport for other realms to which he was denied existence; of course, that particular fallacy was fed by the notion that appearance was more important than essence, as if having a hipper appearance were the equivalent of being truly hip would actually make him more hip! Jesus!

All of the vets he knew denied their service except to other vets; and yet there were those who had never served, or had not gone to the land of blood, shit, and tears, who, counterintuitively and counter-counter-culturally, laid claim to the lineage! What the fuck was the world coming to?

Of course, he totally identified with being a vet, and he was comfortable wearing his jungle boots, boonie hat, even an old-style fatigue jacket with the epaulettes. It was part of an identity he was wanting desperately to have, of being "heavy-duty," jaded and worldly. Sometimes he felt like a sweet gum seed ball, all covered with spiky pointed needles to keep birds and other perpetrators from eating its soft and tender innards. It was all, of course, a reaction to feeling small and vulnerable in spite of all of the extreme experiences he had had. He felt as if he had been plunged involutionally back into some alternate dimension of his earliest life, as if he were starting over on a different level that was vibrationally related to the very beginning of beginnings, the ontogeny of the ontogeny. He believed he was going to have the opportunity to recreate himself in an image more in accord with his own most essential components. Yet he knew there was still so much work ahead, as if paying dues were the actual name f the game and whatever goal might portend, or even pretend to represent THE END wherein there seemed to be no more work—it was quite simply just another illusion.

The weed had worked its magic, first the large muscles relaxing, then the stress and anxiety in his chest, belly, and intestines melting away. It was a life saver for him. Though he still drank alcohol, he preferred good drugs.

The more deeply he relaxed, the more clarity seemed to shine like a primeval sun upon his introspections. His vision of himself had never included wearing his hair short and carrying a lunch box to a factory job—the kind of ideology his father had embraced and tried to infuse in him all of his life, keeping one job for life. his father who had had enough family money and support to graduate from college in the middle of the Great Depression, and from a prestigious school yet! His father who had returned from combat recovering from wounds, and went back to the same fucking job he had had before he went to the war! His father who had remained bitter to his last day of life about former subordinates who had not served and been elevated to supervising him! His father, who had bitterly battled office politics and long daily bus rides in order to toil in corporate trenches, only to drink himself blotto every night to suppress his memories of both his childhood and the war.

Thinking about the convolutions of his parents exhausted him. He went into the kitchen to make a little snack, maybe heat up the other half of a monster burrito he had bought for his dinner earlier, and didn't have time to finish. Then he was struck by the proverbial lightning bolt.

He'd tried LSD with The Toad before he left Northern California, but the man was an old-time tripper and had cautioned Paul to try just half a tab—that resulted in him only getting half-stoned, only "sort of psychedelic," with a few trails and some swirls of color and lights, but he had none of the deep, mind-expanded, other-dimensional effects that he craved. He knew there was another realm, another dimension, out there all around him, waiting for him to open the door.

He had tried one, then one-and-a-half, and finally two tabs at different times. With this last dose, he got that falling-off-the-end-of-the-world sensation for about a half an hour. Paul knew enough about priming doses to understand that he had had a breakthrough experience that re-set the bar, as it were, for his mind to step through fully—to know what was there; to see what was there; and be what was there, to be "far out" and "groovy." He currently thought of himself now as a "wannabe," or a "plastic person," only pretending to belong, only pretending to be hip.

Paul worried that he was so defended, so armored against his own real feelings, that even lysergic acid diethylamide-25 couldn't penetrate, couldn't open his magic doorways. Perhaps he was truly hopeless! He fervently wished he could trip with Timothy Leary!

Just then a line popped into his head. It was from a tune originally recorded as the "The Honey Dripper" by Roosevelt Sykes in 1937: "You know the night time is the right time..." He took this small synchrony as an epiphany, and decided he would take a multiple-tab dose!

Paul procured the small glass vial that held ten hits, and shook the jar, watching the dark-brown speckled beige mini-barrels swirl and rattle with the "Chocolate Chip" acid. He felt both excited and anxious, and hoped for within himself, hoping for some kind of cosmic intuition guidance to give him a clue about the journey upon which he was about to embark. But the intuition that had always warned him about danger was silent. He closed his eyes and held the vial in his hands while listening for a Universal communication. It was without advice too.

He dumped two of the little barrels into his left palm, feeling out the moment—then rolled in three more. He looked into the far distance, still seeking advice, then nodded his head, opened his mouth, popped in the little pile, and swallowed.

Toad had coached him to do deep breathing while waiting for the "medicine" to work. He had heard an unsubstantiated rumor that LSD triggered neurons for a very, very brief period—opened the mental doorways for less than a tenth of a second, before disappearing and becoming totally untraceable in the body. But when he thought about it, he seriously wondered how they (the ubiquitous "they") could have possibly managed the experiment? He shivered in anticipation of what he considered to be the "event" (rather than the journey). It felt more like an event to him, one that he hoped would open him up, and initiate him into a new world, leaving behind forever all of the artifacts that had lived within him forever. He prayed to be freed of the shame and torment of his earliest memories, those he did not seem to be able to shake, no matter how hard he had tried, no matter how many drugs he took.; prayed to be relieved of the emotional burden of the actual memories, to de-fang them through cathartic release.

Paul shook his head as a mild tremor attempted to take up residence in the small of his back, then reverberating up his spine, and wondering if the shit were starting to work. He yearned, burned even, to fully manifest himself completely, to turn his insides out, and feel completely real, and solid.

Purposely breathing seemed so goddamn slow, so he decided to smoke the other half of the joint. Maybe the weed would speed up the process—though he knew he had no idea what he was talking about, even as he thought it. He felt something was waiting, but he didn't know what it was. He had a presentiment of something lurking—and he felt vastly impatient to get there, wherever "there" was!

He lit the large roach, watching intense resins stain the paper dark brown as the resins streaked toward the end he held in the sterling silver roach clip he carried on his key ring. It looked like an Egyptian ankh from one angle, and from another, it was the shape of a face with long jaws that opened to receive the joint end. As the magical smoke turned his muscles liquid, he relaxed further and decided to commemorate this occasion. He retrieved his journal. He was in love with its clean, crisp lines, and the blank pages. He took it from the bedside table, turned to a fresh page, and made a note of the date, time, and location in the upper left-hand corner. Then he sat for a moment, listening to his whirling, swirling thoughts and the images cascading through his head.

He tried to consider what Toad might think. He wanted to emulate him, the first real writer he had ever known. He had lived in the Bay Area most of his life, so that made him extra-hip. They had become instant friends when they met in Qui Nhon, and he had urged Paul repeatedly to keep his shit together around all the lifers, especially that fucking asshole Sergeant Hammonds! He had warned him not to freak too freely in the presence of the long arm of the lifer good old boy network. Paul had ultimately ignored his good counsel, and that led him into danger with the 101st Airborne, getting strung out on opium, and a Court Martial, the last thanks to the supreme asshole of all time, Command Sergeant Major Hoxley. Following his own star, no matter how seemingly misguided it might have been, led him to an awakening to himself for which he was really grateful, and provided grist for his writing that nothing else could have.

He still had contacts to Viet Nam. Captain Magnus Browne had actually written him, congratulating him on being back in the world, and encouraging him again to consider going to college to develop the talents that the good Captain believed he had, and reminding him that he was willing to make a referral for him to a competent therapist experienced in dealing with what was becoming known under the psychiatric rubric of Posttraumatic Stress Disorder. Paul had not yet written back, wanting to delay his refusal for referral, while not wanting to seem ungracious. Dr. Browne had contributed to his getting home with an Honorable Discharge, whole and relatively unscathed when "they" all wanted to send him to Long Bien Jail! His testimony had been brilliant, and chopped the prosecutors into tiny fragments.

A sudden churning in his belly sent spirals of color swirling that seemed vaguely psychedelic. He hoped so. He knew he was investing deeply in the possibility of this drug, and what he was experiencing might just have been placebo effect. No matter how marvelous, it could ever be anything but a heavenly catalyst. Again, he had a vague presentiment hovering.

Seemingly without volition, he scooped up his pen started printing (he had given up cursive a long time ago). Alliterations flooded his brain, and he rapidly recorded the captured images on paper.

*Adrenalized anacondas assault anxious animals as
Beautiful bountiful babies bounce beckoning.
Coruscating coral-colored cetaceans cavort courageously as
Diverse delicious desserts drive droves of diners delusional.*

Oh my God! This was some trippy shit! It was just pouring out of his pen—mind and heart merging, on a primal quest.

*Elegant exquisite equines elaborate excessive equilibrium as
Fine finials flaunt fiery, fabulous, finery.
Gorgeous graceful glamorous girls gaily greet
High hungry hierophants handling hundreds of heavy hunches.*

Damn! More incredible shit! It was all just flowing, released as if from deep inner wellsprings, and seeing light for the very first time!

Innumerable industrious insects inundate invaders as
Jocose jumbles of jejune jacarandas jape joyously.
Kaleidoscopic kabuki kangaroos ken karmic kachinas while
Lithe limber limpid ladies laze languidly luring love.

He'd never been this stoned! Was this what Jimi called "beautiful?"

Mammoth multiphasic mammals murmur melodiously as
Naked nymphs nominate new natural nudes' negligence.
Omnipresent omniscient omnivores offer oblique oddments while
Pundits placidly personify, pandering pronounced perfection.

Wow! He'd always wanted to be a poet—but this was beyond the beyond!

Quirky queens querulously question queer queues as
Restless rhapsodies resound 'round rustic retreats and
Superb serendipities shape-shift, shimmering sinuously.

Streaks of brilliant blue-white light strafed the vault of his head as all his thoughts and feelings blended into one powerful stream.

Tumultuous typhonic terrors tintinnabulate timelessly as
Unctuous unicorns unanimously unify under usury.
Verdant verdigris vies valiantly, vertiginously as
Wending winding waters waft wistfully, wandering willingly.

The sound of the music quivered, etching multi-hued notes and chords in the air as they simultaneously struck his tympanic membranes. He changed the vinyl on the turntable without looking.

Xenogeneic xylophones 'xcite xenophobic xylographs and
Yesterday's youth yen yearningly for yenta's yellow yodeling.
Zealous zazens zanily 'zerve zippy zebras.

Holy shit! A masterpiece! But it needed...something.

And finally,
        the
                acid
                        hits!

He cried in joy, filled by the beauty he had produced, a tremendous elation filling his cells with a splendorous collage of mind-blowing colors, as ancient songs of the hidden wisdom of the ages echoed the perfect attunement of the

Universe in every moment, in every movement, in every now.

The big, round opening notes of the "Who do you Love?" suite cut through the air of his bedroom like a glistening crystal knife. He'd listened to this Quicksilver record before, but it felt brand new now as if he were part of it, inside of it, an osmotic connection made of nothing but air. He picked up the album cover, and psychedelic cover art immediately made the kind of sense that took no words. The music throbbed and bobbed in his head, every single note and tone separate yet nuanced within the gestalt, fused tightly and forever within the flow and thrust of the song. He was stunned by the exquisite beauty of the tune, enriched by it, ingesting the melodious texture of the song as if it were vitamins and minerals dancing along his nerve channels.

His face flushed as a rush of pure white-hot radiance swept up into him as if from the molten core of Mother Earth, inflaming him with the beauty and power of a trillion stars with such power and glory that it would have knocked him off his feet if he hadn't already been sitting. He felt as if he'd been struck by lightning, but had seen no external light, as his head filled with the supernal like a fresh éclair with whipped cream from a pastry pipe. He felt a sudden familiarity with the room, as if he had always been there and the music...he could see the music drafting through him in undulating waves, each note defined as if painted from a palette of vast shades and shapes. He felt simultaneously full and whole, kept expanding as he lay down before he tumbled to the ground. As he lay back, he descended through multiple layers of light and sound surrounding and interpenetrating him.

As he melted, the bed became a part of his body, the music pulsing through him, transporting him to far-off, distant lands filled with delightful beings who all seemed to know him, to welcome him, as if he had been away a very long time and his return was expected! He had hardly a moment to examine this as wave after wave of titanic rushes blasted though him again, as if he were a primeval shore battered by a relentless ancient sea, aged even before the weak imaginings of one-celled life.

He saw/felt as through a portal in time, the presence of innumerable extinct creatures of myth and lore—and knew they had been real, as real as any other "reality" that was palpable. Time opened before him and he saw it as the supreme illusion, perhaps even delusion so well believed it was. A tiny patch of Sigmund Freud echoed in him then: "Time and history are man's only neuroses." He fell through an abyssal hole in his inner eye, as if he were a translucent dot flying rapidly through multiple star fields, time and history simultaneously unfolding as far backward and forward to the furthest horizons, like large rolls of vellum on a wooden staff, unfurling and unfolding in unending waves as rich and detailed historical contents leapt into vibrant life, and then inexorably drawn back to disappear forever. The future magnetically pulled at him, but Paul feared looking directly at it; suddenly felt that this huge awareness that he had released, or had been released through in him, a vessel only, an empty conduit temporarily being filled, and feared for the first time (now that it was far too late to stop it), the power of the magnificent substance he had ingested, a fool's move made out of haughtiness and hubris, now humbling him as if he stood before the mighty numinous Light of the Universe—not afraid of the Light per se, more awed by the immensity of the energy flowing unchecked through him, had attuned to him or he to it, unable to take it all in. He (or at least the "he" that was "he) witnessed a passing zephyr of thought, feeling to immediately vomit up the acid, as if that would somehow stop this incredible journey upon which he had already embarked, one that waited for all of humanity at some point in the evolution and fullness of time. He then chose (he? chose?) to look toward the future unfolding, and it too was sheets of the finest vellum gently falling forward and folding in on themselves endlessly, as images and pictures of future creatures and events, machinery beyond imagining, came forth vibrantly, breathed for an eternal moment, and then was re-captured by the omnipotent pages that glowed with an inner life that was completely unconcerned with the lives of any of who/what inhabited its pages, as if they were simply being transported upon a vast inclusive stage upon which or through which the machinations of a far greater power were being enacted.

In what seemed to be ever-shifting furthest distance, Paul saw an enormous spiraling vortex of energy from his point in space, yet without any effort at all drawing the "he" that was "him" inexorably toward and into it, radiating such exquisite magnetic force that it was impossible to fear and not surrender utterly to whatever the process "he" was experiencing. "He" was totally helpless yet filled with incredible joy, as if all of what "he" had called existence to this point had simply been a prelude, a rehearsal for what was yet to come, for all that was yet to unfold in the fullness and completeness of the cycles in which "he" was immersed—and saw to "his" amazement, "his" total incredulity, millions, billions, numbers beyond counting, of other spheres that were surrounded by their own individual wrapping of colors and rings as if each a miniature Saturn or Jupiter; and all of them undulating, rising and falling in what seemed to be an internal rhythm that was yet a part of a larger theme or scheme that was manifest everywhere, yet pulling it all toward a vast black hole, for that is what it was, "he" recognized it now. It all seemed so very natural, so very perfect, so very attuned with...something "he" could not quite conceive except to call it Wholeness, though it had many names: Creator, Allah, God, The Great Mystery, He She It All That Is, The One. "He" knew in that moment that "he" was seeing the rhythmic unfolding of Time Itself as an aspect, or dimension, of an even greater energy—to say being was to cheapen its power and glory, to almost anthropomorphize It—that filled the entire magnitude of the Universe (perhaps beyond? what was beyond? was there a beyond? how could there be anything beyond the Universe?)—and all of it absolute pulsed with the Great Light of innate awareness of its origins, all of it drawn back inexorably to Source, Origin of All, The Great Divine Mother.

As "he" tumbled into the whirling magnetic field, "his" very atomic structure torn apart by the massive pressure of the forces that called it home. "He" screamed, or thought that "he" had, or someone had, before a great peace descended upon "him" (who was "he" anyway?), and he drifted for eons, eternities, borne along on lucent waves and particles simultaneously filled with light, becoming light, being light indisputably, indubitably, inevitably, forever.

And awoke, if such a term could even apply, in great wonder, confused and disoriented, in a body with which he knew he had had a previous association, knew somehow to be "his" in the sense of temporary occupancy, and was shocked to find himself in an apartment he knew he had rented—yet the information pouring in was so at odds with what he had just experienced (he had, hadn't he?) that he had to shake his head in wonder, confused as if concussed, or coming off the greatest intoxicating experience he had ever had—yet one that was ongoing because he could still feel the electric energy pulsing through his body, so, so different that any other kind of stimulant he had ever taken—and vaguely at first, then more concretely, remembered taking the five tabs and wanting an experience. Jesus! What an experience he was having! Was continuing to have! His body told him it was far from over as he sat up slowly and realized that the album was still playing, the music still dancing along his fully invigorated nerve wires. He picked up the album cover and turned it over, to look into the stoned faces of the band looking back at him. They seemed to know him. Then they started speaking to him, as if they were actually in the room. He shook his head when he heard, or thought he heard, someone (from the album cover?) speaking back to him. No. No. It couldn't be. When he looked directly at the image of John Cipollina, he stepped off the album cover with his 1961 Gibson SG guitar!

Paul gawped as the Guitar God looked at Paul as if it were the most natural thing in the world. This absolutely amazing musician was definitely among those who were "at the vanguard of the revolution," as Stephen Gaskin had said one Monday night at the Straight Theater on Haight. (He also named dope dealers). John was wearing the leather jacket from the album cover, and his beautiful hair (parted on his left) cascaded down his chest. As stunned and stoned as Paul was, he paralyzed by the majesty of the moment, though vivid pictorial images of it would be seared into the neurons of his brain forever.

Paul finally managed some kind of inane comment like "Wow, man, I love your music!"

"Pretty trippy, huh?" said Cipollina, smiling as he looked around the small and slightly faded apartment, a survivor from an earlier area when the neighborhood had been far grander, and a porte-cochere was necessary to accommodate horse-drawn carriages.

"Reminds me a little of Quicksilver's old place on Water Street in San Francisco."

In spite of an aura of unreality that pervaded his perceptions, Paul knew that what he was seeing and hearing was real. His head, though, could not help but question what the other part of him was experiencing. It felt as if he had truly been split in two, when yet a third previously unheard-from part chimed in with the opinion that both of the others were crazy!

As Paul gradually unlimbered from the curare-like effects of his most profound shock, and wanting to take advantage of the presence of this visitor from another realm who had magically appeared in his bedroom, Paul idly wondered if he could manifest a gorgeous, sexy woman as easily!

"What...what are you doing here?"

Cipollina smiled at him and said "You called me!"

"What do you mean?"

"I am here, aren't I?"

Paul had been debating that very topic, seriously questioning his own senses, while enthralled by the undeniable presence of the man standing before him.

"I...I'm not sure. Are you? And how did I 'call you'?"

"You have a very strong mind, but I don't think you know that yet."

"What does that have to do with whether you're real?"

Paul smacked himself on the forehead with an open palm, "I'm talking with my own hallucination!"

"You don't really believe that!"

"How do you know?" Paul demanded angrily, then felt immediately contrite as this all might be really, really real on another dimension to which he was being introduced. Besides, he didn't want to be rude.

The rock master spread his hands and said "Here we are!"

Deciding to trust what was happening, though he still had some reservations, Paul chose to jump in.

"Am I real? Is all of this real?"

"You're real to me. I know that I'm here, so you must be."

"But how?"

"Who was it that said that there is more to life than meets the eye?"

"Just an ancient idiom, or an ancient idiot!"

"Didn't Frank Zappa once ask: 'How can you be in two places at once when you're really nowhere at all?'?"

Paul's brain worked for a moment, and he said, "Bishop Berkeley said we don't exist unless we are in the presence of each other!"

Paul felt overwhelmingly small and humbled, and then he noticed his crisp edges beginning to crumble. Tears fell from his eyes as he looked at the tall, thin man. Was he truly a multi-dimensional creature called through the ethers?

"I really don't care what's real! I'm...just tripped out that you came!" Then he laughed at his own cosmic joke.

John held up two finders in a peace sign, and smiled as he looked into Paul's eyes.

"Don't worry. We'll meet again."

"Wait! Don't go! I'm sorry! I believe in you! I have so many questions!"

With that, the image started to fade until there was nothing left but his twinkling eyes. Then they too blinked out.

CHAPTER SIX
Psychedelic Interludes
Oakland   April, 1970

After he finally escaped from the emotionally barren confines of St. Louis, he, like many others who had been lured in part or in toto, by the immense media-fueled delusion that life in the Golden State was the modern Promised Land, found he would not be able to live easily without working, and enjoy a pleasant, bucolic lifestyle of relative luxury. He almost immediately found out the error of his ways.

The very first portent of occurred on the first night he arrived at Toad's (without calling), and was greeted with immediate hostility by Toad's cousin Nicky, who was sharing Toad's apartment, and playing drums to Toad's bass as they strove to become rock stars. Additionally, Toad was working as much overtime as he could to support a new wife.

San Francisco was certainly the land of free love, and rock-and-roll. It was beautiful, magical, with amazing people doing incredible things. But it was still America, ruled by the same economic terrorism as anywhere else in the "Land of the Big PX" they had all dreamed about in the 'Nam. The reality of it demanded a very high price, maybe even his soul. As Toad had said to him shortly after he arrived: "Brother, you've just begun to pay dues!"

As much as she craved to live a rock-and-roll lifestyle, after a couple of nights at Toad's, he was politely, but firmly asked to find other accommodations. It was one of many hard body blows that his delusional system and his proposed new life, had to absorb.

He begrudgingly applied for Unemployment Benefits to get some cash flow going, but one of the requirements was to make five job applications a week. He made the mistake of excelling on the Post Office test! With his Veteran's preference, he almost immediately landed a job he didn't want in fairly short order—and found himself commuting across the Bay Bridge every night to go to work at the Oakland PO Distribution Center on Seventh and Cypress Streets.

It was one of the craziest places he had ever worked, especially on night shift. There were so many stoners working there! At any given time, Paul could drift out to the loading docks, ostensibly to hit the rest room, and find a friendly face smoking a joint. It made the night pass so much more quickly when he was loaded. And some of the crazy shit that happened, despite the fact that they (the ubiquitous "they") told us we were being surveilled from hidden catwalks behind, and spy holes in, the walls, so much merchandise disappeared from that place—once an entire twenty-six volume edition of the Encyclopedia Britannica! Of *course, Hold Baggage from Viet Nam was regularly plundered since it all arrived in Oakland before being re-directed.*

Commuting back and forth across the Bay Bridge every day, especially when he was exhausted, soon became a real drag. The place where he had been staying was a five bedroom flat occupied by eight itinerant musicians. So, he found a place in Toad's neighborhood. It was a large one bedroom with plenty of windows, and a back porch—and only $105 a month! The Chinese landlord and his wife smoked so much opium on the weekends that anyone walking in the building could get a contact high just walking in the building! So, he started living a block away from MacArthur Park, at 37th and Webster. It was one of the neighborhoods to which many who had fled the rising crime rate and violence of the Haight-Ashbury for other neighborhoods, like the Castro and Potrero Hill in The City, and there in north Oakland, a very hip neighborhood populated by all kinds of artists, musicians, and writers.

Susan Seddons Boulée lived and produced her exquisite art just a few blocks away on Manila Street. On his street, there was an incredible musician who had toured with Miles Davis; a writer who had shot speed with Dylan in the Village in the early '60s; and two dope dealers, who between them were a one stop shop for everything but heroin. The latter had been declared anathema in our little neighborhood.

He often hitchhiked to the Fillmore West, near Market and Van Ness, from his favorite spot to flag rides at the MacArthur Freeway on-ramp. Though he usually caught rides easily, tonight he seemed invisible. Nobody seemed to know him, everybody passed him by.

He had dropped before leaving the house, assuming he would get a quick ride as he always did. He just so wanted to get high, to be psychedelic, that he decided to do so, figuring that it wouldn't come on until he got to the Fillmore. But standing there far longer than he had anticipated, he felt an anticipatory rush, a wave of goose-pimples sweeping up his arms and the back of his neck followed by a Parkinson-like tremor. Shaking his head, he took a deep breath and put on his best smile, sending a silent prayer to the Universe.

It's just a preliminary rush, he thought to himself, when another wave of electric splinters shot through his fingers, and a stream of colored stars shot into the sky from his fingertips. While he was assimilating this, he was struck by the Doppler effect of the freeway traffic noise melting, funneling a greasy smear like a warped wail into his brain.

Jesus! It was really coming on! Then the wind became a compilation of a capella psychedelic tunes punctuated by electronic special effects. His entire body started rippling outward in waves of green, yellow, turquoise, crimson, and violet, all melting and merging, becoming lighter and brighter, more and more ethereal as the energy expanded from his core center in shimmering wavelets, inside and outside amalgamating as he swam on the ethereal waves, with only the slightest connection to his human form, a thin red thread between beingness and nothing.

"Hey!"

A voice called to Paul as through an old megaphone.

"Hey! Anybody home?"

The driver of a nondescript Ford van had stopped, and lowered the passenger side window. He was wearing dark sunglasses and had called out to Paul more than once.

"Where you goin', man?

Paul mumbled *"Fillmore,"* and wobbled as he attempted to keep standing.

"Get in, man. I'll take you there!"

Paul got into the custom-made captain's chair with which the driver had replaced the standard seat. The man looked into his eyes, and smiled broadly. Then he reached over, and handed Paul a set of Sennheiser headphones; and plugged an RCA jack directly into a receptacle built into the dash. Blazing psychedelic music filled his entire Universe as he settled back into the seat, and drifted away surfing mind-expanding waves.

A tap-tap-tapping reverberated through his earphones, and reached up to smack at the irritating insect. When he hit himself in the side of the head, he opened his eyes, and rotated his skull. He was in Hickory Alley, immediately adjacent to the front entrance of the Fillmore.

"Wow, thanks, man!" was all Paul could spit out.

The driver flashed him a Peace sign.

"Glad I could help you make your trip!"

Berkeley   May 30, 1970

Even from two blocks away, Paul could see the almost atomic glow around Shattuck and Allston. Bill Graham sometimes used the Berkeley Community Theater to showcase stars in this more intimate setting—including Paul Robeson, Bob Dylan, Stan Getz, The Grateful Dead, Joni Mitchell, Frank Zappa, James Taylor, Richie Havens, Harry Chapin, and The Band. Tonight, Jimi Hendrix was giving an intimate performance.

Paul was late. Jimi was already playing. Waves of his completely unique ultra-high dimensional tones splashed out into the night sky as Paul half-ran along the side of the building. There were a bunch of thick insulated cables stretched across the sidewalk running into the building through an open side window. As he got closer, the more clearly he heard an unmistakable hiss emanating from the truck.

That sound was almost as compelling as the other-worldly strains wrenched from Jimi's Stratocaster. There were at least a thousand ticketless people milling around trying to buy scalped tickets for the already sold out gig. The audience cheered wildly when Jimi tuned his guitar and then swung into "Fire." The opening chords stimulated his spine and a wave of light seemed to come from both the inside and the outside simultaneously and converged in elongated concentric circles centered on his heart, like a massive figure eight. The distinctive hiss danced like a snake rhythm through his brain, drawing him closer and closer with such demanding intensity that he surrendered to the impulse to slowly open the door, and peek in—first his nose, then his chin, and finally his eyes looking into the complex interior of the sound recording truck.

The entire inside of the truck had been fitted out with the very finest quality sound recording equipment, including a two inch reel-to-reel tape recorder that was methodically turning as its operator—six feet two inches tall, with a beard down almost to his waist and his hair tied back into a long pony tail, wearing a plaid shirt and jeans—checked gauges and switches on amps and soundboards, and then drew deeply on a long red rubber tube connected to a tall, blue-

painted canister. He looked up from the tank directly into Paul's eyes—and far from the potentially hostile glare Paul had been expecting, the grizzled hippie greeted him with a grin, raised both eyebrows in a Groucho Marx imitation, and tipped the tube toward Paul.

"Wow! Goddamn! Thanks, brother!" as Jimi swung into a wild version of "Johnny B Goode."

Suddenly each and every single note from the magic fingers and heart of Music God Jimi soared, shimmered, and raced through him, each one encased in a tiny cocoon yet intimately connected to every other note, the chords weaving a story without words, painting pictures with sound in a perfect dance like a divine transmission of transcendental wholeness obliterating all separateness—and then flew beyond everyday concreteness into entirely new realms of joy, love, and clarity.

Paul fell back, extending the tube in his hand in the vague general direction of the man whose name he still did not know.

"Wow!" was all he could manage.

The Recording Engineer turned the spigot off, and went back to monitoring gauges, pushing slides and twisting knobs, capturing the cathartic, other-dimensional music of the man who would too soon be taken from us forever, except on vinyl, cellulose, and silicon.

CHAPTER SEVEN
Phencyclidine Highway
Sacramento   September, 1974

What a rowdy ass place!

Paul shook his head as he strolled through the now-quiet unit.

Potential psychiatric patients rolled through the door of the ER like a Biblical flood, and quickly up to the seventh floor. To the casual eye it might have seemed that the psych screeners had nothing but severe mental illness diagnoses in their respective kit bags; or had failed to remember that half-way houses and short-term care facilities still existed.

Most of the admits had been pretty damn righteous—only the occasional Borderline Personality manipulating for a place to stay until the next welfare check, or a Malingerer who wanted to get out of a court date. They had been having a rash of PCP admits that had swamped them like the crest of a big wave!

Phencyclidine—originally developed and marketed as an anesthetic to provide numbness and dissociation—was quickly abandoned because of deleterious "side effects." It produced euphoria and was highly addictive, producing hallucinations, distorted body image, and loss of ego boundaries. It was renowned for inducing paranoia (often leading to homicidal impulses and violence), suicidal impulses, and depersonalization.

They had had four or five admits a week all summer, though that seemed to be finally slowing down. Ordinarily, with severely agitated patients, they'd just give him Ativan or some other benzodiazepine to inhibit the agitation and aggression until the temporarily deranged patient de-escalated. With PCP, they were all contraindicated. Even Haldol, when it was rarely ordered, had no effect on the psychotic-like symptoms, and tended to create dangerous effects like dystonia, akathisia, or oculogyric crisis. Generally, treatment was simple: seclude and restrain until the most florid symptoms abated, which might take as long as two days, depending on the purity and the amount of substance used.

Paul rolled his eyes as he looked out through the chicken-wired Plexiglas window in the first steel door that opened into the sally port leading to the unit. This afternoon's admission was the first such in the last three days, and Paul hoped it signaled the end of the tidal wave. He came in half-carried by six Sheriff's Deputies, who despite wearing handcuffs, leg chains, and belly restraints, was struggling, cursing, spitting, snarling, completely-out-of-control, and clearly crazed individual. Another one! Shit!

They had drawn bloods in the ER before they called the unit, but could not get a urine specimen. The patient had been extremely uncooperative. The deputies had previously secured their weapons in the lock boxes outside the ER, and Paul opened the unit door to admit the writhing mass of humans, after one of the deputies secured the outer door.

The man who was the focus of all the attention was disheveled-looking, wearing raggedy, tattered clothes. His body odor preceded him as he came onto the unit. He continued to snarl and curse, then attempted to bite one of the deputies as she put a towel over his mouth to stop him spitting.

The man could not have been more than thirty, but his skin was leathery and severely ravaged, giving him the appearance of someone decades older. He was emaciated, only weighing around a hundred pounds, ribs visible, and eyes bulging like a frightened bull facing the toreador's sword.

Paul led the deputies to the farthest seclusion room on the unit, and queried them.

"Has he been searched?"

"We patted him down, but didn't search the pockets. No guns or knives. Nothing sharp."

Even if they were double-gloved, law enforcement was sometimes hesitant to search vagrant's pockets for fear of encountering uncapped needles or other "surprises."

"No problemo! I'll check his clothes once we get him four-pointed...maybe five might be wise," Paul said, again looking at the belly restraint. They couldn't use chains in seclusion, but two sheets knotted together would work just as effectively when secured to the bed frame.

They kept him controlled while very carefully disrobing him, one appendage at a time. Paul noticed that the man had a large number of scratches under his chin and down his neck. Then he noted other, longer ones running down his arms. Paul immediately diagnosed formication. It was such an odd word, derived from the Latin word for *ant.* It described the sensation of insects crawling up and down the body, triggering the reflex to scratch.

Jim Rivers, the only other male staff on PMs, arrived carrying leather restraints, followed by two of the nurses, all wearing double gloves. They laid the man face down on the bed, leaning heavily on his shoulders and pinning his legs. Two people held him at the waist, keeping him from bucking his hips as they removed the rest of his clothing. Two Deputies attached themselves to each appendage, as the staff members secured each arm and leg with a leather restraint.

"Help me get his head better!" yelled one of the female deputies. "He's trying to bite me!"

One of the male deputies responded with a big smile, "I don't blame him!"

"Fuck you, Jamieson!"

"Any time!"

"OK. That's enough of that! Let's get this done" said one of the nurses.

Paul quickly checked to make sure all of the leather belts had been pulled through the metal bridge on the belts, and secured with the small locking mechanism.

"Everybody ready?"

He made eye contact all around, and they all affirmed.

"OK. Lock him up!"

The man kept muttering and cursing through the towel in his mouth, attempting to dislodge it as he was secured to the bed. Only after the knotted sheets were tightened around his waist and to the bed frame, did someone remove it. Paul stood guard by the door while everyone exited the room. Outside the room, Paul did a further search of the man's pockets—coming up with thirty-two cents in loose change, a sodden pack of matches, and a small, black rock.

"Rehash anybody?"

No one seemed inclined to want one, especially since the procedure had been accomplished so smoothly.

Just then Kathy, the Charge Nurse, stepped up and said, "I need a report from one of you," looking at the sergeant who was the most senior of the Deputies.

"Yes, ma'am!"

Jim made eye contact and motioned toward the staff lounge. Paul followed, and they walked together, in silent company. Then they went to the Men's Room to wash their hands after de-gloving.

Jim was totally straight-looking. Short hair, clean shaven, with a wife and two kids. Only five foot six inches and small for the position, he had nonetheless played guard on his high school team. He coached his son's team, and had invited Paul to watch several times. They did not socialize outside of work, but here on the unit they were a team, a very good team. They had worked together for almost a year now, and had done a lot of seclusion and restraint together. When they were on duty together, they always teamed up whenever any disturbance threatened on the unit. They trusted each other, and knew well each other's' moves.

"So, what'd ya think?"

"Looks like just another nasty guy on PCP."

"Yeah, I know. I meant, is he the end of the last wave or the beginning of a new one?"

"Oh shit! Don't even talk that way!"

"I was just thinking..."

"Well stop it! You know what they say? 'You get what you think about.'"

"The Incredible String Band says that you 'become that which you desire.'"

"Wow! Then I'm going to be a beautiful shaved pussy next life!"

"Jive ass!"

"It's true!"

"No, come on. Answer me."

"I really think we're through the worst of it."

"Yeah, me too. And damn glad of it too."

"Should we have a group tonight?"

"I dunno. Maybe. You think this population is up to it?"

"Maybe. We got some pretty spacey customers here right now."

"No shit! But group would eat up an hour of the shift."

"I know. But then we gotta chart on each one of them."

"Got to anyway."

"I know. But that guy is gonna need fifteen-minute checks. You got a hit that anyone else is gonna go off tonight?"

Jim believed in Paul's penchant for knowing when patients were going to get agitated, an ability that was sometimes disputed by those who to whom it had not yet been proven—until they had seen it proved true, as Paul had, over and over.

"Not tonight, I don't think. We got an open bed. You think we might get another admit?"

"No, I don't think so. I might try to get Tomas to play a game of chess."

"You and chess! Why do you keep playing with him? He always kicks your ass!"

"He's brilliant!"

"Yeah, when he isn't smearing shit on the walls!"

"That's part of what makes him fascinating to me! How he can be so brilliant on the one hand, and so schizzy on the other? I wonder if there's a correlation."

"Have you ever talked to him about physics? You know he has a degree from Cal Tech?"

"Yeah, he mentioned it, but I don't get into it with him like you do."

"I've never seen you go into the seclusion room when he's painting the walls!"

"Not me, brother!"

"You know, I almost got written up for that!"

"I remember. But he's improved so much since then, they had to back off!!"

"My being there with him showed him he that he was not repulsive, even at his worst!"

"But why?"

"I don't know really! He was in seclusion and painting the walls. I just felt I had to go in!"

"Jesus, man! I could never have done that!"

"But I was right! Don't you see? I was right!"

"And you almost got fired!"

"So?"

Jim shook his head, and said "I don't know, man. I've just never had that kind of mind."

"And I always have!"

They both started as a horrendous roar cut through the air like a human sonic boom.

"AAAARRRRRRRRGGGGGHHHHH!!

"What the fuck?"

Next, they heard a rhythmic thumping. They sprang up and ran toward it.

"It's him!"

As they neared the seclusion room, they could hear more guttural groaning, and the sound of chopping coming from the seclusion room.

Jim looked ashen as he turned back from the Plexiglas window.

""Oh fuck! The son of a bitch is out of restraints!"

"What? Impossible!"

"See for yourself!"

Paul jumped back when he saw the face of the newly-admitted man looking back at him through the glass, lips pulled back in a rictus of rage. One arm and both legs were still wearing disconnected restraints, though he had managed somehow—fueled by the PCP "runnin' all 'round his brain" —to pull loose one of the legs of the bed, previously secured in concrete, and was attempting to chop his way to freedom. The high-grade numbing effect of the anesthetic was obviously working both in his favor and to his detriment simultaneously. He could neither feel pain, nor did he realize how badly he had injured himself. He spit when he saw Paul's face in the window.

"Jesus!"

Kathy came running up, and they quickly apprised her of the situation.

"I'll call for Mister Strong!"

The door shivered as if being battered by gale force winds.

He exchanged a telepathic look with Jim, and then nodded as the overhead page went off.

"Mr. Strong! Mr. Strong to the Crisis Unit! STAT!"

By now, a small crowd of staff had gathered, all wanting to indulge in the adrenaline in the air. Unfortunately, many of them were new and relatively inexperienced.

Paul exchanged a glance with Kathy, who spoke.

"I need Charlotte and Antonia to stay here with us. Everybody else get back to the unit!"

There was some grumbling, but they dispersed as the "Go Team" quickly strategized.

"Antonia, open the door and pull it wide. Jim will use the mattress, Paul right behind him. Push him against the wall. I'll be right behind them, and secure the arm with the club. Antonia, you get the other. The Deputies right behind us!"

It went about as smoothly as could be expected when you have a crazed, drug-addled patient trying to chop his way out of the seclusion room, and half a dozen adrenalized deputies waiting to charge in. Jim and Paul were like butter. Antonia unlocked the door, and swung it wide. Paul put himself on Jim's right shoulder and added the force of his body to Jim's as they charged, and slammed the man into the wall like a locomotive with no brakes. The man grunted, exhaling his atrocious breath through damaged, ruined teeth. By the time he got his breath back, Paul had taken the weapon away from him. As he turned to hand the weapon behind him, the crazed patient splattered fresh blood across Paul shirt front before Kathy secured the hand, mashed down with a pile of gauze pads and two towels before wrapping the whole package tight with Ace bandages.

There were two people on each appendage, and two holding the guy's waist as he bucked and squirmed. The Deputies were securing all of the leather restraints before Kathy personally supervised the mangled hand.

"Towel! Need another towel," said one deputy, with spittle sliding off his chin.

Paul watched as another deputy slipped a hand around the man's throat, and started applying pressure. He glanced briefly over his shoulder to ascertain if anyone else could see what was happening, and it seemed no one could. Someone handed in a small pile of towels, one of which was immediately put loosely over the patient's face, as he continued to thrash and sputter, then started to scream that somebody was trying to choke him. The deputy in question looked into Paul's eyes, and they smiled.

"Sir! Sir! You're simply going to have to settle down!"

"Fuck you!" came the muffled voice from under the towel.

"Sir! Please cooperate! We're just trying to help you!" Paul said in my best psych-speak, mostly for the record.

The man kept trying to buck us off of his body, and was spewing a tremendous stream of invective, focused on the nature and quality of our collective parentage, calling all of us "motherfuckers" related to insects or less evolved species. Kathy came back in with a loaded and capped syringe.

"Got some Ativan IM here!"

Though it was not usually given to PCP patients, but by now this guy's blood pressure was probably so high that reducing it radically might be a good thing. Plus, he would have to be going to the ER forthwith, and they needed him calmed down before they could transport him.

"Shoot him in the thigh! I don't want to turn him over!"

"No problemo!" she said, and then proceeded to shoot him. She cupped her hand around the used plastic syringe with the unprotected needle, got to her knees, then her feet, and backed away. When she got to the corner of the seclusion room, she re-capped the needle and left.

"You motherfuckers are poisoning me!!"

"No, sir! We're just trying to help you!"

"Fuck you, and your mother too!" came out, garbled through the towel.

Paul was very used to this kind of invective from patients. He had long ago closed down a certain place in his head that allowed calmness to flow through, and show a placid face.

"I'm sure you'll regret saying that when you feel better!"

After they had secured the man to a gurney, Kathy kept hold of the injured hand, compressing the wrist below the padding that was bleeding through despite the pressure she was applying. Although in severe pain, and alternately cursing them and demanding for narcotics, the man nonetheless kept fighting against the restraints, including with his damaged hand and wrist. A towel was left draped across the man's face as he kept attempting to spit on them.

"If I get out of these restraints, I'm gonna fuck you up!"

Of course, his declarations did nothing but fire the ire of all those attending—giving rise to grimaces, grunts, groans, flushing faces, small jabs to accessible body parts, and even several mumbled comments containing the words "asshole," "cocksucker," and "jackoff." Angry looks flashed amongst them all, and there was no doubt in Paul's mind that, if he had not been there, the drug-induced madman on the gurney would have been given some shots. Paul was himself tempted, but he did not belong to the fellowship of Deputies, and they did not belong to the fellowship of Nursing Staff. There were certain unwritten rules, and lines were not to be crossed.

The staff in the ER, having been alerted, immediately surrounded the condign patient. A very officious doctor insisted that we remove the man's restraints; and when he shifted the towel on the man's face, he was greeted by a face full of spittle and curse words.

"You motherfuckers let me out! I'll fucking kill all of you!"

If he had not already been being held against his will as a danger to self and others, under the provisions of the California Welfare and Institutions Code Section 5150, he would certainly qualify now. Paul addressed this with the ER staff.

"This man is on a 5150 hold! The Deputies will stay on guard here! When he is medically clear, notify the Psych Unit immediately!"

One of the nurses, Adele, stepped up next to Paul, and spoke to him *sub rosa*.

"That was unnecessary. You're not the only professional here, you know?"

"Hey! You're right. I'm just jacked up!"

"Better wash your hands while you have a chance."

"I will. Thanks."

Several of the Deputies had gratefully taken the opportunity to clean up and go back to duty. Several others were lingering on the periphery of the plastic-sheeted enclosure into which the patient had been wheeled, still restrained to the gurney.

While more senior staff scurried about, preparing to deal with his serious injuries, Raymond, a young Certified Nursing Assistant (CNA) was left momentarily in charge of the crazed man. The young man's lack of training and life experience quickly showed. In a very naïve attempt to engage the clearly psychotic man in some form of "meaningful" dialogue, he listened to a simple request—fueled by the sociopathy surfacing from beneath his morphine-mediated pain.

"You're an asshole just like the rest of them!"

"No, sir, I am not!"

"Then loosen up these fucking restraints!"

"I can't do that, sir."

"Just a little! This one is hurting me!" he said, slightly lifting his undamaged right hand.

"I suppose" he answered, thinking, semi-delusionally, that it would help "establish a better rapport with the patient," as he would later write in his report.

As soon as Raymond moved to the side of the bed, and produced the thin metal key that would unlock the leather restraint, the patient began tensing himself in preparation for making the move he was planning.

Raymond let his attention wander during the split-second it took to unlock the lock and release the belt, the man on the gurney struck him in the face, though he did not knock Raymond out. Neither was he able to secure the key from his hand nor stop the younger man from crying out for help.

Nose bleeding, drool dripping, he managed to eke out a tortured cry.

"HELP! RIGHT NOW!"

Two deputies ripped aside the curtain and immediately took in the situation. They secured the uninjured arm and reinserted the belt through the bracket, and tightened it down until the patient screamed and cursed. Paul was immediately behind them, and after verifying that the young man could breathe through his broken nose, he crossed to the gurney and grabbed the injured arm very roughly, and pressed down—eliciting a horrendous scream that brought two more nurses and several other staff onto the scene.

A young female CNA immediately came to him, and started shouting in his face.

"You're hurting him! Stop it right now!"

Before Paul could scream at her and tell her what a useless douche bag she was, the Nursing Supervisor stepped up, and asked her to leave.

"But he was hurting him!"

"She wasn't even here! The man got his arm loose and broke Raymond's nose!"

"He was hurting him!"

"Sheila, go attend to some other duty. Now!"

"But..."

"Go! Now!"

The Nursing Supervisor turned to Paul with a questioning look in her eye.

Paul responded with disdain and anger.

"What? Do you really think I would harm a patient? I was simply securing his arm! He got loose and broke Raymond's nose, goddamn it!"

"I understand. It looked a little rough, what you were doing."

Paul looked at her incredulously.

"You mean you believe that shit she was spouting?! She wasn't even here!"

"I know that. And you know that. But she's young and naïve. She believes she's right about everything. She may write an IR, even file a complaint."

"Just what I need!"

CHAPTER EIGHT
He Meets the Man
San Francisco May 1979

Paul had hit it off immediately with Herb Ballman. They both loved books, good food, fine wine and finer women. And, of course, cocaine. During the course of their first few meetings, they had shared all four.

Herb was bald, portly, and wore round glasses. He smoked ten cigars a day, usually H. Uppman or Partagas, though he wasn't averse to Romeo y Julietta 1875 Churchill Tube. He didn't look intellectually blessed or financially aware, but he ran a string of used book stores throughout San Francisco; and was, by all accounts, extremely well to do. He was outrageously funny. He had what Paul called a 'wacky crack" —extremely erudite and sarcastic simultaneously. He often wore a Groucho Marx like expression including raised eyebrows and a half-smoked cigar.

"Jesus, man! Your shit is so much better than what I've got! Where'd you get it?" Paul couldn't help but comment after seeing and tasting Herb's cocaine.

"A friend of mine in Marin."

"Wow! Great shit! Can I meet him?'

"I don't know, man. He's a very private guy. But I'll ask."

Herb was bopping, gesticulating—amped up and full of power. He introduced the two men to each other, and scurried to the front of the store to "price some new merchandise."

Magnus Du Bre was six foot three, and had massive shoulders. He wore his hair in a short, thick Afro, and was immaculately dressed in taupe linen trousers and a white silk shirt. He closely resembled what he later told Paul of his heritage—French, Chickasaw, and Black. He looked as if he had received the best of his parent's gene pools and features, and was quite good-looking, always getting hit on by hot White chicks.

"Nice to meet you. Herb tells me you're a chess player?"

Paul brightened immediately.

"Yeah! You?'

"Love the game! You play regularly?'

"No. Usually can't find good competition, especially when I like to play."

"When's that?"

"Midnight. Or later."

"Me too. Too busy during the day."

"Me too."

"Let's play sometime."

"Sounds great to me."

Magnus inclined his head toward the back of the store where Herb kept a small office.

"Herb tells me your product could be...higher quality!"

"Whoa, man! That's pretty rude!"

"I've tasted your stuff. You can do a lot better."

He pulled out a large bindle, the center of a centerfold shot—a clean shaven perfect pussy—and dumped several rocks onto the small telescopic lens that Herb used for a mirror.

"Help yourself!"

Paul only hesitated for a moment, then finely chopped two large lines. Then he rolled a hundred-dollar bill and offered it to Magnus.

"No, man. I want you to have a good taste."

Paul put the tip of his baby finger into the small pile and then onto the end of his tongue. The taste was sharper, and had a much more pronounced ether scent than any with which he was accustomed. But, as they say, the proof of the pudding was in the snorting, so...

"WOW!"

Paul's head jerked back as an electric blast shot through him from toes to head, and left him glowing like a neon sign.

"Jesus! This shit is great! Where can I get some?"

"We need to talk a little about business."

"Whaddya mean?"

Magnus stepped forward, snorted the other line, and laid the hundred-dollar bill on the countertop, and then smiled.

"This is my product. This is my business."

————

Within the week, Paul had had several phone conversations with Magnus, who invited him over "after business hours" for a game of chess and a chat at 0200 one Tuesday morning.

Paul went to into his apartment, a two bedroom that included the studio where he painted. The walls were festooned with a variety of paintings and mixed-media collage works-in-progress.

"Your stuff reminds me a lot of the early abstract expressionists."

"Yeah I always liked the early guys—Kandinsky, Max Ernst, de Kooning, Gorky, Rothko."

"Yeah, me too! I like Martha Graham's stuff, and Jackson Pollock, even though he got overrated when he got famous. Klee too was an early favorite of mine!"

"You really do know a little about art!"

"A little. I'm a writer, but I've always wanted to paint."

"I've done some writing. I've had a couple of plays produced too."

"So, how do you end up doing...this?

"You mean the flow?"

"'The flow?'"

"Cocaina!"

"Oh."

"When things are really moving, there's a sense of magic...of flow."

"Got it!"

"So? Want a line?"

"Hell yes! Does the Pope shit in the woods?"

That first line was the beginning of a long, productive business and personal relationship, one that would last more than twenty years, though neither of knew it at the time.

Cocaine acts by inhibiting the reuptake of serotonin, norepinephrine, and dopamine—resulting in a greater concentration of all three neurotransmitters in the brain. Selective serotonin reuptake inhibitors (SSRI) such as Prozac have a similar action, and their legality makes them the source of a twelve billion dollars a year profit for the psychopharmaceutical industry—while the cocaine trade at that same time was estimated to be worth $150-500 billion a year.

Several lines later, and deeply engrossed in a game of chess, Magnus started schooling Paul on the ins-and-outs of the modern cocaine trade. Even though indigenous people have been chewing it for over a thousand years (always with an alkaline substance like lime), it had not been synthesized into a powder form until 1896, after which time it became a highly addictive and transportable product (at first widely advertised by Sigmund Freud).

"I don't know what kind of deal you have now, but I can do better—especially product quality."

"What do you mean?"

"My shit is so much better than what Herb showed me of yours."

"Oh?"

"And I can make you a better price—and you have to do me a small favor with Herb."

"What's that?"

"He...likes to think of himself as a player. He drives all the way over here once or twice a week for a single g(ram). I'm...wanting to unload some of my smaller customers, especially ones in The City. It's just too much traffic!"

"O-K! And?"

"I'll give you a price that's good enough that you can take care of him at the price he's been paying me—$80 a g."

"Shit! I'm paying almost that much! And I have to have half cash!"

"How much for an OZ?"

"Shit! I can't afford an ounce yet!'

"If you could?"

"I don't know! $1800? $2000?"

"How about I give you your first O for...$1500?"

"Wow! No shit?"

"That way you can take care of Herb, still make money on him. There's a few other possible in The City too. You can easily charge everybody else $120 a gram."

Paul was stunned. Wow! What a great opportunity! If he could just keep his nose out of the product...

Paul extended his hand, and they shook. Magnus handed him his first ounce. He would call when he had the required amount, and be given another. He was to bring the money in an envelope, all bills facing the same way with no tears or bent corners—and nothing smaller than a $20 bill, preferably fifties or hundreds.

(Paul found out later that Magnus had a direct connect with the Cartagena Cartel in Marin County. They were moving a hundred kilos a week at that time, and Marin Country was named the "Cocaine Capital of the United States," outstripping even New York City).

Paul stood and they shook hands again. Paul put his ounce baggie, thick with rocks, into a manila envelope inside his leather brief case.

He thanked his new connect for the game.

"We should do this again some time!'

"We will, but I have a feeling you're gonna' be really busy!

CHAPTER NINE
Home Again, Sort Of
San Francisco July 1979

Late a-goddamn-gain! Oh, fucking well! Tough shit!

Paul was thinly disguised as a Licensed Psychiatric Technician, working the night shift at San Francisco General Hospital Unit 7-A—which thought itself was a conundrum, maybe even a paradox.

He was making fifty dollars an hour selling coke, and the same amount for eight hours of mind-breaking bullshit on the unit. And putting up with that fucking Charge Nurse bitch Marty who was far worse than any of the patients—all for the sake of maintaining the façade of having a regular, legal source of income. He had spoken to Magnus about it on a number of occasions, and he kept encouraging Paul to keep his job—the kind of front that many in the trade maintained was necessary. He was always reminded of one of Bob Dylan's famous lines that he cited almost every day: "To live outside the law, you must be honest."

If he were to be completely honest, and admit to his cocaine habit, he would be fired and arrested, thrown in prison, and have what little credibility he had ever had dismissed out of hand. Yet he was bright and articulate, did good, meaningful work with the patients; and according to MENSA, a certified (perhaps even certifiable!) genius. So where exactly was the intersection of the two—being real and being honest?

Paul parked illegally on Vermont Street. He would likely get a parking ticket for parking immediately adjacent to and above the Emergency Room entrance in the lot where only doctors and administrators were "authorized" to park. He decided it could just join the dozen in his backseat!

Although Lombard Street had been designated as a tourist mecca because it was relatively accessible, and in a far better neighborhood than Vermont Street on Potrero Hill—the latter was actually the "crookedest street in the world." When the number and degree of the angles was measured, Vermont beat out Lombard by a large margin.

He dipped the tip of his little finger into the bottom half of his Deering grinder, and had a small sniff as his racing thoughts continued speeding along his neurons. He decided to give himself a few more minutes of peace and solitude before heading in.

He was really feeling his personal split echoed the one with which he was regularly embroiled. Ever since he had been home, anything related to with government duplicity could set him off severely. The process by which citizens were manipulated to agree with governmental mandates as if they were "for their own good," and support actions (like war) without thought or approval. God! It really pissed him off!

Oh shit! Now that it got started, he knew he was going to get worked up. The cocaine was doing a good job of lubricating his dendrites! So, he decided to do a little more!

"Dulce et decorum est pro patria mori."

What a fucking lie! Horace really nailed it when he called it the Noble Lie: "It is a sweet and beautiful thing to give your life for your country."

Enticing people to join the military to support the permanent war economy, to give their lives for the profit motive, was utterly ludicrous! It all drove his assessment that anyone who had the right to send men into battle should themselves have served in combat, borne out by the famous quote of General Sherman in 1865: "Tis only those who have never heard a shot, never heard the shriek and groans of the wounded and lacerated...that cry aloud for more blood, more vengeance, more desolation."

Even though Paul had been home ten years now, he still thought it was ludicrous that anyone with half a brain could expect vets returning home to assume normalcy, as if war had just been a passing phase that should be relegated it to an obscure place in the dusty archives of one's personal history book! Truly absurd!

The longer he sat, trying to convince himself to go in, the later it got, and the harder it got to walk through the doors and go to work. Yet he couldn't stir, he was so lost in his own thoughts and preoccupations.

He made the mistake of thinking of fucking politicians sitting in their upholstered chairs in air-conditioned offices making decisions that affected the lives of thousands who were sweating their asses off in far-away lands risking death and dismemberment! For what? Oil! For the profits of war! The CIA had murdered dozens of duly elected leaders to put in office those who were "more attuned to democratic ideals" —most often placing a right-wing dictator or other fascist in power who agreed with the attitudes of those who occupied the underbelly of the current administration.

Now it looked likely we were gonna have the King of Assholes, Ronald fucking Reagan for President! What a disaster! Anyone who had lived in California when he was governor realized what a totally incompetent, fascist, paternalistic, racist asshole he was! Especially after he called in the National Guard on the UC students! As if his B-grade acting skills qualified him to be President? What a jackoff!

He started to go in, then had another thought. He was fading, so: Another little sniff wouldn't hurt, would it?

The only thing that he and his father had ever agreed on was that they both hated Ronald Reagan! What was worse was that his father always reminded him of that asshole!

Fucking Reagan! He closed Mendocino, DeWitt, and Fairview to put 30,000 "ex-patients" on the street, released as "improved" —most of them loaded up on the miracle neuroleptics like Thorazine, the chemical straitjacket, the chemical lobotomy, the chemical blasphemy! Or worse, Haldol, synthesized from meperidine (Demerol), and even approved by the World Health Organization!

He also eliminated 1700 staff positions, all of it done to make Ronnie Ray Gun look good, to make his stats shine and him as a right-wing wonder! Paul knew the mental health system would suffer under Reagan, even though it didn't really start with him.

In 1962, President Kennedy was hoodwinked by then-Governor Rockefeller and some of his handpicked mental health cronies, including Menninger (of clinic fame), who convinced him of the necessity of "deinstitutionalizing" mental patients, and moving toward a more "community-minded" approach—leading to an investment of billions of dollars to ostensibly build community-based treatment centers and close large-scale institutions like state hospitals, and an even greater emphasis on phenothiazines as a cornerstone of treatment for those marginalized and deemed "mentally ill."

One of Reagan's "cost cutting measures" was the Lanterman-Petris-Short Act (LPS) of 1967, that virtually abolished involuntary hospitalization except in extreme emergencies. It was ostensibly aimed at "stemming entry into the state hospital by encouraging the community system to accept more patients, hopefully improving quality of care while allowing state expense to be alleviated by the newly available federal funds." It was also supposed to protect the rights of patients by allowing them to refuse treatment, unless they were clearly a danger to themselves or another; and it facilitated release of many patients, ostensibly to use community mental health treatment programs funded by the Short-Doyle Act of 1957.

Paul had seen Reagan's perfidy with his own eyes. A beautiful, brand-new such center was set up in Berkeley, somewhere just off Telegraph Avenue, near the campus—on Dwight Way, maybe Bancroft. It was opened with a huge press conference with Ray Gun himself smiling for the cameras. The real problem was that there was nowhere for the "homeless mentally ill" (the vogue term of the times) to keep their meager belongings. The regime place severe restrictions on who could come in. If you were loaded on drugs or alcohol, or had no ID; you were not allowed in, while many who were meant to be "served" either had criminal backgrounds or were actively eluding capture; and they felt violated by having to give up what little privacy and sovereignty they had. Most customers refused to take the brain-damaging chemicals after discharge from the hospital.

The facility closed down practically overnight three months after opening to grand acclaim. All of the furnishings, even the carpets, were removed. They placed a small sign on the door told people to call the local community mental health agency for "further assistance." So much for Ronald Reagan's word!

He decided to have one more little fingertip full! God! This shit was so good!

This inevitably led to the vast creation of board-and-care homes. By 1975, in Los Angeles alone, there were in excess of 11,000 ex-state-hospital patients living in board-and-care facilities, paid directly by the state. Beverly Enterprises was one of the for-profit chains, and owned 38 homes. They were mostly run as "businesses," and squeezed excessive profits out of their operations at the expense of the residents. Five members of Beverly Enterprises' board of directors had ties to Reagan. Financial ties between the governor, who was emptying state hospitals, and business persons who were profiting from the process, would also soon become apparent in other states as well, just as former President Eisenhower's $50,000 loan to buy his Gettysburg, Pennsylvania farm was granted with no interest by a cabal of businessmen, and never repaid. It was a national scandal, yet all the media did was promote Smiling Ronnie as a guru and financial wizard!

Jesus! What an asshole!

And here he was, ruminating about that butt brain when he was already late! And Marty (not "Martha," her real name) would undoubtedly be on this case. Perhaps even rightly so. He was late a lot, but then he had been making money-based decisions lately, a process that had previously been foreign to him. The choice to be late to make an extra fifty or hundred dollars was a no brainer!

Besides, he was only twenty minutes late! Or he had been. Now it was more like forty minutes. Fuck! That was nothing! Fucking "Marty" was like a goddamn machine sometimes! So neat, so precise, so orderly! And never, ever fucking late! Jesus! But he'd been using his nocturnal shifts to good advantage—in terms of notes, narrative, passages, descriptions of characters, even some dialogue he could transcribe on the typewriter when he got home in the morning. There were a lot of people went to bed as soon as they got home, but those hours were precious writing time. As usual, he was working to support his writing habit.

He'd get home by 0800, make a pot of coffee, and write fairly uninterruptedly (with small interruptions for business) until around 1400 when he unplugged the phone and crashed for a while, usually 4 or 5 hours. Then it was a shower, another pot of French Roast, a few more hours of writing, and a couple of lines—interlaced with taking care of business until he had to report for work at 2330. Usually.

Lately the business part of his day had gained supremacy. He'd been getting more and more calls, thanks to Magnus's old contacts. And the amounts were increasing too—which was both a good and bad thing, since he had to re-up more often (not having the capital to buy large amounts), but thankfully Magnus trusted him with fronts for which he paid next time he returned. One new customer wanted half an "O" delivered to Los Altos every Friday night at midnight, and another who wanted the same amount in the Outer Sunset every Saturday night. The guy on San Antonio Road paid the extra freight for the delivery, plus they'd do half a gram or so together before he headed back to The City. Recently he'd gotten another standing order for a half O at 0200 Saturday morning that he would drop off on his way home through the Inner Richmond.

He was using more and more product, which was fine because he both had it, and paid way less than retail. The other side of that equation was that he was becoming more and more dependent on it just to keep going, just to have a "normal" day—whatever that was. Having a job was such an impediment! Having to give away all of those potentially productive hours was a giant pain in the ass, most especially showing up on time. "Marty" had become increasingly pissed, and had threatened to write him up! Fuck! If only she wasn't so butch, well, pseudo-butch, with her key ring slapping against the leather protector on her hip. Truth of the matter was he couldn't read her. Sometimes he thought she was hot. If it weren't for the fact that they worked together, he might offer her a line and see what happened.

Time for a real line, and then: "Hi ho, hi ho, it's off to work I go!"

He locked his beat up-looking, used-to-be chocolate brown 1962 Volvo 122-S. It looked very innocuous, but had a beast under the hood. He kept it well-maintained too. He wanted to have that extra burst of speed, or high-quality brakes that could save your life. He habitually parked nose out so he could escape quickly. He laughed to himself. Same-same reason he always sat with his back to a wall. He hated having his "six" exposed. Even when he sat with other vets, they invariably took seats side-by-side, even if they ended up at separate booths side-by-side.

He walked in through the ER, taking in the disparate (and desperate) sights and sounds that assaulted him. It was inescapable, no matter what inner barriers he constructed. He was invariably affected, maybe even infected, by the variegated display of humanity in the waiting room. It was like a surreal painting by Goya or Dali, but one that had been purposefully smeared with lurid, greasy lacquer so that all of the images clearly represented pain and tragedy, with the edge just enough off that the mind did not immediately register the depth and intensity of the horror represented.

There sat a hugely pregnant Latino woman with blood stains on her beige pants, her much smaller and younger boyfriend sitting by her side muttering in Spanish as she cried disconsolately into a dirty handkerchief. On the bench seat furthest from the door sat a soiled and handcuffed old White guy with a police guard, or at least he thought he was White, buried under multiple layers of grime and a sheen of blood that covered most of his face. In the furthest corner from the cop and his captive huddled a junkie, face pale and diaphoretic, scabs across the backs of both hands, eyes furtively flicking around the landscape. He had no visible injuries, but his disheveled clothing and clotted countenance spoke for themselves.

Paul hoisted his black backpack a higher on his shoulder, and passed through as quickly as he could. He did not want to lose the edge of his high any sooner than he had to. Marty would attempt to ruin it soon enough with her shitty attitude. He did his share of the work, more even sometimes, but lately his bad attitude about having to work at all kept showing. Couldn't help it. He felt entitled to better. As much as he wanted more time to write, while getting more and more immersed in the *cocaina* world. He was allowing more of his precious writing time to get distracted by telephone calls and dope deals. He was still writing his Minimum Daily Requirement of a thousand words a day, writing in the early hours of the morning either at work or at home— "writing ahead" so as to not miss the cadence of production, doing an extra thousand or more when he knew it was going to be busy (like Fridays).

The "problem," which in many ways was not really a problem, was that the shit was so goddamn pretty, especially when he got that occasional batch that was Mother of Pearl with its shiny, iridescent cliff-like layers and that heady bouquet. And the taste! No wonder they called it sweet cocaine! God! It was fucking awesome! He so appreciated the fact that he could do coke and write for hours, though sometimes when he edited portions of "The Great Work" (he liked to think himself akin to Tolstoy) had to be slashed out because of repetition or simply rambling. But still...

He wanted to believe he was getting seriously strung out, but it was far too late. He was a fucking junkie! Why else was there an entire container of fluffy, freshly ground powder in the little mint-green container in the bottom of his backpack being carried into the hospital? And he didn't care!

It was his drug, and he loved it! And he had a right to use it! Fuck them!

On the elevator going up, he remembered that he thought he was smart and oh so hip, when he first started using cocaine.

———————

San Anselmo, California June, 1970

His connect was called "The Captain," whom Paul had met when he lived in North Oakland.

He lived across the Richmond-San Rafael Bridge in Oakland. Paul had a young woman named Dominique, who drove him back and forth to score. She would stash the dope in her panties, in case they got stopped by the cops or CHP, though they never did. He gave her a gram for every trip. She was so lovely and he really wanted to have sex with her, but never did. It was always strictly business. Too bad! (He'd found out much later that she was only sixteen!)

The trade was so much looser in those halcyon days! He bought his first ounce for $875, and had the opportunity to watch it weighed and measured directly off the kilo.

When he first started going to The Captain's house to score, the man greeted by him at the door and led him to a back bedroom. They exchanged a little chit-chat, and Paul laid out the money in fans of a hundred dollars each. (In those days it was mostly twenties). The Captain offered him a line, which he hungrily snorted up, and Paul made a blithe comment about how using coke put him amongst the intelligentsia of the planet. The Captain looked at him, and just shook his head.

"What?" said Paul exasperated, spreading his hands wide.

"You don't know anything about coke until you're strung out!"

"Yeah. Yeah. Whatever! Thanks, man. See you soon!"

Things went along this way for a while, with Dominique sometimes earning two grams a day. Then one rainy Friday night—his third trip of the day—he was ushered into the back room, and immediately started fanning out the money. The Captain just stood watching, counting with his eyes. When Paul looked up, he offered Paul a line.

Paul replied in a rushed/slurred voiced tinged with impatience, almost condescension.

"No thanks, man. I gotta go!"

The Captain looked at him, simply waiting until Paul's eyes steadied on him, and then smiled.

"Now you know what coke is all about!"

It was at that moment that he knew he had "arrived." He was so focused on making money and moving the product (people were waiting!) that he didn't have time for, or interest in, a "free" line.

CHAPTER TEN
"Reality" Intrudes
San Francisco August 1979

The elevator pinged at the seventh floor, and plunged his awareness precipitously back into the present. Paul sighed deeply, and prepared himself for the upcoming verbal onslaught.

Marty was sitting behind the curved wooden desk that separated the office and med room from the rest of the unit. She looked up from a pile of paperwork—chart review, Progress Notes, Doctors' Orders (noted and taken off), Seclusion and Restraint records, lab reports, all needing to be ready to go by day shift at 0645. She simply glared at him, and did not say a word. He glared back at her, and went to leave his backpack in the staff room.

He had to get his head together, wrap himself around all of the bullshit—room checks every thirty minutes; a sufficient supply of linens and all of the various materials nursing staff used, even checking the toilet paper in the bathrooms. But that was all after the chart reviews. They usually shared that task, and split the charts between them before cross-checking their work.

Some nights were worse than others, and tonight threatened to be a monster—mostly because Paul was feeling severely fucking sick of it all. It was all so mundane, having to pretend to be "normal," masquerading as a working man, and having to act like he gave a shit!

Within minutes, he couldn't stand it any longer. He was flagging badly already. He went to the staff bathroom, pulled out the little Deering case, and did a significant snort in each nostril, ran the water, and snurffed some of that too before rubbing his nose vigorously—and then looked in his eyes in the mirror. He saw the sadness leaving and a refreshment appearing. He had to get back to work soon, but then said aloud "Fuck it!" He'd take a few more minutes. Paul was so pissed about his life! There was so much more to be had, so much more to be done, so much more he was capable of doing! Fuck! He just ached to become the man he wanted to be! To manifest all of his freakiness right up front! It was agonizing, living a "life of quiet desperation," about which Thoreau had spoken, so stultifying, so boring, draining away any and all of his creativity! Trying to suppress his rage kept leading him to having nuclear meltdowns and floods of tears! He would sometimes go for long drives on the freeway, screaming the whole time, just to keep him from randomly slaughtering thousands! All he really got was the most momentary relief, of release, of belonging—a second, a nanosecond, of feeling a sense of peace, a glimmer of true value!

He knew he had a hidden greatness in his heart, greatness in his soul. He felt utterly driven to be bigger than the inane empty shell of "reality" into which he had been brainwashed into believing he had to fit. But he'd always been too ashamed, too filled with memories he could only escape in his most altered moments (High on War!). He had always sheltered his initial vision, carried it deep in his heart, lived with it, prayed for it, craved it, yearned for it, wanting it more than anything else, to excel, to have tremendous excess, at last to have the very, very best!

Shame and blame, erosion and derision, intrusion and collusion—always seeking redemption in the welcoming arms and sweet bodies of the next woman, and the next woman, and the next, and the next—all with promises of salvation that were always redeemed only in sorrow.

He believed William Blake had it right: "The road of excess leads to the palace of wisdom... You never know what is enough, until you know what is more than enough." He felt a kinship with Blake, having always been intensely indulgent—food, masturbation, cigarettes, lies, alcohol, stealing, subterfuge, secrets, women, marijuana, power, nitrous oxide, opium, amphetamines, entitlement, LSD, more secrets, money, rage, and now, cocaine. He had always felt driven to have more, to be more, to feel more. There had to be more! Just had to be more! He was not, had never been, convinced that he could be or should be satisfied with being small, unrecognized, pitiable, "normal," stable, steady, hard-working, regular—and "happy," the single most over-rated term that may have ever existed. What a bugaboo word! He despised the entire concept of "adjusting," of "making do," of "letting it go" and being resigned—all of the prescriptions that were flung at him by those of lesser intelligence and lesser emotional depth, as if they were some kind of "fix" that they themselves, in their delusionally "greater" wisdom and life experience, bought and sold as a remedy for being satisfied with a less than a stellar life. He had been told so, so many times that he should be "realistic," or "quit dreaming," and he would then be "a lot better off." Fuck that! Fuck that! Fuck that!

He could see bigger, better, brighter, more evolved worlds and ways to live, ways that were beyond "appropriate" cultural standards, certainly beyond ordinary imagining! Why should he settle for less?

At the end of a long career as benefactor of the poor and downtrodden, and a decided enemy of the state, Emiliano Zapata was offered a reprieve by the authorities when he was captured, if he would publicly recant his previous position. He emphatically told them: "I would rather die on my feet than live on my knees!"

So, why should he, who had always striven for purity, and who had suffered the insensitivities and rude behaviors of others, while seeking a deeper connection with himself, others, and the Universe—why should he simply settle for "normalcy?" Especially if such a state were dictated by the cultural elites and handed down to the masses as the way they "should" live—though the elites themselves passed laws for others to obey, while they themselves lived beyond the law, exercising the power of money to manipulate: to have sex with underage children; to drink and use any substances prohibited to others; indulge themselves in any and every way they might choose, regardless of any harm they might do, regardless of how their inane, narcissistic choices might negatively influence the lives of others, or potentially cause pain, shame, and suffering that would and could reverberate through multiple generations?! They were filled with arrogance and schadenfreude. They simply didn't care!

Many, many times daily he got so sick of dealing with the world and all of its machinations, a world run like a giant private kingdom for the few; driven by insatiable greed, a far, far worse addiction than heroin or cocaine! Greed was directly and factually responsible for every single war that had ever occurred! And continued to do so, *ad infinitum, ad nauseaum.*

It seemed paradoxical that his money from illicit sources was "healthy" compared to his authorized, straight-jacket job of managing the "mentally ill," society's rejected and marginalized. They called it "progress."

Vietnam had liberated him from the need for authority, and he was grateful to be a demi-God in his own world. He was alive, breathing free air, and making a lot of money! He was beloved by many women, and so what if it was only because he was the Candy Man willing to satisfy temporary urges? Paul kept an informal tally in his head of how many women to whom he offered coke, and of those, with how many had he become sexually involved? Currently, it was something like one in five accepted; and of those five, he ended up sexually involved with one point four of them. Not bad! Came out to be something like nine in a hundred, but there were times when it was that many times that on a weekend! Working two full time "jobs," and managing a very active sex life was relatively easy for him. The real crunch was finding enough time to write that first powerhouse novel. Paul was well-acquainted with all of the stats and the pseudo-stats, euphemisms, and folk lore related to first novels, especially: everybody's got at least one novel in them; and write your first novel, then burn it, then write the second. But he didn't care. He had always felt a literary calling in his heart, much like the religious claim to have for their vocation—a calling from "God."

He'd been making notes, creating snippets of dialogue, character sketches, scenes and scenarios, narrative pieces, and even some full scenes. He had three fairly well-developed short stories that he was considering linking together to create a first draft, and calling it "Brotherhood: A Viet Nam Vignette." He like the alliterative value; it was more than one vignette, but figured he could grant himself some literary license.

He had been hanging out in this incredible house in Mill Valley that had only one right angle. Built by a Chinese doctor, it had something to do with feng sheu and keeping the energy moving freely! The folks who lived there were serious old rock-and-roll fiends. Of course, his cocaine was always welcome. The Tuesday night meetings gathering had started as a gathering of writers and musicians—marijuana, alcohol, cocaine, and sharing the latest scribblings or tunes. Some people read poems, or pieces of short stories. Some told tales, or tried out new songs. Paul had captured a rough draft of what became a ten-page short story—and risked reading parts of it on three consecutive Tuesdays. The group had been really encouraging, and he decided to continue mining his mind for more and better material—some retrieved from memory, some pure imagination, and some gathered from other vets.

The Tuesdays kept cascading, and Paul kept writing. His style definitely improved, and he felt the glimmerings of true voice. Hel began to believe that he might be a "real writer," not just some pretend wannabe. The short stories all had a loosely connected theme, but it wasn't until a third consecutive Tuesday night after he had read the third story, when someone suggested that he try to write a novel. It was almost a Biblical revelation! He'd just been telling some stories, and then magically he was a thread to a larger work, his first book—the one he had he had always dreamed he could write!

Despite all his travails, he feared he had not yet been to the very bottom. He tortured himself with not having been a three-tour combat infantryman, or a hard-core junkie with ten years on the streets. No matter how far he had fallen, he just couldn't believe he had been down to the deepest, most dank, most dark, intense arenas of Life. He believed that, if having done so, he would have proved himself more valuable and reliable, more immersed in the truth and worthy of sharing his journey. He had simply to proclaim himself—that was the real revelation!

He wanted was to write a first novel as if from the perspective of "the other side," of having already written an amazing, transcendental novel filled with messages and lessons from his own life. Then he could consider himself credible. It was, of course, the perfect set up for failure since he was seeking the impossible, a perfection beyond human possibility!

The converse side of the situation was that he believed that he harbored whole amphitheaters full of life experience that would and could yield tremendous stories suffused with regrets and sorrow, joy and laughter—all of which might live and breathe, have lives, and even write books of their own! He ached to express them, battled valiantly to so, felt called to channel these stories both as entertainment and spiritual lessons to be passed on through his work to others, for others to savor and digest, to enrich their lives—but he always felt held in check by massive and often overwhelming forces that swept through him with the regularity of the seasons, creating an internal environment subject to the same laws that governed the growth of trees, and the periodicity of the tides.

His biggest question was always: Would there ever be enough? Would he, could he, unfathomably, ever be enough to have the strength and courage to put his words to paper, and commit them to a potentially discerning, even disapproving, readership?

Would he ever be enough? Would he ever be able to stand up before the judgments of the world and proclaim his right to be a great artist? Not necessarily as great or strong or powerful; not necessarily rich and famous, or lauded by the media and the masses of people led around by their nose rings like a hapless and otherwise virile bull. Not necessarily to be acclaimed and upheld in the hearts and minds of others as an inspiration or role model for the ages, but simply strong enough, powerful enough, clean enough of heart and spirit, to finally be enough for himself; to be enough to stand up for himself, and all that he believed in; to deserve love, honor, and self-care; to have garnered enough self-compassion that he could well and truly proclaim that he was worthy of the air he breathed, and had a right to partake of the bounty of the planet without feeling ashamed, or harbor a burning need to run to the Catholic confessionals of his childhood every week filled with litanies of sins he had committed, wanting not ever to burn in the eternal fires of Hell dying unrelieved of the burden imposed by the "Absolvo te absolutam" of the priest who delusionally believed he could actually forgive such "sins" of another!

He and Marty hadn't spoken directly to him any more than was necessary to get the paperwork done, so he simply continued with his own internal monologue.

Beyond glory and fame and riches, it was THE single thing he wanted—to be loved and held in high esteem; honored and honorable in his own body, heart, and mind for who he was, not who he might become, or what he might provide—even though he often believed that he needed to be in an overwhelmingly powerful position financially or emotionally be even be worthy of approaching a woman who might want him, to even be considered as eligible in the Great Game of relationships. He knew (intellectually at least) that it all stemmed from him, from his energy, from his sense of himself as worthy, enjoyable, kind, loving, and sexy. Yet the onus always fell on him to be that person inside that he desired outside of himself, loving and adoring him; having long and extremely interesting conversations with him; taking romantic strolls in the moonlight; eating exotic, erotic dinners by candlelight in far-away places: and having sex in all manner of esoteric positions and locations, always locked together in a love that connected them completely and wholly. People were always telling him that he had to find that kind of desire and fulfillment within himself first; that he had to be his own very best lover, and treat himself that way.

But the task always seemed Herculean, even Sisyphean. He sometimes found it impossible to even like himself, much less slather love himself. It was one of the central tasks of his life, to sort out what or who was truly him, and what he'd incorporated that was not. It was a sticky web that seemed to embrace his every action, his every desire, his every thought and direction. He felt constitutionally incapable of separating the essence of who he was from what he had internalized.

He'd had a similar discussion with a Black friend about racism. Eddie was the only Black man he ever knew who could have belonged to the Ku Klux Klan! He was so racist, very negative about people of his own color. He even arrogantly had designations of Blackness, rated in the number of "Bs" —size of lips and butts, ugliness and other racial characteristics that he personally found repulsive in other Black people. Paul had tried several times to gently remind him of a basic principle of psychology, that he was projecting onto the entire Black race his own hatred, fear, and shame; that like a disfiguring internal crime, he had taken on the worst from his brutal, violent father, and then turned his hatred against himself, blaming all of his pain and shame on his racial background. Paul never seemed to get through to him. He was so guarded and defended that he not could heal the loss of his childhood innocence, and create the soulful alchemic transformation that Paul believed was possible through shedding the toxic encrustations of the past, all of the emotional rifts and reefs.

It was a war he waged constantly within himself—but then, wasn't all war a war against the self, projected onto the world? Were not all unresolved conflicts, seemingly buried and "forgotten," often re-enacted on the world stage? Paul was always torn between what he knew intuitively, and what he believed he had to do to survive. The third leg of his personal triangle was the burning desire to manifest what he felt was his destiny, to become a working artist, with books in print, read by millions, with whom he could share the work of his many years on both sides of the couch; help heal the splits and harms in others that he had himself had redeemed; to be an example, an inspiration for others, so that he might emerge, having lived the life of a wounded healer who had achieved his life purpose in healing himself and others.

When he went to the staff bathroom, he leaned against the wall, and started sobbing while simultaneously chiding himself for being so grandiose! He had always felt so uplifted whenever he went into one of his "mini-trances," so removed from the ordinary, so relieved of the burdens of the mundane. He knew that this other world was real, just beyond the reach of the usual, and he was privileged to go there every once in a while, spontaneously—more so since taking LSD, but it was something he had always seen and done since he was a child; somewhere he had always been capable of apprehending, although it was not a location, or a "place" to which he could travel. He had always known that he had something special, deep within him, that was very different, even alien, buried in his heart, beating with every lub and dub, breathed in with every cool, clear intake of air. He'd always been isolative, apart from others, distant, an island in time as well as space.

His thought train continued barreling down the tracks of his own determination. He knew he had always been a stranger, even in the midst of those who claimed to know him. He'd been called "The Brain" in 8th grade class. It was always his intelligence that he loved the best, that gave him a sense that he had a reason to be on Earth. He clung to it assiduously, held onto it tightly and fiercely, identified with it completely, and always looked for opportunities to express erudite opinions on arcane subjects hoping to impress others.

Sometimes it really sucked being smarter than everybody else. Even more so being more sensitive—castigated, bullied, spit upon, shit upon, hit, beaten, isolated, ganged up upon, split apart from the group, and attacked by others, hurt, shunted, stunted, tricked, kicked, harmed in just about every possible way emotionally and physically—decades of damage, turmoil, chaos, disturbance, trauma, pain, and shame from which he would slowly and painfully have to recover, inch by inch, step by step, moment by moment, as it ached at him, ate away at him, like a slow-burning acid absorbing miniscule portions of his mind and soul, sending streaks of white-hot pain ever deeper into his tortured body, a body he despised as the true source of all of his problems, the body whose improvement and total upgrade would bring about the revolution of joy and wonder, of greatness, love, and honor he had always craved, that would redeem him from all of the shame and sorrow, all the perdition and pure fucking unadulterated shit he had endured for all the years he had been alive—for all that he had been punished, which punishment he had internalized, and used against himself over and over again, his father's voice, the internalized oppressor echoing in his head as viciously as any auditory hallucination, for the crime of being born to parents who used him and tortured him—and left the strained stain of emotional penury and devastation buried deeply in him to fester and spoil, to degenerate and poison his every thought, movement, motion, emotion, wish, desire, hunger, need, dream, and vision.

And he wanted revenge! He wanted them all to pay! Every single motherfucker who had ever harmed him! He wanted to hurt them all! And he would do it gleefully! He had thought long and hard about methods and manners of torture, how he would extract the most excruciating value from the most purposeful harm he could inflict!

His inner clock warned him to go back to work, but he ignored it and continued to drift in reverie, even though he knew he would always have to crash back to Earth, to the vaunted "reality" about which everyone seemed to think they knew so much! Everyone thought they knew what "it" was, but all they knew was their own reality—what clinicians called "naïve reality. He believed that all realities were true, all valid! They all exist simultaneously! He knew there were other worlds, other dimensions, so much more advanced and delicate, sensitive and wonderful, than the goddamn backwash of the Universe here on Earth in the 20th Century! And they were not "drug induced delusions" as some had either implied or had the temerity to say to his face. Fuck them for they know not what they say! That was his motto! Fuck all the hippie dreamers! He was tired of living in penury and obscurity! If he had to be on Earth, he wanted fortune and fame! Despite the fact that Bob Dylan had really claimed it with the line: "On Desolation Row, it's either fortune or fame. You must choose one or the other, though neither of them is to be what they claim!"

Dreams and visions filled him night and day, awake or asleep. He mightily hungered to be elevated from the dust of his life, above the great masses of people and their mundane, banal thoughts and action that so filled him with incandescent rage that nothing could stanch. He felt so helpless, so totally impotent, to do anything about the seeming unchangeableness, the acidic bloated congestion that only seemed temporarily relieved by excess of some sort—never eliminated, never ameliorated, never erased. Sometimes he believed he was born just to suffer in endless expiation for great crimes of which he had no memory; for which he was condemned to forever be alone.

And then, like an ill-wind in the night, Marty appeared as if out of the fog.

"It's 0250. If we're gonna get a break tonight, one of us should go now."

Paul elected to go first. They had a single mattress on a frame at the far end of the break room, along with a small refrigerator, microwave, and storage cabinets filled with coffee, tea, and condiments. He made his way down the hall, and she told him she would wake him in an hour.

He was starting to fade. It had been more than three hours since he'd had a line. He laid down on his back with his left hand across his eyes, and crashed instantly, head filled with frantic, frenetic Technicolor images flashing at light speed; and was instantly immersed in a drama-scape filled with fluorescent dragons, cartoon images with dialogue balloons filled with Arabic script, and huge flows of pastel clouds and charcoal fog. He had just begun walking through a crystal tunnel where sonorous voices echoed from the walls, and eerie voices seemed to emanate from the very air itself. When he heard the distinct sound of Marty's footsteps moving down the highly-polished floor, and the slap of her ring of keys against her hip. In the dream, he watched Marty insert her master key in the lock, heard the tumbler turn, and soft footsteps patter across the carpet. Still in the dream, he heard her approaching, and saw her reaching out her arm toward him. He reached up out of the dream and grabbed her arm in mid-descent. Her scream echoed through the broken silence, and she screamed again as he sat up groggy-eyed from the last vestiges of his oh-too-brief respite from the distracting world of time.

He was curiously moved when he saw how freaked out she looked, and asked.

"You were sleeping with your eyes open!"

"Yeah, I learned to do that in Viet Nam!"

"Jesus, you freaked the shit out of me!"

"I heard you coming in my dream!"

"You are really weird, man!"

Within a week of this strange encounter with Marty, the flow really opened up. He got another drop in his price, and an increase in his front. He was making more money than ever.

The difference between that and what he was earning at the bin was significant.

That following Friday, the flow was really on. The regular order from Los Altos doubled, and he smoked some exquisite ether-base with his client. It was an amazingly sweet batch, transforming the hydrochloric (powder) into an alkaline (base) smokable form. It was one of his first encounters with this high-power version of the drug. He totally lost track of time, and quite honestly, didn't really give a shit! Fuck it! He had made so much money that night! And the first draft of *Brotherhood* was complete! Everything was unfolding perfectly—except for his jive job!

He was totally primed when he showed up for work at 0235—with more than a thousand dollars in his pocket. He took a deep breath, and walked onto the unit. Marty met him practically on the threshold, shaking her finger in his face, and screaming.

"What the kind of shit is this?! You're three hours late!"

Paul's resisted the impulse to punch her. He had a momentary thought to be placatory, but as she continued to shriek at him, wagging her goddamn finger in his face, he couldn't resist the gigantic pulse of hot, bright light that streaked up his spine, sending small orange pinpoints that expanded like lightning trees in his eyeballs. He had enough prescient warning, knowing that of which he was capable, to step back instead of forward—though when he spoke, it was in a low, menacing tone that rasped through his pursed lips.

"Wag that motherfucking finger at me one more time, and I'll break it off!"

Marty lost her breath, and stepped back, shocked, face ashen. She raised her hands in front of her face in a warding gesture.

"Step back, or I'll call Security!"

Paul released his rage in one huge outbreath.

"PAAAAAAGGGHHH!"

He turned quickly, inserted his key into the lock, and turned it. Twisting the key loose from it, he threw it at her.

"I don't have to put up with this shit! I fucking quit!"

CHAPTER ELEVEN

Up

San Francisco May 1979 — August 1982

When he looked back across all of his tumultuous years, it sometimes seemed like they had all occurred a million years ago, even in a past lifetime. Other times it seemed as bright and vibrant as the present moment. He still had extremely powerful euphoric recall of many of the memories—vivid, embracing, raw and powerful; some memories shameful and sad, especially the loss of what had been, or could have been; and the pride and exaltation of having survived, much like he had the war, especially when so many he had known had died, or been otherwise lost to the vast ocean of time.

His hunger for transformation began at the age of seven, when he got dragged to the family doctor (who was five feet six inches tall, and weighed three hundred pounds) to get injected with amphetamines "for weight control!" His father was extremely ashamed of Paul's weight and the sensitivity that manifested as Paul's not wanting to do "manly-man" exercise and sports.

Paul had always been so incredibly driven, totally obsessed, wanting to satisfy the aching hunger of his heart, never sated except in the briefest of moments, when ecstatic rushes blasted through the ancient battlements of his soul, and pure rushes of dopamine and adrenaline surging, surging, surging, he climbed the icy Himalayas inside his brain. Money and women flowed to him, through him, like breath, a gift from the Universe. He was running, running, running, as hard and as fast as he could, usually for five days (though he'd once gone two weeks), running twenty, twenty-two hours a day, sometimes thirty or thirty-six on a weekend, before he had to "rest his eyes" for a fitful couple of hours before it all began again, running, running, running. Cocaine was the most exciting, sexually alluring, multi-talented, powerful woman he had ever known. Cocaine was as close to Steve Miller's famous Quicksilver Girl: "A lover of the world, she spreads her wings, and she's free...She's seen every branch on the tree...If you need a little lovin', she'll turn on the heat, if you take a fall, she'll put you back on your feet, If you're all alone, she's someone to meet, if you need someone, she's a quicksilver girl."

She was so, so much more to him. She was soul mate, guiding light, most boon companion, ally. She was always there for him like no human woman had ever been. If he wanted a lover at 0300, she was there—and she worked to stimulate the real human women who often joined him during these lonely times. She was a burst of power and ingenuity when danger threatened. She was his pathfinder through trouble and twisted waters. She was the most consistent relationship he had ever had! She was always there. Of course, she exacted a high price—but who or what didn't?

There was such power, beauty, glory, when he was flying high, amped out on dopamine, invincible, unconquerable! Excelsior!

He loved the product! To hold a bag of the sparkling crystals in his hand, to feel the heft and imagine the amazing pleasure it would bring—had prompted him to say to people "Your pleasure is my business!" It was so pretty! There were so many varieties, and he loved knowing the countries of origin. He was proud of the fact that he never "hit" any of his product with contaminants like lactose or mannitol (isolated from the flowering ash, and often called "baby laxative"). He knew a woman once who had gotten seriously pissed off at her boyfriend for using up what was supposed to be "their" stash. She subsequently put a big whack of crystal drain cleaner (sodium hydroxide) in the bindle, and was conveniently out of the house when the clown died in agony with the needle still in his arm, and a death rictus on his face. She claimed total innocence and the cops could never break her alibi.

The Flow had transformed, even transfigured Paul, initiated him into a new way, his energy and focus incredibly uplifted.

Of course, it had a lot to do with the substantial amount of his own product he was ingesting. The psychological lift was so undeniably intense, so extraordinarily efficient, at opening up his nervous system, freeing him from much of the old psychological and emotional garbage he had carried. He wished he could get the same effect without the drug, but he couldn't create the extreme and far-reaching power he experienced until he was so under the influence that he could not, would not, even think about walking away. The drug and the effect were so conflated that he was completely unable to separate the two. Pharmacology called it "the placebo effect" —getting high on the belief that you were getting high, while the magic potion effect (Effron would have called cocaine his "selfobject") gave him relief from all of his feelings of being diminished, incomplete, and victimized. He was a king! He was invincible!

Not having to sleep was a decided benefit, an excellent "side effect." He had read about a Korean vet who'd been shot in the head, and had his sleep center destroyed. He survived the war, but was never able to sleep again—though he had to rest for fifteen or twenty minutes several times a day. He managed this routine for a few years, then killed himself because he couldn't stand not being able to dream. For Paul though, the luxury of the "extra time" was the greatest benefit.

Another gift from the Snow Queen was the respite from needing to eat, the loss of appetite and loss of weight—an artifact otherwise achieved only rarely, except when strung out on opium or cocaine (well, there were the diet pills too).

He loved being skinny, even gaunt, free of the shame of being fat, of the memory of being taunted by schoolmates, who thought it was the height of wit and wisdom to hurl epitaphs and slurs at him about his size—until one day, after years of enduring derision, tolerating eons of agony and rage, and oceans of tears, he hit upon a small solution that silenced his biggest enemy (and one of the most popular guys at school).

———————

"Hey fat boy! What's up?"

"Nothing much."

"You on a diet or something? Looks like you might have lost an ounce or two!" he said, and turned to the cronies surrounding him—all of whom, of course, laughed with undisguised glee and relief that it was not they who had not been chosen to be "torn up," relieved that they could be in the gallery that day, and witness my pain, rage, and sorrow. (The term schadenfreude would not come into the popular parlance for many decades yet, but these young men

certainly exemplified it: enjoying the pain and humiliation of others).

"No, Tob, I am not on a diet. But I have a thought to share with you."

"Oh yeah, lard bucket? What's that?" Tob said, smirking, while basking in the spurious glow of his confreres, enjoying as always being at the top of the heap (though at home he was beaten mercilessly by his father as was his mother, though she, in turn, degraded Tob with her rapier-like tongue and small, hard, clammy fists).

"I may be fat..."

His salacious grin increased, as if he were getting sexual pleasure from my degradation.

"Brilliant observation, fatso!"

"...but I can always lose weight."

"That'll be the day," he said, echoing a popular Buddy Holly song of the day.

Then I delivered the blow that seemed at first relatively mild, but as the venom sank deeper and deeper into his cells and tissues, I watched his face implode, almost dissolve, as the import of what I said to him became increasingly evident.

"But you," I said, holding his eyes and looking squarely into his face, "will never be any smarter than you are right now!"

One or two of his little congregation had the balls to laugh out loud into the extremely embarrassed and aphasic silence that ensued.

"Give it up, man! He got you that time!"

"Tore you up!"

He just looked at me, shocked, as if I had stabbed him in the heart—which I had, the pen being mightier than the sword. Finally, he took a deep and shuddering breath, and replied, being verbally violent.

"Fuck you, fat boy!" and took a step toward me.

Paul could not help but throw another riposte at him, even though it was like sticking a banderillo into the bull after the sword has already killed him—a bull who was such a strong and noble animal, full of pride and adrenaline.

"Like Asimov said, 'Violence is the last refuge of the incompetent!'"

Tob turned away, muttering, as he turned and walked away (so no one could see him blushing, perhaps even shedding tears of rage). One or two of the others gave me weak smiles, but they too soon followed their erstwhile leader.

Originally, he wanted to make enough money on the side so he didn't have to work overtime, but the more money he made, the more he wanted to spend. He wasn't spending it lavishly, but he gave away a lot of cocaine, especially to women. It was so easy—and the response was generally the stuff of myth! He had many women hitting on him, and a large percentage of them followed their promises through with sexual favors.

But, of course, the cocaine coursing through his veins and brain didn't bring him any peace—though it did help him feel so much better, so much more powerful! It was the best drug in the world! *Cocaina* took away all of the barriers of shyness and loneliness, eliminated all hesitation to approach women, enabled to offer intimacy, be totally and purely sensual and sexual with no sense of shame!

When he was loaded, he never felt like ten pounds of shit in a five-pound bag! He could go anywhere, and do anything! NOW! Nothing haunted him, nothing taunted him, and no one bothered him. He felt free and open, available and able to give—for the very first time! He felt liberated, released to let go of the toxic boundaries and bindings that had always encased him! He felt released, almost enlightened, no matter how otherwise ludicrous that it might seem, scaling the spiritual peaks when every fiber of his body was crying out for the exquisite dopaminergic boost of more cocaine!

CHAPTER ELEVEN
Down
San Francisco May 1979 — August 1982

When he looked back across all of his tumultuous years, it sometimes seemed like they had all occurred a million years ago, even in a past lifetime. Other times it seemed as bright and vibrant as the present moment. He still had extremely powerful euphoric recall of many of the memories—vivid, embracing, raw and powerful; some memories shameful and sad, especially the loss of what had been, or could have been; and the pride and exaltation of having survived, much like he had the war, especially when so many he had known had died, or been otherwise lost to the vast ocean of time.

Though he had had an almost textbook childhood history, and filled with what Laing would have called "ontological insecurity," he had always hated feeling victimized. His suspicions sometimes erupted into strong flashes of paranoia, and the accompanying shades of self-repudiation, of feeling as if he were being punished for the crimes of past lifetimes. And then, inevitably, the always worst aspect of waking up after a run, feeling like the crumpled poster boy for "crash." He had been known to fall out wherever and whenever he was—on a couch, a chair, while on an open telephone call, on the floor, unfortunately behind the wheel of his car once, on the 280 Freeway at 0321 coming back from the last deal of a long, long day. Fortunately, the "wake up bumps" on the edge of the asphalt surface did their job, summoning him back from the land of "nod" long enough to get him to the next off-ramp, and to a motel. Opening his eyes to the glaring reality of being awake—eyes crusty, throat raw and desert dry, breath that would melt a fire hydrant, stomach tighter than a ten-year old anorexic, every single nerve twitching and twanging a tortured refrain, body leaden and just wanting another six or eight or ten hours sleep—yet his brain was already beginning to zing with plots and plans, appointments to keep, phone calls to make, despite the fact that he was considering putting his open mouth directly under the feeder spout of the coffee pot to get some caffeine quicker, totally aware from long experience that he had to eat a meal of some magnitude before that first line of the day in order to get the whole cycle going again full steam. It was the purest agony of being awake, having to feel every moment of it, and do nothing about the pain and agony, much as if he had been paralyzed with Pavulon or curare. He knew he had to just hold still and endure it, the interminable minutes until he could jump-start his body again, stumbling around smoking a cigarette while the coffee brewed. Then it was an entire pot of the thickest, richest brew he could manage before the hottest shower on Earth, a long and scalding interlude before getting to one of his favorite restaurants that served breakfast and good coffee 24/7. These were simply the basic requirements. It there happened to be beautiful waitresses, it was a decided plus for the eyes and hearts.

He loved Hopwell's on 24th Street, La Cucina on Union, or Dish at Haight and Masonic. If he were to awaken in a "foreign" locale (it happened, but rarely, that he fell out in Los Gatos or Mill Valley), then it was The Golden West in Santa Cruz or Tiny's in Aptos. If he was in Marin, anywhere within striking distance of The Peppermill in Corte Madera, that was his destination for good eats and eye treats.

Breakfast was usually 6 eggs basted, triple order of sausages, double order of hash browns cooked crisp, and four English muffins with extra butter and lots of jam (and/or a waffle or a large stack of pancakes). Usually another pot of coffee to finish off the meal, followed by two or three cigarettes—and a couple of gigantic lines immediately afterward to smooth out the rhythm of the machine before the cycle started in earnest again.

He and Magnus had sat down together for a meal of similar magnitude. One of the pretty waitresses told him she made a bet with one of the other women, who had bet $25 that they couldn't possibly eat it all—and, of course, they had! (He gave her a $25 tip on top of it!)

Having slept for twenty-four hours, starting a new run seemed like the natural thing to do. His answering machine was jammed with desperate messages. He would prioritize the calls, return them in order of importance (based upon how good the customer was), and then settle back to get a start on the day's income. If he were at home (having cooked a massive breakfast with the phone still unplugged), his loosely written rule for himself was that he wouldn't leave the house without at least $500 in his wallet. While waiting for people to arrive, to visit the "Candy Man," he would break out the digital laboratory scale and start weighing amounts into precut bindles, usually made from the most delicious shots of pornographic magazines, or into Zip-Lock bags for larger quantities. He remembered one Christmas when he had sold a half-ounce in a bright red bindle to a very good customer, who tucked it into the inside pocket of his sport coat, and went on his way—only to totally freak out when he pulled it out an hour later to share some toot with a couple of women—and discovered he had a hot pink stash! He immediately wanted Paul to give him a free replacement! When Paul got up off the floor, having collapsed from laughing so hard, with John John sputtering at the other end of the phone, he agreed. The man was a good customer and a friend.

Having exhausted all physical and mental resources, the ultimate downside was the huge and inevitable crash; and the huge and inevitable crash; and the huge and inevitable crash; and the huge and inevitable crash—it was like being in a hall of mirrors and echoes. This portion of the ride was akin to living in Hell, and being constantly tormented by Hades' Minions. He had never succumbed to heroin, barbiturates, or benzos to get down, as many had—often developing secondary addictions. There was no escape. He was often reminded that he believed he had come from another planet far more advanced than 20th Century Earth. If he felt alienated, maybe he was an alien!

A doctor friend (a fellow fiend), had told him that the cocaine actually took five days to be completely excreted, while benzoylecgonine, the carboxylic acid of cocaine, (its methyl ester formed by metabolism in the liver that was catalyzed by carboxylesterases) stayed in the body for as long as a month, and could be traced in a urine sample.

Money and women flowed to him, through him, as if they were his breath, a gift from the Universe—running, running, running as hard and as fast as he could, usually for five days (though he had once gone two weeks), running twenty, twenty-two hours a day, sometimes thirty or thirty-six on a weekend before he had to "rest his eyes" for a fitful couple of hours before it all began again—running, running, running.

––––––––––

He knew that part of what he was experiencing as lassitude, disinterest, melancholy, depression, anergia, was intimately related to the mourning he had been periodically experiencing due to the loss of his cocaine life—all of the thrills, the hyper-adrenalized, extraordinary states of intoxication, of just plain being high, but more the loss of the underlying accoutrement of back stage passes for rock concerts (where he always had a ready supply of "party favors," and to which he had often been invited to supply his favorite product); of expensive and expansive dinners at excellent restaurants where he was in the company of others like Herb who were not fearful of spending two hundred dollars for a bottle of exquisite wine; he flashy clothes he never worried about buying; the shows and gallery openings to which he was invariably invited; and the amazing panoply of women—God, he fucking missed them! Not even the sex per se, but the intimate companionship through some amazing times that would never be, could never be, repeated. And, though there were many women he thought of fondly, there were none of them in particular he remembered as anything more than different sets of body parts, personality quirks, branches of knowledge and intelligence, emotional allure, or just plain companionship. They had always just been there, even though frequently it had been the allure of the product—and they used him as well as he used them. The plain fact remained was that there had been hundreds, and he had come in his time to take their presence for granted. To some extent he had measured his value and even intrinsic quality in the mirroring presence or absence of, as Peter O'Toole once said, "The ladies, always the ladies."

All these prime experiences had disappeared from his life, and it resonated with even earlier times he had not mourned, as if they had just been put on hold, awaiting this newest awakening—his decision to continue to live and move forward along the glorious, shining journey of his evolution. They reminded him of the long path he had stepped upon so many decades before, and the utter impossibility of ever turning back to any level of a former life. In part, because it would be so boring. Once having been to the heights, it would just be insufferably boring, bland, and empty. Of course, the flight to the heights might simply have been just to escape the dismal dankness of the lower levels of his own mind.

CHAPTER TWELVE
...And All Around
San Francisco May 1979 — August 1982

Jesus! In having a very intimate affair with sweet sister cocaine, strung out and hopeless to quit, his entire life revolved around the precious powder—the taste, the smell, the power of the rushes, the sense of being fully embodied and alive with crackling purpose, the extraordinary money—even though that was only to keep going to get some more! On the run, he didn't have to think about any of the shit! Nothing ordinary mattered—not his weight, depression, food, sex, sleep, not even his fears and shame. They were gone. Erased. Non-existent (for at least a little while).

Of course, there were thousands of problems, not the least of which was how he was destroying his body on a daily basis, though the weight loss and lack of sleep were like gifts from the gods! But he had to stop once in a while (everybody did!) —usually every five days, when there was the inevitable payment due from the Universe. He felt like a clinical specimen for an epidemiological case study: sinuses aching, bleeding; caked cocaine inside of his nostrils (no matter how much water he snorted); eyes itchy and watering; headache splitting his brain ; mouth drier than a desert sirocco; belly repulsed at the thought of anything but coffee; asshole puckered from lack of use (who cared about food when your head was lit up like the finest Bally pinball machine?); body aches from head to toe (used to be from days and days of acrobatic sex; in the latter times, just from utter exhaustion and a gritty unwillingness to quit); scalp itching constantly, no matter how many showers and shampoos he had had; and the goddamn twitches, sometimes his fingers or toes spasming uncontrollably, even his whole arm (usually the left). Jesus! He might be developing Parkinson's!

And the paranoia! It would just fucking eat you alive! It was constant pressure around the eyes, scalp taut, belly roiling, nauseated as hell waiting for the hammer to drop; eyeballs dried out from the constant scanning and rotating, searching everywhere for potential dangers that could come from just about anywhere—a footstep behind you coming out of a bar; the cop car that scoped you out going down Union Street; a suspicious looking seedy character you've seen three times in the last two days; any one of your customers who could end up being a low-life motherfucker, and decide to rip you off because they were strung out too; any of the many chicks who had spent time at your house, maybe even during business hours—or any of them who might have their "real" boyfriend rip you off; or decide to help themselves to your stash, when you had trusted them enough to leave them alone in the bedroom while you had a shower; and the constant driving sense that your life was in danger, and you could be fucked with at any time by any number of malicious people, all of whom meant you no good.

And all of it all driven by the overriding, completely-embodied, absolute need/desire/compulsion/obsession to get free of the shittiest, most horrible pervasive sense of self-loathing, like a second skin, or toxic body armor that coated his epidermis and needed removing frequently. Until "She" came into his life, the black magic woman, liberating him for small bits of time, granting him a sense of false freedom and the temporary ability to move within himself.

———

Of course, he was attempting to escape his depression! He got so fucking tired of people telling him he was "just depressed," as if it were some kind of Einsteinian genius assessment to declare such a banal and ludicrous ideas as new, fresh and brilliant—as if he were unaware of the massive depredations and utter shit storms that raged within him, giving rise to titanic miseries and utter self-repudiation, dunning himself, slathering himself with gallons, buckets, oceans of self-hatred and shame—shame on many levels including shame about being ashamed, shame about still carrying as living events the essence of his childhood that seemed to have set a template for his life and times. He had always suffered "the slings and arrows of outrageous fortune," and managed to survive. It had been enough at the time to survive, to keep slogging through the emotional storms and the semi-formed molasses passages of his soul because he had a vision, of a bright, shining, beautiful future that had been promised to him, that kept him keeping on. Even in his darkest moments, he always believed; even when he felt abandoned by the entire Universe; when the voice he had come to know as Divine Mother came to him in those scintillating, disintegrating nanoseconds of immanent self-destruction; when he could stand it no longer and wanted release from his earthly vessel; where the whole web of illusion/delusion hung in the balance like a razor-sharp blade readied to be plunged into his sick-to-death-of-just-surviving heart; wanting, needing, craving, ready-to die in order to thrive instead of simply tolerating less than that for which his discriminating tastes longed, ached, hungered mightily, just to feel OK, just to feel "normal" and right being in this body, being on this Earth; having to put up with uncountable amounts of emotionally indigestible bullshit; innumerable, impossible-to-assimilate, and why-should-he incidents; insults, and injuries that most people took for granted, that shook him to his foundations; and gave rise to tremendous rage that often led to fantasies of vast destruction and slaughter. Some days, he needed more just to continue breathing. There had to be more. He had even lost his belief in "the perfect woman," having been ripped off so many times by parasitic bitches who only wanted to use him, and/or betray him.

Conversely, he had become quite accustomed to hot sex with wild passionate women. It was so much easier than looking for any kind of lasting relationship. He was totally obsessed with sex, and refused to look at it as some kind of pathological condition. Having sex with a hot loving woman was the best thing on Earth. There was nothing else so exciting, inspiring, uplifting, enriching, comforting, and awe-inspiring all at the same time. It had to be Creator's ultimate answer to the myriad miseries of human life. Even sharing the illusion of love, for whatever period of time, was the closest he had ever come to feeling whole and real, complete and fulfilled.

It haunted him that he had such a difficult time learning to love himself. It was, of course, the greatest barrier he ever encountered in finding a loving relationship. How in the bloody hell could he ever find someone to love him if he were unable to do so for himself? In many ways, it was a Holographic Universe where any fragment of the whole reflects the whole. It all boiled down to the simplest of equations. One attracts what one is—though for him there was no real comfort in the thought.

Paul had read a lot of the literature; absorbed millions of words related to addiction and obsession, pathology and withdrawal, dependence and habituation. Most of it pointed to the process whereby taking greater amounts of certain neurochemicals from outside the body actually gave rise to the body stopping its natural production that, in turn, led to the need for more, ever more. He had read a study about heroin and the endogenous pentapeptides that bind to morphine receptors in the central nervous system. Then when one quit using, there were no reserves, and the body took between two and six weeks to start manufacturing them again. The suffering was amplified because there was no buffer against the withdrawal symptoms that obliterated the body's ability to ameliorate everyday aches and pains (enkephalins), or the ability to feel pleasure (dopamine), after the euphoria of the initial upregulation that created the intoxication.

CHAPTER THIRTEEN
Flashback
San Francisco August 1982

Paul's $1000 a day habit had progressed over time from snorting to free-basing, and thence to shooting. He had abandoned himself to the specious ecstasy of his sweet lover, and quit caring about clothing, cleanliness, food, or sex. He only quit because he completely self-destructed when he stopped caring about having enough money to score—using all of the money from fronts to pay off other fronts and finally just using it all up in a kind of Gotterdammerung blast that left him broke, unable to pay back anyone's front, physically damaged, and with his reputation in tatters.

The rent was overdue (the manager was one of his connections); gas and electricity were turned off for lack of payment—and he had, at that point, totally alienated everyone he had ever known. Yet the only thing he could think about was cocaine. The only thing he wanted was cocaine. The only thing he needed was cocaine.

When all of the struts and supports of his world disintegrated, he slept—it seemed months, but was likely only two weeks. Sleeping and delirium 16-18 hours of the day. Most of the rest of the days (and nights) were spent in bed reading, or ruminating and castigating himself for the mess he had made of his life (oh the glorious familiarity of self-loathing!) Whatever else he might have done during that fog he catalogued as officially "lost." Even his delirium dreams were related to cocaine craving and scheming— none of which had any effect on his having to dodge two different people wanting to cause him great bodily harm for money owed from unrepaid fronts.

Paul realized now that he had been dazed and confused for many weeks. When he finally surfaced, leaden with extreme lethargy and anergia, it was with an intense craving (of course!) for cocaine. Since he had people watching his apartment building from the park across the street, he had to come and go carefully through the basement service door. Since he had totally ruined his reputation as a stand-up dope dealer, no one would even give him a single line. In the aftermath of one delirious sleep-and-dream sessions, he awoke with the most severe craving he'd ever had. As he lay in bed crying, shaking, totally depressed, and exhausted, he threw his hands in the air and said "I need some coke!"

As he started to stumble around, disoriented and despairing, a woman's voice spoke to him out of the corner of the ceiling. He knew instantly that it was The Voice. Divine Mother was unmistakable. He only ever heard from her in extreme situations, the first time in 1970 when he was on

chest until he almost blacked out, seeing purple stars against a black background.

When he was finally able to breathe again, he got to his feet, and threw his hands in the air.

"Please help me!"

Almost instantly, a flood of soothing syrup flowed through his body, and the intense craving eased instantly. In that scintillating moment he decided he wanted to live! He wanted to live! No matter what a shitty mess he had made, he wanted to live!

CHAPTER FOURTEEN
This is the End
Sausalito December 24 1982

He had managed to get through the previous few months without cocaine by dint of steel will and perseverance—or at least that's what he told himself. It made for an especially great myth-defining fiction for him, about him—he saw himself as the valiant knight struggling gloriously to maintain abstinence and sanity, though perhaps not necessarily holding them in equal portions.

The truth of the matter was that every single day was a monumental struggle. He had had plenty of opportunities to use in the previous few months, but he had demurred—not out of nobility or a trenchant desire to stay clean, but because the amounts offered had been, first of all far too small, and would have only ignited what he knew would be his already proven gigantic appetite; and secondly were offered only as "a line," never in a context wherein he could have scooped it into a jar, added baking soda or sodium hydroxide, and based it up to smoke—in his also non-existent glass pipe with nine screens.

When he burned out his nose, he started smoking alkaline form. And, given his very deep incursion into the lands of penury, there was absolutely no way that he could manage even a one-day binge of any size. Paul knew he would not, could not, be satisfied with anything less than a quarter, more likely, half "O" to have all for his own. But thinking like this only led him down potential pathways of great misery, self-derision, and tremendous longing. He was not clean long enough to have stopped having euphoric recall (despite all that had gone wrong; despite all that had been graphically proven to him that was pathological and extremely self-damaging about the drug and all of his relations with it; despite the fact that he was beginning to regain some small semblance of "sanity," whatever that was, since he had stopped using one hundred twenty six days previously).

To some extent it was the euphoric recall; to some extent it was the rather extremely isolated lifestyle he had adopted (he favored saying "forced to adopt") due to straightened circumstances, and the fact that almost everyone with whom he has previously been associated either was or had been in the trade; was or had been owed money by him; or was or had been seeking some kind of revenge or pay back from him. The other category was the large number of individuals who wanted absolutely nothing to do with him, either because of his intense and frequently blunt, overbearing or irritable personality traits; or because he no longer dealt in the highest quality product. To some extent it was a combination of all three.

Tonight, he had the opportunity to hang out with two of his favorite people from the halcyon days of being a prominent figure with money to spend, able to afford good restaurants, high-level carousing with wild and crazy people, and had a brief fling of seeming to belong in those worlds that he had frequented.

Tonight, he was at a very small gathering with two of the people who belonged to both categories, and who had the added distinction of really liking him, having shared numerous adventures with him, even when he didn't have money or product. He had somewhat reluctantly agreed to attend this small soiree in Sausalito, after half a dozen telephone invitations—despite the enormous amount of cocaine that would undoubtedly be on offer. He knew it would be an occasion of temptation, but also an opportunity for personal growth.

Though promised a sumptuous repast, and invited to indulge in it freely, Paul decided to pass on the meal—his stomach was too upset anyway, with his accumulated anxiety—especially since the food would be superfluous when the real centerpiece of this evening was presented for selected friends and associates—a "big bag" (pound) of cocaine. It was the kind of grand gesture as a party favor he had come to expect of Magnus, a quicksilver bright, erudite, literate renaissance man of the Twentieth Century, who embodied many of the traits and characteristics that Paul despaired of ever himself having—powerful, bold, sophisticated, urbane, a great businessman, sharp dresser, and incredibly suave and knowledgeable with women, all on top of being extremely buff and handsome in a most "manly-man" way. The only personal dissonance the man had ever exhibited was around being a Black man. Magnus felt that in many ways this was the distinguishing feature that set him apart in a racist-oriented world, but that (he believed) hobbled his "making it" as an artist.

Paul loved watching the man work in his studio, surrounded by completed works and works-in-progress, as well as the accoutrement (or detritus) of a working artist's studio: crinkled up tubes of paint, broken or worn brushes of many sorts, torn canvases, stretcher bars, rags and turpentine in abundance, sketch pads, boxes and boxes of various materials, textured and patterned, boxes of pastel and oil crayons, easels of different sizes and heights, jars and jars of brushes soaking, and inevitably, a grand variety of items of women's clothing, usually brightly colored panties (some of which ended up on canvases), lipstick cases, mascara palettes, as well as scarves and handkerchiefs. It was the first times in his life that Paul had been invited to working artist's studio (initially for purposes of business, but also for chess matches). He had become enthralled with the vibrancy and level of activity Magnus contributed to his art work (intense, but less sharply focused than with his major business).

Herb was dressed in his usual attire: worn blue jeans, white dress shirt with the sleeves rolled to mid-forearms, and a well-tailored vest, open. He seemed in full roar when Paul arrived slightly after 9 PM. In attendance were one of Magnus's girlfriends, Janet, the owner of a restaurant in Corte Madera, and Herb's ex-wife Barbara with whom he was still friends and lovers. She was a rep for a distributor of boutique wines, and usually provided two or three bottles of very fine pressings. Magnus did not usually drink, though he would have an occasion sake or cognac; Paul was not able to afford his longstanding habit of drinking 100 proof Stolichnaya, though he was grateful to see that Magnus had provided a bottle of the former in the freezer. There was a small retinue of women—all good-looking and clad in different upscale combinations of silks and denim. He was too depressed to even make the effort, though in previous times he had managed to become quite well acquainted with the women he met at Magnus's.

There were a few other people there, mostly from the many businesses Magnus had established at least in part to maintain the façade of being an successful entrepreneur, though they also provided services Magnus needed: a pickup and delivery company; a small boutique art gallery that mainly featured his work; a lithography and art print company; and, of course, a very discrete and thriving high-end escort service that functioned for him personally to provide for his "after hours' needs." Working hours for the cocaine trade usually ran to the latest hours of the night (or the earliest hours of the day) —or even occasionally longer.

Paul felt grateful to have escaped "the Great Wheel" of that kind of insanity, staying up all night, night after night, pursuing the elusive but always seductive allure of "just a little more," seeking some kind of revelation or redemption just around the bend of the next line, or the next altered state. Conversely, he had never been a very good businessman, in spite of really good tutoring from Magnus. Paul had always been too trusting to really crack the whip as he had seen Magnus do numerous times, ruthlessly cutting people out of his life and business, or both, for transgressions against the code of the craft or his personal beliefs. In the cocaine trade, there were just things that were not done—the old 'loose lips sink ships" had been reborn!

He felt somewhat ashamed at having been invited, in part for having "failed" to make his fortune and getting out (despite celebrating his recovery and harboring pride that he was not using). He felt somewhat emasculated in the company of successful persons from different levels of the cocaine trade—though he and Magnus were the only two who had really been down and dirty in "the trade."

"Want a hit?"

It was Magnus being munificent, gesturing broadly toward the big bag that was festooned with many small glistening chunks.

Paul hadn't even gotten his jacket off yet.

"Uh, no. No thanks. You know I been clean since August!"

"Thought maybe you might have changed your mind!"

"None for me thanks!"

Paul looked longingly at the bag, thought just for the slightest moment of how it might be to have just one line, one little line. But he knew better, far better than to take that one 'sucker line" —knowing he would not be able to stop, one inevitably leading to another. He didn't really want the snort anyway. If Magnus had offered him a gram or two, and a pipe, he might have fallen for the nefarious offer—and abandoned all of his hard work.

He decided to have a Stoli, with two cubes of ice—to see if he could manage a conversation that did not involve cocaine, or the "biz" in some form. But he was distracted by Herb's frequent and loud visits to the table, followed by his little manic dance, vaguely reminiscent of a Three Stooges hop, accompanied by a wild spray of hooting and howling, and an occasional spew of Hebraic homonyms and homilies.

Paul had promised himself to have only the one drink, but by the time he'd been there an hour, he'd already had three—and had kept refusing invitations to have a line. The more intoxicated he got, the better the bag looked, more enticing, more inviting, more seductive! He kept digging into the inner well of his strength. He had to keep reminding himself how excruciating had been his detox! He'd never had to titrate a detox off of any drug he had ever used. He just used until he burned out, and then quit. Cold Turkey. That's exactly how he had felt too. But with the base, he had had to back his dosage down and keep extending the amount of time between binges until he made his final pilgrimage with the glass pipe.

He retreated to a quiet corner from which to observe, and nurse his anxieties. Again, and again he questioned why he had come, and kept arriving at the sad and depressing conclusion that he would rather be in some kind of company than spend Christmas Eve alone. He had kept a loose contact with both Herb and Magnus after he'd gotten clean—but their relationship was never been again like the good old days when they'd all partied hearty.

"You look pretty isolated. Are you sure you don't want just a little line?

"No. I think I'll just go home."

"It's not even midnight yet!"

"I know. I'm just kind of...bummed out, I guess."

"How about a game?"

"Naw. I'm not up to it."

"Are you sure you don't want just a little. This is the real mother-of-pearl."

"I know. I saw."

Magnus put his arm around Paul's shoulder, and they turned toward the table. Magnus took what appeared to be about a gram-sized rock out of the bag and placed it on the mirror, procured one of several Deering grinders sitting around the table, dropped the rock in, and turned it several times, before twisting the bottom open to reveal a fluffy pile of perfect rainbow–scaled powder glistening. He dipped the edge of a credit card into the mound, and quickly laid out a hefty pair of lines, then shifted position, aligning the glass straw, and took a deep, intense snort, before handing it to Paul, who—feeling the brotherhood of the many shared memories of earlier amazing times—allowed it to overwhelm his sanity, as he applied himself to the other sparkling line, and snorted it.

And immediately started cursing, holding his index finger against his right nostril, that, despite the beauty and purity, started burning with sharp and intense pain.

"Goddamn! Goddamn! Oh, that fucking hurts! I'll never do that again!"

And he never did.

CHAPTER FIFTEEN
A Meeting with "The Master"
San Francisco February 1983

Cherise had recommended two docs. James Farraday, M.D. did not have an opening for another two weeks (plus he sounded snotty and arrogant on the phone). The other was Johann Augustus Frederich, M.D., who was not only Board-certified as a psychiatrist, but as both a Child and Adult Psychoanalyst. As such, he brought an enormous depth of field of his therapeutic foundation, and its variegated applications. Besides that, he sounded empathic on the phone—and, miracle of miracles, he had just had a cancelation, creating an appointment that very afternoon, if Paul could make it by 1630.

Cherise had agreed to get one of the on-calls to take his place on the PM shift, but he'd had to agree to fill in for a Day shift Tech who'd called in sick. For the first time in living memory, he'd agreed to work the day shift, and would walk directly there after work.

He began to anticipate potential glitches and other possible issues that might surface working with the day staff—not knowing how they would react in a takedown; not knowing who was the more verbal, and who might be best counted upon when things got physical, as they inevitably did; not knowing who would respond first when he called for assistance, and who would melt into the woodwork instead of assisting; and which of the nurses would quibble and dither, and which would respond immediately with the needed leather restraints and injectable meds.

Even though he frequently functioned as the "med nurse," he was almost always involved in the takedowns. He had found that many of the female nurses tended to congregate in the Nurses' Station, while he and the Techs (mostly male) tended to roam the floor and have both more contact with the patients, and a much greater presence and availability for immediate action, when and if the need arose.

Staff who worked together regularly knew each other's strengths and abilities, knew each other's moves in potentially dangerous situations, and were often able to act like one person in several bodies, using silent eye contact to communicate their intentions; knew that each takedown was different and always dangerous, though the primary purpose was always to contain the patient with as little force as necessary to keep him or her and the staff from getting hurt. When he stepped onto the unit, he had some small trepidation about these issues. He was early as was his wont, to do his usual pre-assessment about the quality and condition of the clients. It wasn't that he distrusted the opinions and assessments of the staff on this shift—he simply trusted his own intuition more.

He locked the outer door when he was in the sally port, and stepped through onto the unit. He could immediately smell/tell that someone had been incontinent during the night, and the noc(turnal) staff had not yet gotten the individual cleaned up. As he strode through the dayroom, he had an encounter with one of his least favorite patients of all time, Ted Meinz (who insisted on having his name pronounced "Mains," not "Mines), who was always quick to hector the staff when they did not comply with his idiosyncratic demands. Of course, they extended to almost everything in his life, around which he had erected minefields and barriers to keep what he saw as a hostile world at bay. Even given his social history, there was no excuse for his preying on the weaker and more debilitated, especially fragile older patients. He also had a history of becoming violent at a moment's notice. Paul and he had had enough run-ins before that Paul had selected him for membership in his (unofficial) All Time Hall of Shame as one of the worst patients he had ever encountered.

"Well, good morning, Paul!" said Meinz, as a grin split his pock-marked face, and a glint in his eyes that hinted at hidden agendas.

"Mr. Meinz."

"And what are you doing here on this lovely day?"

It was one of those amazingly gorgeous "Indian Summer" days of September and October that San Franciscans got as a reward for enduring the fog and chilly temperatures during the "summer months" of June through August.

Paul immediately went on guard, so he threw back a little verbal riposte of his own.

"I had nothing better to do today, so I came in to visit with you."

"Oh really? How thoughtful!"

"I expect you'll be on your best behavior today since I'm making this special visit!"

His grin deepened, if such a thing were possible, and Ted cackled when replying, "You can count on it! Yes sir, you can!"

Paul went to check on Tony Baskoff, the only geriatric patient on the unit. The old man greeted him as he greeted nearly every experience in his life now. He smiled his vacuous smile, one that carried neither joy nor enlightenment from his uninformed, undiscriminating brains cells, as he daily lost further ground in his battle with Alzheimer's. He would ordinarily have been sent to a specialty unit, certainly a less acute care unit, but as "Mr. B" became increasingly confused and disoriented, he became more violent too. His grieving wife of fifty-three years could no longer handle his mercurial behaviors and his four children too distanced themselves from him and his unpredictable antics. They were only keeping him until his insurance ran out. Then he would be transferred to a less expensive, Medicare only, unit. Since he could no longer care for himself, or administer his own money or affairs, he was considered to be gravely disabled under the provisions of the Welfare and Institutions Code Section 5150. The family was in the process of acquiring Permanent Conservatorship.

"Mr. B" always gravitated to the bathrooms. Perhaps the brightness attracted him like the proverbial moth. That's where Paul found him—water running full blast, and about to overflow. He had taken the toilet paper off the roller, and was blissfully, brainlessly, soaking strips of it in the sink, plastering the mirror and walls with it as a kind of demented paper-mâché art project.

Paul entered swiftly, and turned off the tap. He was immediately and acutely aware that Mr. B needed continence care that the Noc staff should have provided. He leaned out the door, spoke to one of the night staff, and apprised her of the situation.

"Well why don't you clean him up yourself?" she replied snottily.

Paul made a show of looking at his watch, and then said, "You've still on duty for the next twenty-five minutes, and I have to go to report!"

She scowled, and agreed she would "Get to him as soon as possible," and moved off to another task. Paul did a quick cleanup of most of the damp paper, threw it in the trash can, removed "Mr. B's" soggy pajamas, and settled him contentedly on the toilet, just in case there was anything else coming out of that end of his alimentary canal.

Paul washed his hands for the first of perhaps a hundred times that day. He went into report, and apprised the Noc shift nurse about the situation, who immediately scrambled out of the room, muttering to herself.

Paul had just expressed his premonition about Meinz when a ruckus broke out. It was perfect time for a psychopath like Ted Meinz to go on the hunt for the weakest prey, when the night staff was dragging from exhaustion and the day staff was in report. By the time the assembled staff got there, Meinz was standing in the middle of the dayroom, loudly announcing his innocence while trying to look as sheepishly virtuous as he could.

"I didn't do anything! I swear!"

Lulu, one Noc Techs, immediately contradicted him.

"I found him in Mr. B's bathroom! With his penis out!"

Meinz whirled, screaming "You fucking liar! You wouldn't know a hard-on if it slapped you in the face!"

"I walked in, and he was standing in front of Mr. B., waving his dick around!"

"OK, that's enough! Mr. Meinz, please go to your room!"

"Fuck that! I didn't do shit!"

"NOW! Sir!"

"Fuck you," snarled Meinz, and stepped back, preparing to battle and continuing to curse.

"That's it!" said Paul. He pushed the alarm button, and stepped toward Meinz.

"Take him down!"

Meinz stepped back, still protesting.

When Paul and Loretta approached, he swung on her, but she pulled back just enough so that his swing only glanced off her jaw, but sent her reeling.

By then, a veritable phalanx of staff was pouring through the door and flung themselves at the florid, agitated man. Paul, who was a veteran of at least a thousand takedowns, immediately asserted his authority.

"Grab an arm! You! Get that leg!"

Staff ended up sprawled around the man like a bunch of crazed Lilliputians on a fallen Gulliver. Meinz went momentarily still, condign after they pulled him to the floor.

"Don't let go! He'll go again any minute!"

The warning was almost too late, as the cursing snarling Meinz started bucking like a berserk bronco, then slammed his head from side to side, chomping madly at any body part close enough, and spitting until someone finally, mercifully, covered his face with a towel.

Meinz kept calling out to his "Master," what was later determined to be an auditory hallucination that they added onto his long list of symptoms—and changed his diagnosis to Schizoaffective.

"Give me Your Power!" implored Meinz.

Loretta came running up with four leather restraints, and handed them quickly into waiting hands. Her jaw was swollen, and there was dried blood on her blouse—but her eyes were clear and angry.

"Shout out when you have your limb secured," Paul ordered, as one by one all of the patient's appendages were accounted for. He did a quick visual check to assure that each limb had been properly shackled and was in readiness—leather belts pulled all the way through, each held firmly by someone other than the person immobilizing the limb.

"Somebody get him by the waistband! If he starts to struggle, take him down again! Keep him face down and watch his mouth! OK! On three!"

He made eye contact all the staff around the perimeter of the group.

"One! Two! Three! Lift!"

Curses and more invective poured from Meinz like a steady mountain stream. One staff member held the towel firmly around his face. Two other staff members wrapped their arms around his upper thighs and arms, as Meinz raved at them, threatening lawsuits and their jobs.

"One at a time! Don't let go of the straps!"

The mass of staff got temporarily jammed up at the seclusion room doorway, but soon had their quarry placed on the bed with the straps secured through the metal bedstead where slots had been machined to accept them. He was positioned face down to prevent his aspirating his tongue or vomitus, and cutting off his air supply. Meinz continued to struggle against the restraints as they were applied, necessitating that a staff member lay across his back to hold him down.

"He's trying to fuck me in the butt!" screamed Meinz.

His obscene references continued as the staff filed out of the room. Though they all theoretically understood that he was trying to provoke their negative attention, even violence, it still took a lot of self-control to not respond in a less than professional manner. No one wanted to "prove him superior" by doing anything his twisted mind could interpret as "inappropriate," and thus reinforce Meinz's opinions.

As they were leaving the seclusion room, Meinz spoke of Paul's mother having sex with various kinds of animals and insects prior to his birth. It drew an inappropriate laugh from one of the nurses, and a scowl from Paul.

"Just settle down, sir. We're gonna get you some medication."

"Fuck you! Fuck your mother! And fuck your medication too!"

As the other staff members filed out, Warren, Paul, and Loretta were left behind briefly. Loretta met their eyes, and then approached Meinz who was now crying and mumbling, begging forgiveness from his Master. They nodded at her simultaneously, and she swung her closed right fist into his rib cage.

"Goddamn bastard!" she said, then turned on her heel, and left the room. Paul closed and locked the door as they exited.

Several of the staff requested a rehash of the takedown, done at least in part to give people a chance to settle their adrenaline. Sometimes there were clinical issues, even criticisms, involved.

"Paul, I think you acted too quickly! You just came out of report, and the next thing I knew, the patient was on the ground!"

This was from a new Tech who had just started working there. It was, in fact, her first real assignment.

"OK. Let me break it down. Lorraine reported that Meinz appeared to be acting sexually inappropriate, maybe even contemplating sexual assault, with a demented man in his bathroom. Are you with me?"

"Yes, but I think..."

"I don't care what you think! We're rehashing the takedown now! This is not a theory session! Got it?"

"OK."

"Then he tells me to 'Fuck off!' That's assault! Understand? No one on this staff ever has to endure an assault! No one!"

"But I think you reacted too quickly!

"What do you suggest I should have done? Let him hit me? Spit on me? Attack me? Ain't gonna happen!"

"Well you could have tried to talk to him!"

"He was witnessed being sexually inappropriate! And then he defied authority! If we let him get away with it, he would have just gotten worse. I know this guy."

"But you could have…"

"What? Asked why he was waving his hard on in Mr. B's face?'"

"Well you reacted so quickly!"

"And you saw what happened! He attacked Lorraine when I asked him to go to his room!"

"Yes, but…"

"Let's get back to the beginning! Lulu reported that he was 'waving his penis around' in Mr. B's face in the bathroom! That was potentially sexual assault! Do you think I should have offered him a 'second chance' at that point?"

"I still think you might have overreacted!"

"I'm sure glad you aren't in charge here! I'm the Senior Tech! You're brand new! You're here to learn! So, then we took him to the floor, hooked him up, and got him to the seclusion room. Any other questions?"

Paul could feel the young woman seething with righteous indignity. He took a deep breath, and turned to her. He addressed her in a very quiet tone that was the antithesis of what he was feeling.

"And how exactly would you have handled it?"

"Well, I, that is, maybe we could have talked to him some more."

"And?"

"Well he might have obeyed if you gave him another chance!"

Loretta looked at Paul, and took another deep breath before speaking.

"So. Meinz told Paul 'Fuck you!' Then Paul asked him to go to his room. Do you have a problem with him asking the man to do that?"

"Well no, it's just that..."

"And legally, telling Paul 'Fuck you!' constitutes an assault. Ergo, it was right to order the takedown."

"But we should have talked about it!"

"No! Not in that moment we couldn't! We don't have discussions in front of patients. There's only one leader in a potentially dangerous situation—the most senior person present! That was Paul! And you don't know Meinz like we do. If we hadn't reacted immediately, he would have had the entire unit in a frenzy! I've seen it before! He thrives on that kind of shit!"

The young woman just hung her head.

"It's our duty to protect every person on this unit! We have to back each other up! If we had allowed him 'a second chance,' it would have just gotten worse. It's part of why I'm

Charge Nurse. That's why I get paid the big bucks to make these kinds of decisions."

Meinz stayed in seclusion, verbally vomiting his foul-mouthed garbage any time anyone approached. Since he continued to refuse oral meds, he kept getting injections until he finally quieted down. They checked his vital signs every hour on the hour. Mr. B went to the ER to assure that he had not been injured, and the Incident Report supported Paul's version of events—but, of course, he wrote most of it!

CHAPTER SIXTEEN

A New Therapeutic Encounter

San Francisco March 1983

I.

Paul contemplated as he traversed The City.

Releasing the toxic contents of his heart was the single most important thing he did for himself in terms of self-care. Yet he had strong resistance to letting down his psychic shields enough to allow his chronic discontents fresh air. It wasn't fear of pain as much as it was fear of exposure, or, even fear of exposing his shame to others; of putting it on view, and potentially making himself available for re-shaming. He even had shame about being ashamed—shame being the least talked about topic in psychiatric and therapeutic circles, even though to him it was the key element in all dysfunctions from addictions to "mental illness." He felt like a poster boy for shame, even carrying his shame of shame to the extent that he was ashamed of letting go of the shame!

He walked down Parnassus, through Ashbury Heights to Masonic, across the top of the hill where Fireman's Fund had excellently placed their offices.

He had heard many therapeutic approaches called "re-traumatizing," some of which he had experienced firsthand, including Primal Therapy wherein he yelled, screamed, and cursed without fear of being "too loud," or suppressing himself in any other way! It had been awesome! He always came away from sessions feeling so relieved! The naysayers were almost always those who had not experienced it, or were so fearful of their clients being "re-traumatized" by the work of being real and releasing the toxic waste that they themselves had built up huge theoretical and cognitive walls against it. Paul believed that they themselves were fearful of being real—and supported suppressive therapeutic protocols in order to maintain their own therapeutic opacity.

He reached Pine, and walked down the hill three blocks where the august offices of Dr. Johann Augustus Frederich, M.D. were located in a refurbished three-story stick-Italianate Victorian, up a set of stairs on the ground floor where his brain kept the train of associations about therapeutic interventions rolling.

Once he had experienced the pure Dionysian delight of being given permission to respond from the core of his injury, without fear of retribution or any culturally imposed limits. It was so wonderful to feel the wonder and power, the beauty and joy, of releasing his rage in a directed manner against appropriate targets! It was what he had always sought and had experienced. He could only call it redemption.

So many people went into therapy and didn't really do the difficult work required to truly heal. Some people seemed to think it was chic to say "My therapist says...," or to advertise the fact that they were making "progress" in their lives, like putting a fresh coat of paint on a house without cleaning off the old layers of dirt and grime. He knew it might be pathological, but he did feel superior to them, since he was intensely focused on letting go of the many old burdens he had for so long carried.

His new therapist shared the building with two other mental health practitioners, one per floor. There was set of buttons to push to let the various practitioners know that the next client was waiting. The only real drawback was the single waiting room, so that all of the comings and goings of all of the various clients were visible to the others, though Paul judged that it would, over time, not be an impediment. Actually, the ambiance of the waiting room facilitated his further mental meanderings.

He felt very strongly that a clinician should provide nothing less than a full-on opportunity for a client to emotionally release. It had always been his own best favorite personal approach. Doing so allows for the release of old memories and any attendant emotional bondage that the client has been carrying.

Beating the shit out of pillows with a tennis racket for an hour and a half each week had always left him hoarse and exhausted when he first did Primal Therapy. It had opened up what Arthur Janov had called his "armor" that had kept all the more profound and salient issues addressed by straight "talk therapy" safely buried, allowing the only surface to even be touched.

Sometimes he hated his shame, even as he served it, nurtured it, kept it fat and entitled like the haunches of an obese sultan—as it, in turn, perversely served him by shutting down his awareness of his deepest injuries. He kept a vapid hope alive, hoping one day to capture what he called his "keystone" or "cornerstone" memory, the very first building block of trauma upon which the template of his misery had been successively layered like geologic strata. He believed that if he could capture that moment in its fullness and release the gathered emotional pressure—catharct or abreact it, in clinical terms—he would be more relatively free to move ahead, to clear the "defensive constellations" he experienced as symptoms of PTSD.

He wanted the same thing from a therapist for his own personal work. For him it was imperative that he have a sanctuary wherein he could come and put down whatever burdens he was carrying. He needed to know that there was somewhere totally safe where he felt protected and welcomed enough to be completely honest. He had for too long protected his perpetrators as if they were sacred and necessary to his spiritual unfoldment, rather than impeding it. Now that he was clean, he decided to really commit himself to unravelling the Gordian knot of his heart in therapy this time, releasing eons of old rage, shame and recrimination. He wanted so badly to learn to embrace himself completely, to lavish his own most precious love all over himself like the most exotic soothing balm that ever was, assuaging the agony of his heart and letting his love shine.

Outside of deep emotive therapy, it was only in the throes of sex that he was ever able to temporarily release his most private fears and shame. Having sex was the closest he ever really came to experiencing the intimacy he so deeply craved. In that sense he went "to the well" as often as he could, seeking from women what he could not give himself—a level of love, honesty, safety, and ultimately, forgiveness that would allow him momentary respite from the aching, burning flames of his own heart. Such occasions opened the doors to his inner world without embarrassment, washing away some of the internalized poison, excavating his heart as if it were an ancient civilization being revealed by the tender ministrations of an archeological crew.

II.

Dr. Frederich was a tall, dark-haired, slender man in his early fifties. He appeared at first glance to be self-effacing, almost bland. For a man with such an enormous reputation, he appeared friendly and not terribly flashy, the opposite of what Paul had been expecting. As he came through the doorway, Paul could see that his years showed well on his face, adding a light patina of sagaciousness to his features. He was wearing charcoal colored slacks, a blue Oxford shirt with a psychedelic tie. (A Jerry Garcia?) He was clean shaven and looked to be about ten years older than Paul.

"You must be Paul Marzeky," he said, and held out his hand to shake.

Paul liked his clear gaze, and good eye contact.

"Yes, I am. Thank you for fitting me into your schedule, and so quickly. I...I really need someone to talk to."

In the inner office, there were Arica palms in colorful clay pots scattered around the large rectangular room that channeled the client's attention toward the far end of the room where a set of French doors opened into a small courtyard. Paul spotted a well-manufactured wooden bench, a small table, and a couple of canvas-back chairs out there.

There was a small pond, with what looked like koi splashing. (Paul wondered idly how they survived the winter). The art on the walls was all framed, and seemed to be high quality art prints of theatrical openings from San Francisco and New York as well as 1960's rock concerts that looked original.

He gestured Paul to the seating area, set apart on a small Persian rug that sat atop a much larger, older looking rug in the center of the room. There was a pair of chairs with a small table between them facing what was clearly his chair and another small table. The entire wall to his right were floor-to-ceiling bookcases filled with an incredible collection of books, many of them hard-bound. Paul glanced quickly at them and saw many of the expected clinical tomes, but there were also titles on history, art, and archeology, as well as a large selection of medical books in several languages—English, of course, but also French and German, and what might have been Russian. At the far end of the room on Paul's left was a large mahogany desk with a multiple line telephone, and several small *objets d'art*, including what might have been a Zuni figurine of an eagle carved out of some white veined stone, and another of a bear made of turquoise. There was another door to the right of the desk that was closed. (Paul would later find out that it contained a private bathroom, a small kitchen, and an extensive array of filing cabinets as well as yet another desk, this one devoted only to transcribing his case notes).

"Well then, let's get started. There is, as you well know, the inevitable paperwork. But we'll try to keep it to a minimum."

"I really appreciate that."

Paul mentioned being severely depressed, and almost immediately broke down crying. When Dr. Frederich did not intervene as it turned into deep, chest-racking sobs of anguish.

Paul grabbed the tissue box, wiped his eyes, and blew his nose several times.

"Sorry about that. I've just been so depressed. I must...believe I'm gonna get some relief here," he said, and then tucked his head as if to hide his shame. "Don't mean to be presumptuous."

"I think it is a valid assumption. Otherwise why would we be here?"

Paul laughed, very acutely aware of the use of "we," as if they were already forming the therapeutic bond that was at the heart of all healing, the "alchemy" that Argüelles had referred to as an "inner technology" —something severely overlooked in the "modern" world with all of its emphasis on lab tests and machines for diagnosis; with chemicals and surgery replacing human contact.

Paul looked at the opposite wall from the book cases. There he had displayed his various degrees and honors, all framed in what appeared to be burl wood. Paul had expected this, but also knew he would be put off by an ostentatious display. This arrangement though looked to have been done for the purpose of simply displaying credentials rather than inducing cowering in the less educated. His respect deepened even before they had really plumbed any of the soulful topics he wanted to explore.

The good doctor offered Paul a cup of tea, which he declined. He then produced a sheaf of paperwork from a small leather portfolio on his table, and handed them over.

"Let's get the paperwork out of the way up front. Then we don't ever have to deal with it again, and can talk freely. That's why I scheduled two hours with you today, so we can have plenty of time for an initial session."

Paul was greatly relieved. He had come to the session filled with an admixture of shame, pain, fear, and rage, marinated in dank depression, and flavored with suicidal ideation. Therefore, he approached filling out the required forms much more graciously than he ordinarily would have. Dr. Frederich addressed a first, broad question to him even as he wrote on a clipboard that held several sheets of blank paper.

"So," he said, his accent tempered by many years in America, though clearly Germanic with a French influence, "I know what brings you in today, but I would like you to add some more color to your canvas, as it were."

Paul immediately started crying again, and then, as the power and the rhythm caught him, sobbed for several minutes. He felt embarrassed, and, after wiping his eyes and blowing his nose, he tried to deflect his emotions by making a bad joke.

"Wow! You are one hell of a therapist! One question and I'm already crying!"

The doctor assumed the look of a detached observer (what Paul came to call his "psychoanalytic look"), and replied after a moment of silence and reflection.

"Are you ashamed of crying, here, in my office?"

Paul was taken aback a bit, because he had nailed it so perfectly, asking his question in such a non-shaming manner. He decided to plunge in and answer candidly.

"Yes I am. My father used to shame me for crying, telling me that 'real men don't cry.' Sometimes he'd call me a 'pussy!'"

"So, he was sexist as well as cruel?"

"Absolutely!"

"You work as a Licensed Psychiatric Technician, correct?"

"Yes."

"That is both an advantage and a disadvantage for our work."

"How's that?"

He steepled his fingers before speaking.

"The advantage is obvious. We share the uncommon language called 'Psychologese.' We can use clinical terms without a lot of explanation, though anytime I use a word you might not recognize or understand, do not hesitate to ask."

"Thank you. I'm really hungry to learn!"

He continued as if Paul had not spoken at all.

"The disadvantage is that you may know too much."

Paul started, and then interrupted him.

"That's what they told me in Viet Nam when I tried to get out!"

"Yes, well it should be obvious that you are an intelligent fellow, and, combined with the 'insider information' you had, I can see why. We face a similar issue here."

"I understand."

"So, as much as possible, I want you to keep an open mind, though you may question anything I ask. OK?"

"Yes. Thank you."

"So, let's try it again. What brings you in today?"

"I'm really depressed! And really, really pissed off! It's gotten to the point where I'm not motivated to go to work.

I...don't really even want to get out of bed. I just want to sleep a lot...and read. And write, of course!"

"And?"

"I cry every day, sometimes for hours. I have to work really hard to get motivated! I used to love my job, but lately I get so irritated with the patients...and the staff. Plus, I almost made a serious med error the other day!"

Paul went on to tell him how he had almost administered a hundred milligrams of Haldol that had been ordered as ten.

"So, you have someone on the unit prescribed ten milligrams of Haldol?"

"Yes, and he's one of my least favorite patients anyway. He's angry, depressed, demanding, and entitled!"

"Who does he remind you of?"

Paul was genuinely puzzled at first, then got angry, and finally started to laugh.

"Well me, though I don't believe I'm entitled. I don't feel like I deserve anything, not even...love."

"Do you still use drugs?"

"I smoked weed until last year, but I quit. Haven't done any cocaine since 1982!"

"You should be proud of that! Congratulations!"

"Thanks. But my depression has gotten much worse since I stopped using."

"And this surprises you?"

"Well, yes and no. I used to believe I used stimulants to lift my depression. I believed it was all real, even life-changing, in a permanent way."

"And now?"

"I understand that they just kept me from being aware of how truly fucked up I was."

"I see you took quite a lot of LSD. Did you believe in your visions?"

"I did," said Paul emphatically, "for a long time. Now I call them my 'LSD delusions.' I believed I was being permanently altered, re-shaped into someone who didn't have to carry all the sadness and sorrow that Paul did."

"Do you consider yourself to be psychotic?"

Paul had considered this at various times, especially when his behaviors were stranger than usual, or particularly reprehensible. He decided to roll the dice, and tell the whole truth; to use these sessions as a doorway to being more real.

"When I was loaded on a large dose of LSD. Or in the 'Nam, where totally crazy shit just passed for normal—because totally fucked up shit took place all the time!"

Paul drifted off into a soft reverie, and began to recount an experience at LZ Sally, near Hue City, in 1968—a memory still as fresh and vivid in his mind and heart as if it had happened yesterday.

The entire perimeter of the chopper pad was well-armed and extremely dangerous—fifty people, all locked and loaded. The electricity of the gathering was crackling, with a constant influx of new arrivals bringing both new drugs and renewed energy. No one even considered the possibility of lifers fucking with them. Someone passed me a baggie full of multicolored pills he called "fruit salad." I passed on it, just as I passed up heroin, barbiturates, a sticky wad of opium— even LSD sent from the world on the back of postage stamps by somebody's sister. I was smoking weed and drinking beer, and someone handed me a bag of large orange tablets.

"What the fuck? Chlorprimaquin (malaria tablets)?"

"No, man. Preludin," said one of the battalion medics, "diet pills. Guaranteed to fuck you up!"

I momentarily lost my resolve, and took two of the bitter discs with a swallow of my beer.

We shook hands and dapped.

"Paul. Paul Marzeky."

"Doc Roach."

""What's up tonight? I've never seen this many people getting loaded."

"I'm hip. We got some First Cav guys, Marines, even Seabees from Phu Bai."

"What's the latest poop (rumors)?"

"First of the O-Deuce lost a bunch of guys in the A Shau. Second of the O-Deuce captured four tons of rice and a whole bunker complex. 'Course, they only found three dead gooks."

The first rush of the diet pills blasted into my brain like a billion electric splinters, obliterating any memory of ever having experienced pain in my life. The exhilaration was so immense, so enhancing, so entrancing, that I totally forgot who I was, that I had ever existed. I was a newborn Sun Child. When I took off my glasses, I could see perfectly, though my vision was surreal, even psychedelic—the film projector of my brain gone berserk. Minutes (hours?) later as the rush subsided, and I began to feel I had a body, crimson flames of scathing paranoia rang in my ears—and I was suddenly aware of being surrounded by this mass of people—and totally freaked, as my true existential position was painted for me, etched sharply in my heart and mind! I was blasted out of my gourd!

But something was seriously wrong! How could there be this many of us here without some lifer fucking with us? I started gnawing rapidly on a large wad of chewing gum along with the insides of my cheeks. Fear and anxiety rushed through my feet like steaming rivers of molten lava.

They were coming! They were coming! The fucking lifers were gonna bust us!

I had to tell Roach!

"Roach! Roach! They're coming! They're gonna bust us!"

He grabbed me, and forcibly pushed me down as every cell in my body strained to run. They were coming! They were coming!

Paul tripped on a comment of William Burroughs' about an over-amp: "I got the fear! I got the fear! I got the coke fear! Ten thousand Chinese policemen are chasing me!"

"It's just the rush, man! You're tweaking!"

He handed me a bottle of vodka, and said "Have a hit of this."

I didn't want any, but I had to trust somebody. Liquid fire burned down my throat, as yet another rush shook me like a grand mal seizure. My skin was splitting open, unable to contain my light and heat!

"WOOO-EEE!! This shit is a motherfucker!"

I extended my hand, and we slapped palms.

"This place is getting a little too freaky. Wanna play some Hearts?"

"Abso-fucking-lutely!"

We drew the shades, and prepared two separate decks for play. I could barely sit still. My stomach was jumping. My cheeks were shredded from my manic chewing. I had an unmistakable feeling that someone was standing behind me. I kept whipping my head around, but there was no one there—and my back was against the wall.

Paul had gotten excited while retelling this tale with pure euphoric recall.

The doctor met his eyes, and stated, rather laconically, "You were, of course, under the influence. So that makes possible the diagnosis 'Drug Induced Delusional Episode,' not something more organically psychotic."

Then Paul responded, in a burst too long suppressed.

"Sometimes I think I might be a multiple!"

It was Paul's deepest fear that he might be so severely dissociated that his personality had fragmented into discreet alternate personalities, each handling different aspects of personality organization as if by separate beings—hence, Multiple Personality Disorder (MPD).

"MPD is not a psychotic condition. It is a Dissociative Disorder."

"I have done some things in an altered state that were very strange."

"That is to be expected, no?"

"Yeah, I guess so."

"But we should take it up when we have more time. Is there anything else you want to address today?"

"Hell, yes! Something very important!"

"OK."

"I've been so depressed that even my co-workers have commented on it. And then Cherise Rosenbaum, the Head Nurse—she recommended you because she thought I might be having some old issues from the war re-surfacing; that I might really need 'professional help.'"

"OK."

"And personally, I think it goes back a lot further."

"Certainly."

"And, well," said Paul, lowering his head in shame, "I've been having serious suicidal ideation lately." Then he jerked his eyes up to meet the doctor's, "But I don't qualify for a 5150! Don't put me in to the hospital!"

"I understand. And this ideation—do you have a specific plan and the means to carry it out?"

Paul knew he was definitely on the griddle now. This was the delineating question that drew the line in the sand, as it were, between voluntary outpatient treatment and involuntary in-patient treatment. He had asked the same question of patients hundreds of times.

"I...have moments where the intent is strong, even times when I want to jump off the top of a building like the Transamerica Pyramid. But it's never gotten that far."

"OK. So, what do you want to do?"

"Keep working on my issues."

"And medication?"

"I'm generally opposed to psych drugs."

"Medication can be quite efficacious."

"I have heard so many docs tell their patients 'You're going to have to be on this the rest of your life!' I don't want that!"

"I was definitely thinking short term. An antidepressant. You're severely depressed. Why not?"

"Can't we just do the work in sessions?"

"Maybe if we had five years, and you could come in five days a week, we could do classical psychoanalysis. Your insurance only covers an hour every other week, so that's not feasible. Besides, the latest studies show that the combination of medication and therapy is more effective than either of them alone—by something like 13% with a base of a thousand cases."

"Really?"

"I will never lie to you."

"Can I think about it until next time?"

"Of course. And we can also talk about your going on disability."

"How did you know?"

"Clearly, you're having trouble functioning, and Cherise recommended me. The obvious conclusion is that you might benefit from six months off to do some intensive work on yourself."

CHAPTER SEVENTEEN
The Beat Goes On
San Francisco March 1983

The session had lifted some of the burden off his shoulders, and Paul felt a certain amount of his hope restored at the thought of getting six months off work! How exciting!

Even though he badly wanted it to last, the sense of relief couldn't possibly! He knew it was just a taste of the possible! He knew this kind of relief was always transitory, a special kind of altered state! But the severe edge of his depression had lifted for the first time in weeks! And fuck anybody who tried to mess with his head!

He felt as if he were being seen and heard. He had been craving it so much, the emotional equivalent of vitamins and minerals, proteins and nutrients. The old adage of Hermes Trismegistus, "As above, so below," seemed so related to Paul's interpretation, "You can only have what you already are," or the old "like attracts like." Paul really did not believe the popular adage that "opposites attract."

Even feeling this deficiency did not stop him from being sexually magnetic. *Au contraire!* Magnificent lifetime memories! Sweet beautiful encounters of feeling greatly loved, and memories of orgasms that shook him like a Force Five hurricane curling his toes (which he had always thought a myth!). Despite all of this, there was always a narrow margin in which he was separate from himself, distanced from the marrow of his own experience—watching himself as if he were a spectator at a hockey match, a disconnected doppelgänger as from the ceiling of a surgical suite. Always aware of his deep-seated need to be a "people pleaser" —wanting, of course to get his own needs met roundaboutly through others—pounded into him repeatedly by his mother's incessant needs and demands, as if failing to please were the cosmic equivalent of being wiped off the roll call of love. Paul continued to constantly excavate his personal history, and it sometimes, even often, it triggered flashbacks, and not always about Vietnam.

Of course, some of them were.

The more Camp Evans shaped up its physical plant, the more the lifers seemed to think we should embrace the bullshit notion of "military discipline," wanting us to shine boots and brass, and get regular haircuts—in order to make themselves feel righteous and more important. This seemed proportional to the troops becoming more aware of Mental Hygiene, like the relationship between caribou herds and wolf packs. Most had a completely wrong take on what I did, or what they thought I could do. I had even resorted to triaging an enormous pile of referrals to determine those in most need and urgency. The one rare, and major exception drifted in one day while I was busy writing up more than a dozen evals.

He was medium height, with gaunt, sallow cheeks that defined the planes of his weather-beaten face. His blond hair was crew cut, and he wore camouflage Screaming Eagle patches on both shoulders of his sun-bleached tiger stripes, with an "LRRP" tab on the left. I was surprised. Usually the Long-Range Recon Patrol guys kept themselves to themselves. They were an extremely tight bunch. They had to be. Spending days, even weeks out in the most isolated locations with only each other to depend on to guard each other's backs in small bands ranging from three to eleven, they were traditionally very closed-mouthed around anyone else. He had a banana clip inserted in his AK-47; what looked like an old K-Bar in a sheath worn handle down on the left side of his chest; and a 45 caliber auto on his right hip. Usually the guys who appeared at my door disarmed themselves first, but I figured, if this guy is LRRP, he deserves to be a little freaky. He'd rather give up a body part than his weapon!

He stood just to the inside of the tent, scanning left-to-right, front-to-back, his eyeballs swiveling like marbles in olive oil. Conversely, he appeared defocused, as if looking inward a thousand yards, and had lost contact with the reality to which most of us subscribe. Then, perhaps unkindly, I had *the thought that he was loaded on some new substance I hadn't tried.*

"How can I help you?"

"You can't, man. Nobody can."

"Then why are you here?"

He shook his head in genuine confusion. "I don't know, man. I really don't know."

I squirmed a little deeper into my seat, suddenly paying much better attention.

"Why don't you have a seat? Let's talk about it."

CHAPTER EIGHTEEN
Aftermath
San Francisco April, 1983

Gray slashing sheets of rain fell from the dispassionate sky, drenching all and sundry. Paul sat in one of the window seats in the dayroom, contemplating. He had always loved the rain—the petrichor, that magnificent smell, the fresh ozone-like refreshment the Earth released just before it rained, clearing away pollutants; the feel of the rain, especially when he was walking in it well-protected in his London For greatcoat with the hood nice and snug, and his waterproof boots; the sound of the rain as it pattered, or smashed against windows and roofs; and the taste of the rain and its effervescent promise of new life.

He was flooded with remembrances: during childhood, playing in the back yard in the rain with his plastic soldiers, immersed in a fantastic journey through enemy territory—while his mother screamed at him to come in out of the rain, and he refused; a snippet of a Janis Joplin song where she was "looking out at the rain," reminding him again of her loss, and Jimi Hendrix, and Jim Morrison...just terrible, terrible losses to the revolutionary culture they had embodied, an edgy, powerful movement that was dying a little more each day, as the entire planet got swept up, directly or indirectly, in "Reaganomics" and the full tilt boogie of greed and capitalism: and finally, and of course, the many, many days he had sat sodden in canvas tents, or plunged through the smashing slashing rains to board a chopper to a distant fire base to interview a man where the rain was omnipotent; ubiquitous, the rain ruling supreme; and it had never had any qualms about destroying the best laid plans of humans.

Paul sighed. Thank all the gods that at least it was quiet tonight! The last thing he wanted was another rowdy night! After all of the personal roiling turmoil of the last year, he really longed for what Henry Miller had spoken of: "Even a bad novel needs a place to sit and a bit of privacy." It was so true! He was grateful to have finally (he most fervently hoped and prayed) come through the darkest days of this life relatively intact. But even relative was a relative word! It all related to that with which one was comparing for quality or intensity or severity. Compared to a year ago at this time, his life was far, far calmer and much, much improved in many dimensions!

Paul had been suffering ever since he had stopped using, as if he had lost his very best friend; had been in mourning ever since, with massive sadness, huge bouts of crying that he thought might never end, and whole days when he had cried for twelve hours. Some days he could barely walk, or talk—felt so sodden, so weighed down by sadness and sorrow he couldn't get out of bed; so terribly encumbered with the terrible weight of the living memories he carried in the very cytoarchitecture of his body, enmeshed and embedded in the vascularity of his cells, nerves, veins, and arteries. There was no part unaffected, no aspect of his beingness untouched by the blinding saturation of his soul, his psyche, with the artifacts and elements of his personal history that could not be, could never seemingly be, erased or ameliorated. He wanted so much for his personal history to no longer haunt him, torture him, causing great shame and sadness with the remembrances, that shattered his night dreams and polluted his daydreams—for which he had previously expended so much of his life force, seeking relief and expiation for which he had vaingloriously saturated himself with chemicals to create a foothold on a specious peace.

Sometimes he felt as if he were drowning in a sea of unction, lungs filled with unbreathable potions and balms intended to heal, but that were actually killing him. He then had to make a point of taking deep breaths, afraid that he would not, could not, get a breath, all of the vitality snatched from his body, and vacuum sealed—accompanied by angina pectoris, and the fear that he might experience a myocardial infarct (heart attack). Sometimes he would become faint, short of breath, vision faded to black and filled with purple spots—feeling he deserved to suffer in payment for the abuse he had inflicted on his body, as if by a sweaty, grossly overweight, leather-clad sadistic tormenter in a dank medieval dungeon.

His writing had suffered through the three years of his being strung out. It had decimated him like the Black Death sweeping across Europe in the 14th Century, sparing only random strangers. Soon after compiling a rough first draft, all he had managed since was a batch of poems written during highly-altered and amplified states. Very occasionally he had brought forward fragments of a dream character here and there; a burst of dialogue; even one memorable dream sequence in which "thick, slab-faced men said "All men must be free!" The "biz-ness" and pleasures of cocaine in its myriad forms and functions ate up all of his time, stemming from to his delusional belief that he could work four hours a day selling coke, live the high life, and write extensively!

Of course, he loved exotic substances, what he called his "delicatessen" —unique psychedelics, like DMT (di-methyl tryptamine), STP (2,5-Dimethoxy-4-methylamphetamine (also called "Serenity, Tranquility, and Peace"), even a revival of what they used to be called MDA (methyl di-oxy amphetamine)   or   MMDA   (3-methoxy-4,5-methylenedioxyamphetamine   5-methoxy-MDA),   later became known as Ecstasy. He had once encountered an oddball friend of the chemist Owsley, who had a stash of the original produced LSD for the early Bay Area rock bands, including the Grateful Dead and the Jefferson Airplane. Paul had also experimented with altered compounds of LSD, like LSD-8 and LSD-13, for which he had eagerly been a "tester." A new connection had been re-kindled, a connection a bit like of the lost energy of the 1960's, amongst the fellowship of dealers, though not as loose and far more cut-throat. A notable exception was a beautiful LSD source named Maya with whom he traded cocaine, always hoping to get another level of relationship going, but to no avail. Cocaine was far more expensive and did not lend itself to navel gazing or far out adventures of the sort that LSD and marijuana did. Until about mid-1980 when Ronnie Ray Gun maneuvered the extremely racist "powder versus rock cocaine" law through Congress ostensibly "to stem the flow and use of crack." It was actually genocidal, locking up young Black men who were the most frequent users of small amounts of crack. Paul had known a group of White dealers who regularly based up an ounce at a time in a giant pickle jar with baking soda or sodium hydroxide.

It was all so easy at first. He was never paranoid talking on the phone about product, or having fifteen or twenty people coming to his apartment every day. It was just no big deal. But in short order, he got completely burned out on dealing in small quantities, and with dilettantes who thought doing lines was chic—and quickly moved up as quickly as possible in the biz.

The rain continued slamming down against the side of the building and jolted Paul back into the present. Tonight, he was working the Alcohol Detox unit. Most of the patients came with Blood Alcohol (BA) levels two or three times the legal limit (1.0). He had even seen a guy once with a 5.19 who was still walking and talking, though severely impaired. The unit protocol had been designed to keep serious drunks from going into seizures and getting brain damage. After they were given medical clearance, usually at one of the ERs, (St. Luke's was nearby), but it could be any of The City's hospitals, the patient was admitted swiftly, had his or her vital signs taken and noted; and was then given an immediate IM (intramuscular) injections of thiamin, and folic acid (two of the essential B vitamins destroyed by chronic alcohol use). They were put into hospital pajamas, and loaded with either four or eight milligrams of paraldehyde—chemically related to formaldehyde (embalming fluid), and was quite potent. It had to be given in a glass container as it melted plastic on contact. This would "snow" the patient, lowering the seizure threshold significantly, and put the patient into a deep sleep. The rest of the night was then a simple matter of making frequent rounds, assisting patients to the bathroom as needed, and taking vitals throughout the night—followed, of course, by the ever-pressing and necessary paperwork.

He wished, sincerely and dearly wished and prayed, that he could just go home and write, sit down and put pen to paper, or even better, open up his little Olivetti portable and knock out a thousand words or so. He was still afflicted by what was called PAWS, or Post-Acute Withdrawal Syndrome, which affected ex-users who remained clean, but continued to have withdrawal symptoms, sometimes for a year or more after stopping active use.

It was most noted clinically with benzodiazepines, though Paul still experienced a myriad of symptoms: the expected strong and almost irrepressible desire to use; to feel the surging electric rush like taking off in a jet without the plane; and the usual severe depression and mood swings; but then his recovery tacked on anhedonia, the extreme loss of interest, and he felt like he had lost the ability to think or write or feel—felt betrayed and abandoned, as if he had never had any ability, or had had to sacrifice it to the gods/demons of cocaine for the extremely altered states that made ordinary experiences seem so utterly bland to a brain that had long ago transgressed the culturally-approved brainwashed neural pathways.

Mostly he thought it had been worth it, the price he had to pay in burnt-out brain cells and the lingering sequelae. It seemed that he had been destined, even pre-destined, to walk the path he had taken, to have the experiences he had had, to become the person he had, to fulfill the future he had not yet seen or lived, as if there were a fate he had been assigned, a destiny given to him, and him alone. Paul often vacillated between the poles that defined his existence; and when he attempted to escape this orbit toward the other dimension where he felt he belonged, one that seemed beyond his reach. On rare occasions, he "saw" aspects of that more rarified, gentle, and beautiful world. A sea breeze could trigger it, or the scent of a flower, or a woman's smile could transport him—and he would fly away to that other place, so far away, yet as close as the feathered touch of grace.

Despite this joy and wonder, flashbacks recurred.

After doing another quick scan of the tent, he pulled a chair against the side of the desk so that he could keep constant vigil on the tent flap doorway. He draped his weapon casually across his knees, and kept his finger on the trigger guard. When he began to speak, it was as if he were speaking into the air, talking to others only he could see.

I felt completely disarmed, as if I had been transported to another reality in which none of the old rules applied. I stuttered and stammered a bit, trying to get some coherent words to form. I felt intuitive alarm bells going off in sequence and series as my nerve endings fired at hypersonic speed. Psychiatric nosology and diagnoses poured in montage-like, and I started sweating even more profusely along my hairline, under my armpits, and my crotch. The recon man sat stone still, watching and listening. I had a moment of the purest paranoia, believing for a moment that he was reading the wild thumping of my heart. I was I freaking freely, sending out copious prayers to gods known and unknown, asking for the tools to handle what I knew somehow was about to transpire.

"So, uh, what's going on?"

His eyes blazed with fire and hatred, a palpable sense of danger and pain emanating from him, his aura markedly erratic. Then he turned his focus on me.

"We're all gonna die, man. No one here gets out alive."

I knew I was in deep shit, and sinking fast. I recognized the last as part of a Doors' tune, but he'd said it in such a flat tone that I knew he was not hearing rock-and-roll in his head.

"What do you mean?

"Shorty and Roscoe," he said, followed by a long pause. "McNeer, Hurdley, Jones, and Schwartz—they're all dead, man. The LT, and the cherry. They're all dead—and so am I."

CHAPTER NINETEEN
The Changes Continue
San Francisco April, 1983

Everything that had ever happened in his life had pushed him to ever more deeply explore his inner workings, his faults and foibles, the pathological underpinnings of his dysfunctions and aberrant behaviors—and the tremendous spirit that lived within him.

He really didn't give a damn about anything except writing. He regularly wrote poetry because it kept the fires of his emotions burning. It got him higher any drug.

Paul had vowed as a child that he would one day be "Dr. Marzeky." He had wanted it, craved it, needed it, lived and died for it—as if having multiple college degrees would or could change him into someone he could love. When he was young, and bullied at school and battered at home, he often fantasized, wishing he were an asshole, one of the schoolyard bullies. As he got older, he was tormented when he saw the asshole "bad guys" get the girls he wanted—especially when he was always on the sidelines, wishing, hoping, praying that he might one day measure up to the hidden standard these other young men had, that was so attractive to the girls he wanted.

He wanted to be somebody; to be recognized for his brilliance, charm, sophistication, manners, grace, eruditeness, wisdom, and knowledge of the world. He wanted women to flock to him, throw themselves at him. (It took many years for Paul to realize that he was seeking the kind of recognition healthy mothers imparted to their children as separate and sovereign beings, not simply making them into lifelong emotional appendages still attached by an invisible umbilicus). He had felt lonely all of his life, like an ulcerated, leprous urchin. He longed for unconditional love. It had only rarely occurred to him that he could home himself that way, so strong was the proscription that he had to earn love. It was as if he were from another planet where the rules and social etiquette were so different that, in the words of Van Morrison, he was "nothing but a stranger in this world."

His earliest desire had always been to go to medical school, but it no longer appealed to him, though psychology did. Vietnam had shown him where his skills and abilities lay. On psych units, he had suffered through having to watch Masters students—even Psychology Ph.D. interns—completely bumble interactions with patients with their inept attempts to intercede, coming out of theoretical contexts they had been taught that were not backed up by real life experience. When clinical students treat patients like aberrant creatures, instead of injured individuals harmed by the cruel treatment of a violent society devoted to greed and avarice, using everyone, parasitizing everyone, for money, it only contributes to the problem.

Often the most difficult-to-reach patients seemed to respond to him the most readily because he had a more open approach and really listening rather than regurgitating old, stale maxims and rigidly held principles pushed by formal schools of psychology and their turgid ideology. Adhering to brand loyalty defeated what a more empathic method might achieve.

He'd learned a long time ago that he had an ability to heal people's headaches simply by laying his hands on the person's head. He always knew where someone's pain was, and the tracks it took as it started to recede. Knowing his innate abilities drove him to get more education so as to get the hell out of the trenches. He needed academic validation so that he could use the skills and abilities he already had in order to practice healing his own way. Of course, he could charge a hell of a lot of money too, but that was not, and never had been, his goal.

Nevertheless, he believed that he was an amazing healer of souls; and could help many others gain entrance to a new way of life. He wanted to share the beauty, wonder, and joy of the work could do, utilizing the import of his own healing, though his road might look unorthodox to others. Healing himself and others were intimately tied. It wasn't rock and roll, but it was the music that lived in his heart.

When he looked at some of the chronic cases with whom he had dealt, he despaired of humanity. He actually held very little hope for the human race as a whole. He thought of humanity as a kind of blight, even a cancer, silently and indiscriminatingly eating its host alive from within. It certainly reflected his own despair about the future. Emotional and psychic enmeshment seemed to cut across gender, racial, and economic lines. He considered using the topic as a research study at some point. There were so much to know, to explore, that was needed to provide a more infinite fundament. It was a taste of schadenfreude, a guilty sense of enjoyment, not so much in the pain of others as a sense that he was so much better off than them—especially in that he had the keys to the asylum and could go home at night!

He always felt drawn to the most extreme situations and the patients in the most extreme danger, distress or need. It seemed to ignite, or best facilitate, his ability to help healing from the compendium he carried in his head. The trippiest thing about it was that he seemed to know what to do intuitively—and it fed his personal growth as he felt his way into the *Terra Incognita* of his immense gratitude.

And for some reason, unbeknownst and perhaps unknowable, Camp Evan intruded.

I thought at first to attempt a "reality orientation," but quickly changed gears. I needed some fucking help, but anyone who walked through the tent flap was likely to get wasted. Or he might decide to make me dead too! I wished myself far away in the arms of a loving woman on a beach where they had never heard of war. Instead I made my first big mistake. I asked who all of those men were.

Brother X stopped breathing, and sat like a stone statue. Then he took a very slow, measured breath through his nostrils. I remember thinking that if this cat smoked dope, he could hold a hit for <u>three</u> minutes easily. Then he breathed out, "Bllaaaahh!" all in a rush that startled me. I jumped back, making a little screech as goose pimples raced up and down my arms, and the hair on the back of my neck stood up. He scrunched his head down further into his fatigue jacket, then flicked a steely-eyed hawk-like look at me before he froze again, looking very much like a fossilized turtle.

"You know who they were, man."

Oh shit! Now I was being written into his fantasy, or delusion, or whatever he was experiencing. And I didn't like it. It was the last place I wanted to be. I felt paralyzed, unable to do anything sane like get the fuck out of there. I felt hypnotized, as if he were a snake or bird of prey. I froze too, aware of the nearness of danger. I experienced the vagrant impulse to leave a thousand times, but I knew I could move neither fast nor slow enough. He would definitely grease me! Then I made another big mistake.

"I've never heard of them before."

His head swiveled toward me as if it were operating with a disused set of gears in an ancient monastery. Then, again, he shot me "the look."

"Come on, Doc—they were in our platoon."

Jesus! What next? And how do I get myself out of this alive? Those guys were obviously people in his platoon. And they were dead. I warred with myself about being therapeutic or just being human, even humane. My quandary was exacerbated by the fact that I had to piss like a motherfucker. I didn't think he would be terribly affirmative about me going out to the piss tube!

"Why don't you tell me about it anyway?"

"They're all dead, man. And so am I." His mantra.

Clearly traumatic dissociation; probably delusional. Combat Fatigue. Shock. Possible fugue state. I didn't know—maybe Multiple Personality! This was some kind of bizarre psychotic reaction, but I had no experience with anything like it. I swore I would never again complain about writing up 212

Discharges! I listened, then decided to trust the flow of directions that seemed to be coming from a higher authority.

"How do you know you're dead, brother?"

He answered in the same flat voice, one that emanated from a safe place devoid of emotion, pulling the words from a deep and painful place he could barely touch.

"Dead people don't feel things."

CHAPTER TWENTY
Changes Redux
San Francisco The Next Day

The following morning, Paul awakened excited, even euphoric, with memories of the previous day's session. He felt so good that he called in sick, deciding to languish in the comforting glow of the feelings that had surfaced, the post-adrenal release of grief.

He decided to give himself a cherished day off in bed. It was something he only managed once or twice a year. His apartment was comfortable. He had plenty of food in the refrigerator and pantries; and, best of all, absolutely no good reason to have to go out. He decided he was going to read in bed, write, rest, reflect on his life's experiences, and nap. And later he would bone and butterfly the leg of lamb he had taken out of the freezer the night before, stuff it with garlic cloves, roast it with onions, and make mashed potatoes, and gravy, and have cranberry sauce with it. How delicious! It would only need an hour and a half to come out crisp on the outside and rare on the inside. That would be his big project for the day. He rolled over and opened the novel he was reading, the latest in the Burke series by Andrew Vachss, *Hard Candy.* For a backup, he had James

Lee Burke's first Dave Robicheaux book (how he had missed reading him before this was beyond belief!) *Neon Rain*. Jesus, this was going to be exciting!

That first day off was marvelous, a day without real responsibilities or pressures, without schedules or chores or errands, still rippling with the psychedelic echoes of the day before. So right, in fact, that Paul decided to call in sick again the next day. He had rarely taken a sick day, so there was no rumbling or grumbling when he did so, just a reminder that, starting with the third day, he would not be paid without a doctor's note attesting to his illness. This, of course, would generate more income for the doctor because it would require an office visit.

He had cooked the leg of lamb yesterday, and had a meal of the tastiest parts closest to the bone, as well as the crispy skin, along with several roasted onions, and a thick gravy made from pan drippings. Today he would cut up the more roasted portions, and create a sumptuous lamb stew with potatoes, onions, carrots, turnips, garlic, thyme, and bay leaves, finished with a cup of hearty red wine. It would cook for three hours on low heat in his trusty cast iron Dutch oven, and fill the house with savory aromas.

He called Dr. Frederich's office, and left an impassioned plea on his answering machine, appealing for his official support in taking the rest of the week off; and see him early the following week. He explained the situation from his point of view, and stated, rather boldly, that he thought he deserved to be qualified for State Disability, and wanted to pursue it forthwith.

Of course, what was hidden in all of this potential bureaucratic manipulation were the real and very dangerous nadirs of a dark and fulminating depressive episode to which he was susceptible, as if he were a little boy's fragile paper boat caught up in a suddenly stormy froth. Even though he felt resilient, powerful, alert, aware, even brilliant at times, at other times he felt totally incapable of getting out of his own most foul and dark moods.

He had even had to give some weight to, horror of horrors, acceding to his new therapist's repeated "suggestions" that he might benefit from "a short-term trial" (whatever that meant) of anti-depressants! There had been times lately when he couldn't pull himself out of the corkscrew tail spins that his anger, rage, and self-hatred had created—with the inevitable result of his frequently seriously considering suicide. He had witnessed how often some people got a lot of attention about a "failed attempt," or showing off the scratches on their wrists. What utter borderline, narcissistic bullshit! His would be dramatic and final! He would fly off a thirteen-story building, or jump in front of a BART train. (He had been on the verge of both at different times, and remembered the immense power, the incredibly magnetic draw, attached to what he perceived would be the cessation of consciousness—no longer having to carry around 24/7 the burden of his own torturous thoughts!)

Today though, he was feeling safe and sheltered like a pupa in its cocoon. When Dr. Frederich returned his call, though, it shattered his mood. He was quite brusque, even short, with Paul, until he realized it was 1935, and likely the end of a very long day for his shrink. Nonetheless, he found himself pulling back, the glorious aura that had surrounded him all day receding. Though he knew it was ridiculous to feel abandoned, even repudiated—it was just what it was. After he endured a short reiteration of what the limits of his medical insurance were, a tentative silence ensued.

"I'm really sorry to bother you, but I'm not doing too well. I called in sick because it's just not worth it enduring another eight hours of the bullshit!"

"If you quit, your insurance won't cover your visits."

"I know! I know! But my health is more important! Every single bloody day I go in there, something or someone sets me off. I am a bundle of nerves, like I'm trapped in a minefield, and anywhere I turn, I'll get blown up."

"Is that a real memory?"

"No, it's just how it feels. I could say that I feel like people are just waiting to mess with me, but I know that's not true either."

"We haven't really explored you experiences in the war. I want to get into that during our next session."

"Perfect! Me too!"

"Your insurance only covers one hour every other week. Which would mean that I cannot see you until next week."

"And I'll have to go to work, or lose the pay!"

"I don't usually do this, but let's say, theoretically, I were able to create an extra slot in my schedule."

Excitedly. "Yes."

"And again, theoretically, if I were to offer it to you."

"Yes!" Emphatically.

"If I were to do so, I could see you for half my regular rate, but payment would have to be in cash."

"And that would be?"

"A hundred dollars."

"Absolutely! But I'll need a note from you, excusing me for the three days I took off sick!"

"What day would you be nominally returning to work?"

"This is Thursday. I'm calling in again tomorrow, and I am off the weekend. So, Monday at 1500."

"Can you come in at 0900 on Monday?"

Paul groaned, and said, "I'd rather it be noon!"

"0900 is the best I can do."

"I'll be there. And thanks for working with me."

"*De nada.*"

"By the way, do you know a psychiatrist by the name of Martin Browne—with an 'e'?"

"Why do you ask?"

"He was living in San Francisco in 1968. And I know that the psych community here is so tight that!"

"Do you know Dr. Browne?"

"He testified for the defense in my Court Martial trial fifteen years ago!"

"We have a lot to talk about, young man!"

Talking about Martin Browne brought back thoughts again of camp Evans.

I leapt intuitively again, into thin air without a parachute.

"It looks like you're feeling pretty sad."

His neck almost creaked as he answered.

"I'm scared, Doc."

He was talking to me now, not the platoon medic. I had to keep him going.

"What are you scared of?"

A single tear ran out of the corner of his right eye, and dripped down the front of his fatigue jacket. I really didn't know what to say.

"Is it something to do with your guys?"

"No! Yes! I don't know."

I was momentarily tempted to offer to smoke a joint, but it was me that needed the smoke, not him. I realized I no longer needed to pee.

"What can I do to help?"

"Nothin', man. I'm dead."

"I'm sitting here talking to you. I know you're alive."

Fiery liquid tears filled both his eyes, and he replied "I'm dead...inside."

"Inside?"

"I can't feel anything."

"Like what?"

"Nothing. Everything."

"Isn't there anything you like doing?"

"Killing gooks."

Great. What next?

"When I get pissed off, I'd just as soon kill people as look at them."

This is progress?

"But don't you feel something then?" Wrong question.

His eyes shot fire at me as he jumped up, weapon at port arms.

"Pure hatred."

Oh Jesus! In the sudden silence, he sat again.

"And now?"

He quieted, rifle again across his lap.

"Now I'm dead."

I debated, then decided to take a risk.

"Would you to please put the safety on, brother? Just in case."

He looked at me for the longest time, his empty stare suddenly focused entirely on me, filling me with dread. Then he blinked and looked away, before hitting the safety.

"Thanks."

Now what? I really needed Captain Magnus Browne, wonder psychiatrist, right now! Where in the fuck was he? I had no idea. This cat obviously needed hospitalization, probably to be shipped back to the world for long-term treatment. But I had no idea how to get from here to there!

"Look man, I'm gonna be completely honest with you. I think you're really suffering. I think we should walk to the Battalion Aid Station so you can get some rest."

"I'm not tired. I just need to go back to my platoon. Then I'll feel better."

"Feeling dead inside must be really scary for you."

"Yeah it is," he said quietly. Then he jumped up and screamed.

"I keep seeing 'em! In my dreams! It only stops when I'm smacked out!"

"Will you come with me, to the Aid Station?"

"I don't wanna die! Please Doc, don't let me die!"

"I won't. I promise."

Just as suddenly the storm passed, and he was again angry and suspicious. He dropped his rifle barrel until it pointed directly at my belly.

"That's what you said to Shorty! And he died!"

I don't wanna die either! Help me Lord Jesus! A warm trickle of long-suppressed urine ran down my pants leg as my intuition fed me, words tumbling out in desperation.

"He was going to die anyway. Would it have been worse to tell him?"

Stifling a sob, he dropped his rifle barrel, and sat back onto the chair.

"You're right, Doc. I'm sorry."

I took three deep breaths before I knew I could speak without squeaking.

"Look. Let's get to Battalion Aid. I want to talk to the doctor there."

CHAPTER TWENTY-ONE
Manic Depression
San Francisco April 1983

"Manic-depressive" was yet another of the terms that Paul believed were either misused or entirely overused by non-clinicians—though Paul used the term to describe his lifestyle as such, because he always fluctuated between the extremes of the emotional spectrum, going through intense and extraordinary changes of mood, perception, and just plain life experience.

Although he might qualify clinically for the diagnosis as "Depressive Type," he also considered: Posttraumatic Stress Disorder (PTSD); Major Depressive Disorder (MDD); and Polysubstance Abuse (in remission). Since no one can spend 100% of their time in either mania or depression, there were always elements of the former mixed with the latter. Most of the mania he had experienced in his life had been purposefully induced, a result of ingested substances (amphetamines, LSD, and cocaine), aimed, in sometimes obscure or oblique ways, to alleviate his periodic depressions, the thick, black grungy clouds of his moods that felt like the sky before a major hurricane makes ground fall.

Paul had always carried what he called a "negative vision." Where others might have dreams or visions of ascending higher, or accomplishing great things, Paul always felt he had been born embodying the burden of many former lifetimes. Therefore, for him it was always a matter of quitting something (cigarettes); or changing behaviors (being obsequious with women), as means of demarcating his progress. Everything was measured in eliminating, not gaining, and hence "negative vision." (Though for every loss there is a gain, and vice versa). Overall Paul felt he had made significant "progress," though that was yet another specious term, like "reality," about which "everyone" spoke, but which few knew how to define, lost in the manufactured dreams and mandates of the planetary oligarchs as if such were the highest spiritual tasks. For the longest time, Paul had gone in the opposite direction and embraced the so called "New Age" Dionysian mantra of complete abandon— and had repeatedly tried to convince himself was actually working.

The thought that he was "getting a little bit better" in a variety of arenas was a vital measure, sometimes the only thing that kept him from blowing his brains out at least once every day. The almost infinitesimal slow-crawl was the only visible movement of his personal pedometer. He so often felt driven not to surrender to the great dominant repetition trance-inducing mediocrity like a gerbil on a wheel, continuously running in place and going nowhere—though he had always so deeply indulged in addictions of every stripe to fill the empty spaces inside, and now embraced the next in his personal line of dominos—and he did so with the unspoken promise that one day he would no longer have to do so. It was destiny or fate that drove him, especially when he was severely flagging, reserves low, running out of fuel—and just wanted to be relieved of the necessity of any further work, even though he was always reminded that he was not yet done; that there was still so much work to be done, required of him to channel or produce to be made real in the world of illusion and fantasy; to not give up either harming himself or others because it seemed right or necessary, but because he had gotten to the point where he no longer needed it; to dis-create a world wherein all violence was seen as a substitute for being loved, wanted, valued, needed, appreciated, admired, and cherished.

He believed it to be the only real "cure" for all human misery, for all addictions, for all "mental illness." Only genuine human care could ever heal the horrible machinations and manifestations, medicalized for profit, that were called "mental illness." There was simply nothing more powerful or more beautiful in all of Creation. Everything else was aberration, illusion, and delusion. Love is all there is.

CHAPTER TWENTY-TWO
Commitment
San Francisco May 1983

Paul was walking slowly—there was no need to rush, was there? —as if he were walking through semi-hardening liquid gelatin. Suddenly the sky looked different, brighter, and more alive; and the air seemed cleaner, less smoggy, and even more saturated with ozone, if that were at all possible on a sunny day. He decided he would walk all the way up Divisadero to the top of Broadway to take in the sweeping view from the Golden Gate and its magnificent bridge, down through Pacific Heights, Cow Hollow and the Marina, sweeping all the way over to Russian Hill, North Beach, and the Embarcadero. A million dollar view indeed!

And it cost him nothing, other than the price of living here in the city of his heart! San Francisco inspired him with its literary, musical, and artistic history, and all of the manifestations of its effulgent beauty so very visible everywhere. Oh God, how he loved her!

It only takes a tiny corner of
This great big world to make the place we love;
My home upon the hill, I find I love you still,
I've been away, but now I'm back to tell you...

San Francisco, open your golden gate
You let no stranger wait outside your door
San Francisco, here is your wanderin' one
Saying I'll wander no more.

Other places only make me love you best
Tell me you're the heart of all the golden west
San Francisco, welcome me home again
I'm coming home to go roaming no more!

Sung by Jeannette McDonald in the 1936 film, it was the closing theme of KOFY (formerly KTZO), San Francisco's innovative, and independent television station run by Jim Gabbert, one of the very best stations he had ever had the opportunity to watch—with diverse programming and Perry Mason re-runs five times a day!

He had visited the State Disability office, and had provided all of what he had been told would be needed including a note from a licensed, board-certified psychiatrist attesting to his inability to work, since he was claiming for psychological reasons. His disability payments had started arriving three weeks after the paperwork had been filed, and every two weeks after that. His medical insurance remained active since he was, in effect, injured on the job (though was not eligible for Workers' Compensation). Cherise had been generous, and happy for him that he was taking the opportunity to truly nurture himself! A gigantic relief indeed!

He saw it as a grand opportunity to heal, to explore the subterranean trenches and marine canyons of his psyche, and clean them up, integrate them, and not waste a bunch of time getting stoned, or other faux activity that would distract him from his real work.

There hadn't even been any argument after they had finished talking about Martin Browne and PTSD. It turned out that Dr. Frederich had actually known him both socially and professionally in San Francisco. Dr. Browne was still married to the same woman, and they had moved to Vashon Island, Washington where he had a small private practice and continued his research and writing of clinical articles. With my Release of Information in hand, they had spoken about me for over an hour, the clinical issues involved, and the propriety and necessity of my being granted medical leave. Dr. Browne also forwarded his strong suggestion that I go back to school and apply what he called my "wealth of talents" to getting credentialed as a Mental Health Professional!

Paul mulled over his agreement to "do a trial" with an antidepressant, one they had talked about at some length, especially after Paul rejected several of the ones he mentioned—having either given them out as med nurse, and hence had read about them so he could answer questions definitively; or having researched them on his own, ever since the topic had first been broached. Again, it was a case of him "knowing too much." Some part of why anti-depressants worked was "placebo effect." Simply put, they worked because the client believed they would. There were those who went even further, and said whether it was a "real" drug or an inert compound, the effect an individual felt was due to his or her innate healing power; that the client was inspired to believe that it would work! Paul had read a number of clinical studies, the conclusion of which were that antidepressants were effective for depression about 31-70% of the time; while placebos are effective 12-50% of the time—for an average antidepressant versus placebo difference of 20%. So, when Dr. Frederich mentioned the "latest and greatest," Prozac, Paul was immediately suspicious because of all of the media hoopla surrounding it. Paul had heard an unsubstantiated rumor that the former head of the American Medical Association had been paid a million dollars by Eli Lilly for a one-hour speech endorsing the drug at the American Psychiatric Association Annual Meeting! It was enough for him to say, "None for me thanks!"

Paul argued that if—and a mighty big one it was too—he were to take an antidepressant, he would prefer the old style, tri-cyclic Imipramine that he had taken for a year approximately five years earlier. Dr. Frederich argued against it, citing the severity of side effects such as constipation, and dry mouth.

"And don't forget loss of sexual desire! Doctors never tell their clients about that!"

The doctor reluctantly agreed, and Paul laughed.

"Just messing with you! I would rather be less depressed and less sexual for a little while than take any of the new shit! Just as long as you give me a 'script for stool softeners! That was the worst part for me!"

"You didn't tell me about this before. What was your response to the medication?"

"I've been trying to avoid taking drugs, but I seriously need some help. But it cannot be just the drugs alone! You have to help me work through the memories...to facilitate all of this goddamn rage and hatred! I want to be...a gentle man!" Paul blurted, and started sobbing, flashes of angry outbursts floating through his head—sometimes almost as if he were carrying the hallucinated haunting, taunting voice of his father! It was clearly his memory, but he wondered if auditory hallucinations weren't deeply imprinted shaming voices that had been dissociated and amplified by the psychotic process?

"So, you did well on the Imipramine?" Dr. Frederich asked, bringing him back into the present.

"I took it for a year. It was the first time in my life I knew what it was like to not be depressed. It was kind of shocking actually. One day it just hit me: Hey I'm not depressed!"

"Why did you stop?"

"Two reasons really. I did not then, and do not now, intend to take any drug for the rest of my life. I'll only take it to facilitate my natural healing process. And two, I had a strong intuition that it was time to stop. So, I titrated myself off of it!"

"And now?"

"Two things. First one is, it seems like I need a tune up. I'll do a year max."

"And?"

"The other thing is, I trust you. I really feel like you are going to help me!"

He gave Paul some sample packs, which he accepted reluctantly.

"Is the loading dose still 75 milligrams?"

"It surely is!" answered the good doctor, and they made an appointment for two weeks. Paul pocketed the pills, and stepped out onto the small porch at the front of the building, contemplating all that was before him, both literally and metaphorically.

Spread out before him was a pie slice of one of The City's many incredible views—Cathedral Hill, Transamerica Pyramid in the far distance, and a piece of downtown. He contemplated several possibilities. One of which was to go get a drink. Even though he had essentially quit drinking, there was still some skeptical/delusional aspect of himself that was really and truly convinced that he was not an alcoholic, and in that moment, he was really craving a Drambuie, as if capitulating to taking psychiatric "medication" were either a gateway for him to use again, or the drink would be, somehow could be, a reward for doing so. In either case, by the time he had trudged slowly up Divisadero, he had decided "Hell no!" though he was still considering walking all of the rest of the way down Broadway, through all of the changing neighborhoods—Pacific Heights to Russian Hill through the Broadway-Stockton tunnel, through the edge of Chinatown to North Beach—just for the flavor and texture and the zest of vibrant city life! To feel the pulse and glow and excitement he always felt just being a part of this great urban adventure!

He always felt so proud to call himself a San Franciscan, even when putting his address on an envelope with 94127, or 94108, or 94133, or 94115 was uplifting. He always felt a swelling in his chest when he did so—and realized again how identified he had become with being in the Bay Area, as if living in one of the hippest, most artistic, most culturally advanced and aware areas in the world would rub off on him, and dissolve the residue of what he viewed as his tainted past, the living, Technicolor past, as if it were an indissoluble imprimatur that could never be erased! Once a Catholic, always a Catholic! Once a junkie, always a junkie! He fought so hard against such rigidity and displacement because he believed in the goodness of his heart and the righteousness of his path! He would never recommend that anyone else follow the roads he had chosen. He only knew that they had been right for him; had always led and would always lead him to where he needed to go to achieve his own form of "redemption." He always had to remind himself of the origin of that word from the Latin, meaning to "buy back." In that sense, it was all perfectly designed and perfectly manifested, if only he could embrace a large enough time frame from which or through which to view it.

Fighting against the given had sharpened his personal tools sufficiently that he had hopes that he would one day "arrive," reborn and triumphant, shorn of the past and shining forth in numinous glory. That sounded so goddamn Christian! It was repulsive to him in that sense, yet that was the way the vision painted itself, with him having dropped or used up all that had retarded the golden beauty that was truly him, and being allowed (how passive!) to shine forth in his native glory, unencumbered by naysayers and sycophantic usurers claiming some part of his development or might, as their own—for he would have worked every single inch of the way, as his bleeding fingernails would show! He lived for the day! Not that there wasn't some level of personal victory in it! He was not, and would never be, a saint! He was just a full-bodied man living out his destiny.

Having eschewed the idea of a drink, so too did he put aside the walk to North Beach. He ambled down Broadway to Octavia, then turned south to cut over through Lafayette Park where he lazed in the sunshine, relishing the fact that he did not have to hurry, did not have to worry (too much), and most especially, could look forward to the evening alone, listening to some good tunes and journaling for hours if he pleased; or new poetry; editing a more solid version of *Brotherhood*; perhaps even starting a manuscript for a book about a confused and depressed recovering addict Vietnam vet who's too depressed to work—and is given the opportunity to read and think and write while making perambulations through San Francisco, the city he loved above all others.

CHAPTER TWENTY-THREE
Yet another Loop
San Francisco June 1983

Paul awoke without cursing of the day, but with a soft sigh of gratitude, and a sense of emptiness and relief—as if an eight-pound tumor had been removed from his chest. He had always ashamed to cry in the presence of other men, especially with all of the existing cultural condemnation designed to suffocate the emotional and psychological catharsis that could free all men of the internalized oppression. For the longest time he had blamed himself for being deficient, lacking testosterone, damaged by his mother's influence, or, in lock-step with his father's judgments of him. All in all, he had worn his damage in the way most people wear clothing, as a signal to others of status, power, strength, and place in the world. He had to admit he had attracted more than his share of the downtrodden, scammers, manipulators, and thieves than he felt was his due—though they likely only reflected his own bad attitude about himself.

He had endured beatings, harsh words, derision, and imprecations of his being homosexual because he cried when he felt the need, washing clean his internal slate of all the clinging emotional vomitus he might otherwise have suppressed. It had been his salvation. If he had not been able to cry and to write, he would never have survived his childhood. It had served to make him stronger, more resilient, and more capable of dealing with the crass and the crude. It had been a kind of foreplay, in a sense, for him to enter the healing professions.

Remembering and integrating this required devotion as well as a great deal of time and attention. Some portion of his daily journeys, his "San Francisco Perambulations," were devoted to this, to the big "Why?" and to his gradually diminishing sense of abject depression as it got sorted, re-hashed, and ruminated about every single day of his sojourn, leading to his "re-orientation," as he walked through the sylvan glades and towering eucalypti of Golden Gate Park.

He had mapped out a number of trails that were designed to suit his moods, the weather, and the contents of his mind. There was an eight-mile walk, a nine-mile walk, and two different five-mile treks, all taking in the wonders and splendors of his favorite park in the world. Additionally, he loved walking to and from all manner of appointments all over The City, routinely enjoying the views and vistas that San Francisco bounteously provided. He loved San Francisco totally and irrevocably—and yet his affection managed to grow more steadily and steadfastly than in any relationship he had ever had. He was committed to spending the rest of his life here, and finally have his ashes released near the Farallon Islands. It seemed an appropriately romantic gesture. The Ohlone people named them the "Islands of the Dead" because they were considered to be the abode of the spirits of the departed. They were only thirty miles off the coast, yet the locals rarely, if ever, travelled there. The voyage and the currents were extremely dangerous, and the spirits palpably ruled there.

It was during his meanderings that he contemplated long gone, both in fine detail, in swaths of agglomerated memories, or in pastiches of small segments sewn together into a multicolored and mellifluous quilt of thoughts, dreams, and bitter-sweetness. He often felt his chest heave and his belly roil, and his heart convulsed with tremors and tremolos that rejuvenated, him, following the oceans of tears filled with prolactin and cortisol that accompanying his psychic release.

He was so proud of being a San Franciscan, having joys unexpected as he walked endless miles, burning off the energy generated by his continuing recovery (now coming up on two years!), and the dissipating sadness and depression. Walking had become the third leg of his troika of recompense and reconciliation with himself, added to crying and writing as instruments of his redemption.

He had found that the loneliness and isolation he had previously cursed were actually a blessing, allowing him to write without having to pay attention to the needs and deeds of others. He frequently found himself wanting to be alone, to try to express the inexpressible; to clarify his thoughts and feelings; to distinguish them from what he had been programmed to believe was real and true; and develop the smallest wedge of sanity against the might of the North Atlantic winter storms pouring over his starboard beam. His isolation was the only solid, three-dimensional lodestar he had, anchoring him in the vast sea of unconsciousness that seemed to be populated by souls with no bearings or anchors—driven hither and thither by the vast currents, the primal energies of the Universe, without any concern or consideration, swept away by the cosmic winds like the shriveled wings of a butterfly that fails to make it out of its cocoon case.

It was writing that sustained him, gave him an anchor in the world, no matter how tentative or fragile his hold otherwise. It was the most "real" thing he experienced, outside of sex, the most true and steady connection with his inner world. It was the only arena wherein he could express his distilled and digested thoughts and feelings, and allow their fruiting, creating a more coherent worldview of his own construction. (He had a fantasy of writing a book called "Memoirs of a

Visitor to Planet Earth," in which he would expose "normal" daily activities as being the completely insane orientation they must appear to anyone not indoctrinated into the violence and brutality of this planet). His journals had always been his best friends, the repository of his greatest joys and flights of fancy, and his lowest and most profound moments of being ready to leave the planet. He had even written a suicide note disguised as a poem called *Guru* in 1970.

Writing was always there for him, no matter what mood, no matter what moment. It was his true work, while anything done to "make a living" was simply a job to support his writing habit. In terms of the literary, he was a stone junkie. There never had been, probably never would be, anything that he wouldn't do to keep writing. Just as when he had been actively using, he took enormous risks to guarantee himself a steady supply of whatever he needed. No matter what mood he was in, writing welcomed him, made him comfortable, cooked his dinner, gave him his pipe and slippers, watched a video with him, and then made mad, passionate love to him at the end of the night. Writing was his compensation for putting up with the daily deadly bullshit imposed by the owners and producers of the "spectacle reality" provided by media and government—though which one owned which remained a good question.

Having thought of the "Big G," as he called it, brought back Camp Evans yet again.

Momentarily surrendering, he simply nodded his head. I very carefully came out from behind my desk, staying immediately in front of him. He seemed completely done in, depleted, as if he had gone as far as he could under his own power. Now I would have to take over. My fatigues were completely soaked with sweat and piss. My brain was operating on a wavelength that I hadn't even known existed before, and I was reminded of Nietzsche: "That which does not destroy me makes me stronger." I knew I was gonna be a strong motherfucker after today!

I parted the tent flap, and we walked out slowly, taking tiny shuffling steps. He carried his weapon with a finger in the trigger guard. I walked beside him, talking to him in low, soothing terms.

"Don't worry about anything now. Just walk with me. OK?"

He nodded his head again, shuffling his feet, eyes downcast. Out of the periphery of my eye, I saw Rush coming our way. Oh, motherfucking shit! Not now!

We called him Rush because he would drink, shoot or smoke anything for the rush. I had seen him shoot speed, heroin, and whiskey, even water. He was the only person I had ever seen put a cubic centimeter of air into a vein to get high.

Lately he'd been walking around babbling, a rambling monologue of garbled poetry. Nobody seemed to know what he was doing at Sally, except maybe he worked a permanent night watch in S-4 (Battalion Supply). He always seemed to know when to keep a low profile; but he had been known to be extremely intrusive too. This could be a very dangerous time for him to act out.

I tried to steer the pair of us away from him, but he locked on like a fucking guided missile.

"I am the chalice of the mendicant...lost in the great and gravid graveyard of old dreams and schemes..."

Oh, fucking Christ! Now what?

"...I am ages of medieval penury and deprivation...with no vision or purpose..."

His monomaniacal mush of words preceded him like the droning intonations of a mad monk. I could see an otherworldly light burning in his eyes. Oh, Jesus God protect me!

My client—God, I didn't even know the cat's name—must have sensed Rush's alien energy approaching. He tensed up, and started walking pretty tall. Though his eyes were still glazed, his weapon slipped naturally into his hands, and he whispered, "Don't worry, Doc. I got it!"

I was afraid I might fragment into a thousand shards of broken crystal.

"...the hangman is shadowing my dreams, but I am again denied..."

Click!

The sound of his safety switching off broke through my reverie. My brain went into high gear, preparing a miracle crisis intervention—various scenarios running at nanosecond speed from conception to rejection. Rush and Brother X halted, peered deeply into each other's eyes—and smiled!

What the fuck? Over.

Rush made a peace symbol with his right hand, and moved on as if this were just another chance meeting with an old friend.

Brother X's face looked slightly less ashen as he slipped the safety back on. His attempt at a smile was as eerie as a rictus as he slouched along at my side

"Some people just shouldn't take drugs!" was all he said.

I laughed, massive pressure easing off my chest.

In my most soothing voice I asked, "What's your name, brother?"

"Arrow."

"Great name!"

He smiled his secret smile, though his eyes were far, far away, deep in his own dream.

As we neared Battalion Aid, I spoke soothingly again.

"OK, Arrow. We're gonna be talking to the doc here pretty soon. You're gonna have to check your weapons. I'll make sure I get a receipt for them."

He stiffened at the mention of having to give his best friends to a stranger, so I spoke harshly into his ear to get his attention.

"Listen man. I'm on your side. You have to trust me. Dig it?" He nodded weakly, and I continued.

"These are very good people here. But they're a bunch of REMFs."

"I'll trust you with my weapons."

"Roger that."

Arrow tensed as a Spec Four corpsman stuck his head out.

"I gotta see the doctor right away. It's Paul Marzeky, the Psych Consultant." He disappeared inside quickly.

"OK, brother. I am not going to desert you—no matter what these folks want."

The doctor came through the tent flap accompanied by the corpsman, and an E-6 Clinical Specialist. Fortunately, it was one of the doctors with whom I had become acquainted on my fairly rare visits to Battalion Aid.

"Can we get this man settled please? He's a psychiatric casualty!"

Arrow allowed himself to be assisted onto a gurney, but insisted I stay in close eye contact. He very reluctantly pulled the clip out of the breech, dropped it on the ground; then pulled back the bolt, and ejected the round in the chamber before he snapped on the safety, and finally handed it to me with a look of sadness. He went through the same procedure with his 45, as if on automatic pilot, implying that no matter how bad things otherwise were, there was still a proper way of managing weapons. Then he unstrapped his K-Bar rig as if it were a bodily organ.

"I'm the only one he trusts at the moment, sir," I said to the doctor, holding Arrow's personal armory as we shifted slightly to speak privately and still keep an eye on the brother.

After a quick glance at Arrow, he met my eyes, and said, "What's up?"

"Sir, I believe this man is having some kind of psychotic reaction. He does not appear to be on drugs. He's reporting that his entire team has been wiped out. I have no details about that. For a little while, he thought I was his platoon's medic. He seems dissociated, completely stressed out, possibly delusional. He is very suspicious, easily startled, and has razor sharp reflexes. Don't move too quickly around him, and speak softly."

"Why do you say 'psychotic'?"

"Mostly I believe he is delusional. He stated that he thought he was dead." (Paul found out much later that this is a rare *symptom called Cotard's delusion, named after the man who discovered it in 1880).*

"Well clearly he is alive!"

"Yes, sir."

"What do you want us to do?"

"See if you can raise Captain Browne on the net. He's the most qualified to deal with this. In the meantime, keep him as quiet as possible; and in as quiet a place as possible. He looks dehydrated. Maybe it's just his electrolytes. I'll talk to him see if he'll take some meds, maybe a Valium. Could be he hasn't slept. This may all be transitory, but it surely looks like Combat Stress Syndrome" (the old name for Posttraumatic Stress Disorder).

The doctor was tall, heavily fleshed man, with thick bushy eyebrows and black hair above a very Semitic nose. He conferred with the Clinical Specialist, who then disappeared further into the tent. And then he then did a very uncharacteristic thing—he agreed with me without asserting his authority!

I stayed by his side as the orderly took his vital signs, and the Clinical Specialist got a line running with normal saline with 5% glucose. Though Arrow seemed comatose, I stood by, whispering quietly, giving him constant reassurance.

Doctor Jacob Mieszcowitz ordered some labs—electrolytes, complete blood count, serum toxicology screen, liver function tests, and a couple of other panels—and then, at length, spoke to me.

"Do you think he'll answer a few questions?"

"The basic bullshit will probably agitate him. I just spent the last two hours getting him to trust me enough to get him here."

Arrow started screaming in his comatose/fugue state "I'm dead! I'm fucking dead! They're all fucking dead!" The doctor ordered five milligrams of Valium through the IV lock just as Arrow shouted, "It's all my fault!", and started sobbing, pulling at the IV line, and attempting to get off the stretcher before we applied soft ties to secure him and give the meds time to work.

CHAPTER TWENTY-FOUR
Reflection or Regression?
San Francisco August 1983

Paul awoke from yet another of the continuing series of dreams of Vietnam (now the politically correct way of spelling it), wondering if he would always be haunted by spectral images from the past. This was actually the least problematic aspect, compared to other symptoms that sometimes showed up: bursts of rage triggered by seemingly insignificant words or odors; overreacting, jumping even, when startled, as when a waiter approached the table too quickly; the seemingly unavoidable shudders and shakes when he dwelled too long on a touchy topic; and the goddamn nightmares! Almost fifteen years! Did the shit ever really end? Or was this just part of the price he had to pay to evolve, to keep working on his material until he could integrate it? At least that was what the literature on PTSD indicated, a process of gradual desensitization leading to the virtual extinguishing of the traumatic materials and the attendant reactions.

Paul felt exposed, as if constantly on public view, as if he had eviscerated himself, and plastered his innards on a wall in a kind of performance art, like a quasi-Rembrandt painting of a surgical theater or an abattoir; as if all of his nerve endings were on the surface of his skin, so exquisitely sensitive to every movement of the air, or touch of any sort; that he had to consciously examine very moment carefully for content and potential impact in terms of enrichment or harm. It felt as if his pre-frontal cortex had been removed from the equation of his processing, without an autonomic nervous system to screen out the multifold possibilities of every moment.

Gautama Buddha ostensibly said that during the time it took to blink your eye, thirteen trillion sense impressions were available to the brain. If the autonomic nervous system were highly evolved, one could easily deal with the filtered essence that came to conscious awareness. If, on the other hand, one were in either a highly altered, or lowered, state of awareness, one might find oneself overwhelmed and battered by the massive onslaught—and feel rightly inclined to withdraw as a sort of protection, fending off the offending thoughts, pictures, and ideas—attempting to do the best one could do in such a circumstance simply to survive.

He considered the possibility that he was, in fact, "mentally ill," of which he had been accused many times. It was a term bandied about most especially by those who had no idea what they were talking about—a hundred fifty years of trying to "prove" the biological basis of mental illness, and no concrete evidence! No lesions! There was one study that found correlations with organic changes to the brain with schizophrenia, but the researchers withheld the fact that their test subjects had been "medicated" for ten to fifteen years prior to the study! So, of course they had brain damage!

The highly regressed, almost feral, behaviors that some severely psychotic people exhibited was in marked contrast to the dulled and apathetic mien of those whose pre-frontal cortex had been injured by lobotomy or ECT. There was an equivalence to be found, to a lesser extent, by the emotionally traumatized. They often presented as individuals in whom the thin veneer of socialization had been stripped away. Paul considered that it might relate to the question about how the subconscious might have originally developed as the storehouse of old memories, fears, and traumas; and why the terrible injuries of early life often did not manifest sometimes until decades later. And had a connection to the world of dreams, so explored by Freud and Jung, as the "royal road to the unconscious."

This line of investigation was certainly beginning to fit in with his own dimly glimpsed conceptions, his *weltanschauung*, based on what he was experiencing; and he wondered if it was his destiny to experience such altered states in order to develop more compassion for humanity, and thence for himself? What if everything were exactly right and correct all the time; and that he was supposed to make sense of it all, and create an ordering of it with his own mind that might ultimately make sense to others?; that he might be creating some kind of illuminated path through the darkness that others could follow; that he might have an evolutionary spiritual instinct that had driven him his entire life, through all of the shoals and shallows, through all of the reefs and retribution, in order that what had always seemed to him a massive struggle, might prove itself to be his own personal shining path of reclamation, of redemption, his own personal Hero's Journey? Or, he had to ask, was it simply another aspect of his delusion, created to comfort him through the many excruciating experiences, and the stranglehold of his own thoughts? Was he, in fact, truly grandiose, a "dreamer" as he had so many times been called; or needing "professional help," that strident accusation that had been flung at him like a handful of goat dung, shameless invective projected onto him by those whom he considered to be pitiably deficient in both courage and brain power, immersed in the stifling, petty dramas most people called "reality"?

There were, of course, periods of time when he did not feel as deeply depressed or withdrawn, like commas and periods in a paragraph; and he was even considering adding

Agoraphobia without Panic Attacks to his personal diagnosis. Although it translated as "fear of the marketplace," it was used to denote individuals who were fearful of open spaces, even though it might also include fear of being too close to, or around too many people (though he was definitely not xenophobic—yet). It wasn't exact science with him, though he was feeling an increasingly stronger aversion to human contact; he often did not go out of the house for days at a time if he could help it—even resented having to go out when he inevitably did. He had even taken to shopping at really odd hours, usually 0300 at the Marina Safeway. (It had changed from being one of the top pick-up spots in the "good old/bad old" days when cocaine was plentiful, and shopping there was a hunting ground at the end of a long day's labors). He generally found most people rude, loud, smelly, or obnoxious. He very rarely felt any need or desire to extend his boundaries by reaching out, or even to expend the necessary energy to withdraw even further. The former seemed a particular waste of time, and the older he got, the more realized the latter was simply regression.

None of which was to discount his real and genuine depression. There were times when he could easily have been the poster boy for what was now being touted as "Clinical Depression." His sadness was huge and encompassing, global in depth and breadth and width; and felt as if it were eternal, despite whatever best efforts he might contrive to put forth to stanch the intense emotional bleeding he felt. Sometimes it just took too much effort to do all of the little things required by daily life—showering, cleaning dishes, housekeeping, even having social congress, maintaining social relations—it all seemed false in many senses, having to put on airs of affability, maintain social etiquette and manners, tell lies when the truth was so much easier and obvious. What was the point? He asked himself this a dozen, a hundred, times a day. What exactly was the point of all these things that would seem so easy and important if only he were not so depressed?

He sometimes thought that other people were just better off emotionally, more well-adjusted, but then maybe that was an illness in and of itself! Maybe others were actually more fucked up than he was, but they lacked the awareness or sensitivity to realize it. Maybe what Krishnamurti had said so long ago—insanity is the only sane adjustment to an insane world—was on point? Ergo, those who were the most adjusted were actually the ones who were the worst off! But that was no real comfort to him, for all of his suffering, for all of the work he had done, unravelling the toxic mélange that he had endured as an intimate, intricate part of what he derisively called his "socialization," the role inversion he had practiced to take upon himself the mantle of responsibility for his parents' needs—and yet be egregiously punished when he dared assert even a fingernail's worth of effort to be himself, to ask for what he really needed and wanted, to become a relatively free and independent being, and finally escape the concentration camp of their control.

CHAPTER TWENTY-FIVE
If you're not Working on Yourself,
you're not Working!
San Francisco September 1983

Paul slammed his right fist on the arm of the chair, as his hair flew back against his face. His eyes were wide and focused as he repeated his demand for an answer.

"If I'm so goddamn smart," he fumed, gripping the paper in his left hand, "then why the am I nor rich and successful?"

His psychiatrist simply shot his cuffs, and looked at him benevolently, unflustered by Paul's display of emotion. He had become quite accustomed to it in the previous months, and, today was rather mild by comparison. He had been expecting the rant that usually followed such an expression of deep disgust and self-questioning, a rant that combined prayer and a challenge to the Creator of the Universe. It was Paul's usual way of deflecting the extremely ingrained shame that was so pervasive that it might have been built into his DNA.

Paul took yet another tack, pursuing the same direction.

Shaking the paper in his left hand again, he said, "It says so right here! Certified by a California State Licensed Psychologist in a monitored test! '150 IQ score' on the Wechsler Adult Intelligence Scale! I'm a fucking genius! But what the good has it ever done me? If I'm so goddamn smart, why aren't I rich?"

"There isn't any direct correlation between intelligence and 'success.' Success is a culturally-freighted word, and means something different depending on the context. If you were a Laplander, having fifty reindeer might make you a very successful man. You would accrue cultural credits in that society. It would make you a potentially good mate. Young women would seek your company, and wrongly reading your reindeer herd as a sign of your good genetics, might want to have your baby!"

This cool, rational response completely unmanned Paul's anger and the thrust of his rant.

"But, "he sputtered, in a significantly altered tone, "What does that have to do with me?"

"You've conflated the idea of intelligence with 'success' in such a way that you believe that being one should lead to the other, whereas the thrust of your question revolves around feeling worthy and valued."

"Wait a minute! Wait a minute! So, what you're saying is that what I really want is to feel loved and wanted, not necessarily that I want to be successful in the contemporary mode—because I don't! I despise the trappings of success as they're measured in this society! I especially hate the fact that it's all defined by money!"

"Money is gained or granted as a result of a certain...recognition, and certain agreements within one's cultural context, as a sign of acceptance both of oneself and the society."

"What? Wait a minute here! So, you're saying my aversion to the mechanistic ways of this society is why I don't have success?"

"It all depends on how you look at 'success.' Some people might look at you and say that you were successful because you survived the war!"

"Big fucking deal! So, what? I survived all of that bullshit, and then I come home! I get treated like shit because 'we lost the war.' By implication I am a loser because a bunch of politicians found it more expedient to keep the war going, and cause millions of deaths just to make shitloads of money?"

"Is that how you view your military experience?"

Paul sat up and took a deep breath.

"I'm very grateful I went into the service. It broke me out of my parent's house forever. But I don't support the patriotic rah-rah. I don't believe for a moment the bullshit that we were 'defending America's best interests' being in Southeast Asia. We were only protecting America's riches, and making billions of dollars! War is always good business!"

The psychiatrist merely flicked his fingers in encouragement for Paul to continue.

"Do you know about all of the 'patriotic industrialists' who invested heavily in Germany and Japan's buildup of infrastructure both before <u>and</u> during the war—Goodyear, Carnegie, Rockefeller, Morgan, Ford—all operating through the Nazi-controlled Bank for International Settlements in Basle, Switzerland.

"And?" asked Dr. Frederich with a raised right eyebrow.

Paul slammed his right fist onto the chair arm again.

"People don't matter, just money! We're constantly lied to, and nobody does a goddamn thing to stop it! We're taught to support this corrupt system without thinking about it! We're supposed to act like our lives depend on it!"

"You obviously have a lot of energy invested in this. Where's all of that coming from?"

"I...feel ripped off! I was used, I have been my whole life, all simply to benefit other people! I'm super pissed about it! And I feel powerless to change anything! I want to be loved and valued and honored! I'm a bloody genius! But nobody respects that! Nobody gives a shit about that!"

"So, what have you done with your 'genius' so far? What have you ever done that should give rise to generating respect?"

That question brought Paul to a grinding halt. The truth of the matter was, not very much. He knew he was really smart; that he had a pretty damn good handle on psychology; and his writing was really coming along. But he always got sabotaged by his emotions. He was jealous of people who had a lot of money, who could manipulate the world with their credit cards; who could have all of the women they wanted simply by dressing well and spending a lot of cash. He wanted that! He was sexually and emotionally frustrated! He wanted to feel loved and wanted! He wanted to feel powerful! He wanted to feel as if he mattered!

"Acceptance of yourself." Could it be as simple as that? Perhaps his rage was just a cover for feeling diminished? What if that was what all his symptoms really were? Not feeling worthy of love and intimacy! Maybe he rejected traditional "success" because he couldn't seem to have it—wouldn't allow himself to have it! Because he would have to sacrifice his precious time for it! Fuck that completely! He wasn't built that way! He never would be, try as hard as he might! The very thought of it was an abomination!

Paul then expressed this to his shrink.

"You feel you're out of place in the modern world. You don't feel like you belong. This may be related to your...belief that you come from another planet where the local time is far in the future. But that's material for another session. I want to give you a little assignment to work on, and bring with you next time. I want you to write about your genius: what you believe the nature of it is; how it might further you and maybe even humanity; and write about the nature and quality of your frustration at failing to be recognized for your genius. This will help you better focus on how you might manifest it in the world; and be more satisfied with yourself."

"Wow! OK."

"I know we usually do this first, but you seemed so ready today, I didn't want to divert you! I want to take a few minutes to check in around the medications. It's been six weeks now."

Paul had to stop so he wouldn't just have his usual knee jerk reactionary response. He <u>was</u> feeling better, less filled with rage, experiencing far less suicidal ideation—and he was still actually crying shitloads every day. Sometimes even watching a television commercial could trigger him into a gibbering spasm. The emotional release had nothing to do with cognitive functioning or reshaping thoughts. It had only to do with what he called his "vault," where he had stored countless pictures and film clips of abuse, horror, and shame, all of which, in turn, magnetized him to attract even more! No matter how hard he worked, the cycle continued.

He just couldn't shovel the shit out quickly enough to make a dent. He had to admit that his global opinion about psych meds might be just a little off.

Meds were not the answer. He had never believed in the "broken brain" or "chemical imbalance" ideas—or that medications were necessary to correct some kind of biological damage. Never! It was the utter height of bullshit! Traumatic experiences induced emotional damage that manifested as behaviors called "symptoms," conveniently adopted and medicalized. Paul was now feeling his feelings without being overwhelmed by depression. He was sorting through them, cleaning up decades of built-up psychological grime. He was feeling what he really felt, no longer driven by torrents of anguish and rage. It was the key piece for him. He would only take them as long as they aided his healing.

"I believe they've kicked in. I don't think it's simply placebo effect. I'm drinking lots of water because my mouth gets really dry. And the stool softeners help with the constipation."

"I really want you to apply yourself to your homework. There're many layers of purpose involved. You'll see."

"Thanks! Two weeks? Same time, same place?"

CHAPTER TWENTY-SIX
Loneliness is a Toxic Flower
San Francisco October 1983

It had been hard for Paul to keep his word about immediately doing his homework assignment for two reasons: the first was that he honestly could not enumerate too many things about which he should have garnered respect. This led to the rapid conclusion that much of what he was upset about was a more general lack of respect and his own collusion with the degradation he had suffered. The second reason was that he had spiraled out after the session into a whirling swirl of thoughts and memories, prompted at least in part by a flood of memories of Jimi Hendrix, and the lost era that he had been so blessed to experience.

It was a veritable cascade of remembrances mixed with equal parts of longing and hope. He remembered all of the wonderful, loose, hip, beautiful, and enticing women with whom he had been, some of whom had genuinely cared about him. Having a lot of sex was such an aberrant measure of "manliness." It really annoyed him. It was like value being measured by how big your bank account was, or how many cars you had. Such bookkeeping methods completely missed the mark as far as real value was concerned. Just another aspect of contemporary "civilization" that equated quality with quantity, and tallied spiritual growth with acquisition. The accumulated psychic weight of the contemporary expectations, especially having to carry it around, or deal with its effects every time he had to have any kind of contact with the "ordinary" world, made it hard for Paul to stay on Earth. It was very hard for him to relate to humanity most of the time. He really resonated with Jung's ideas about men projecting their internalized feminine nature onto women and expecting amplified emotional feedback from them, especially sexually. Look at all of the insanity surrounding "breast enhancement!" Mostly this was done by mentally unbalanced women who actually believed they would be more desirable to men! Most guys were aberrant anyway, wanting to create something about women that was just not natural. Jesus, it was sick—as if greatly enlarged mammary glands really made a woman more truly sexy in the soulful sense. Paul considered it to be a huge turn-off!

Conversely, Jung postulated that many women projected their animus (inner male) onto men as well, and looked for returns in big muscles, sports cars, and bigger wallets! This was in lieu of doing their own personal work sorting out their felt-deficiencies and inner disfigurements; and acknowledging all human beauty and qualities within themselves. He wondered if women pursued questions like this from their own angle, questioning their projections about men in such a way as to discover in themselves everything they thought they wanted in a man. And whether this was perhaps a key for him—to find in himself all that he sought in the mythical, mystical embrace of the perfect loving woman—all the love, kindness, compassion, and recognition he sought, and in his very own heart? But that would require him to be genuinely loving of himself first in the ways that he sought to love in another! It would require him to change his entire life, all of his attitudes, and relinquish his fears, his shame, and his pain!

Paul had always believed that he would find love for himself through loving another—hence the intense lifelong search for that one perfect woman, "SHE" somehow being the key to revealing his inner treasure, and furthering his spiritual evolution. It seemed impossible that any woman in her right mind would ever want to tackle the messy, chaotic, often violent inner world of any man? It actually did not make any sense. Why would she? Paul knew it was his work, his assigned task to arrive at a genuinely loving position vis a vis himself and his life, and have this as a more-or-less completed picture or assignment with which to exist, and to be in the world—and then, and maybe only then, start the search for a compatible companion with whom to share life on a totally different level, opening vast new vistas and incorporating huge new possibilities to share.

All the half-baked and sometimes completely crazy women he had known were all perfect reflections of where he had been at when he'd met them. They likely felt the same way about him in retrospect, if they thought about him at all. Not having an intimate relationship was a poignant lack of fulfillment in his life. He often spent time trying to suss out the cosmic paradox contained in and underlying this mystery that allowed him a glimpse that this undying hunger, this awful ache in his gut for completion with and through another, was in actuality a hunger for his own personal wholeness, completion within himself. He could never mediate it through drugs or alcohol, sex, work, or any of the other ways he had ever investigated. Only through being, sitting in selfness, naked and without artifice, could he ever get there—and he had no idea how.

His loneliness and his genius all seemed related. Paul had always felt that great conversation was the best foreplay. It provided a foundation for relatedness on the highest level. He admitted that he an intellectual snob, and had often used this as a way of keeping himself separate from others; or rather "screening" them for intelligence, awareness, and understanding, so that he did not have to waste time getting deeply involved with someone to whom he had to too often explain what he called "the ABCs" when he wanted to have a conversation about something much further along in the alphabet. He could admit that there were whole arenas wherein he was a novice or journeyman, but he was open to learning, not to just passively sitting back and absorbing other people's truth and nodding his head, but actively questioning them about details and history. He always loved it when he met someone who could expand an area of his already existing knowledge bank, especially in medicine or psychology. He often dreamed of having a relationship with a female doctor or psychologist—another writer would be amazing. Of course, they would have even higher standards, especially financially; and in all likelihood want more from him intellectually than he might be able to provide—although, and this was yet another crux, he knew he had the potential to be an excellent partner on those higher intellectual levels. But he could not, probably never would, be able to participate in terms of money and the world. It always came to that basic question: If I'm so smart, why aren't I rich?

In the contemporary world culture, the two arenas had become intimately tied in many ways, and Paul had (rightly or wrongly) conflated his happiness with being able to attract the kind of woman about whom he fantasized. He believed he had to "qualify" to be loved. He had to be rich, fit, and smart in order to have a chance at being loved—yet there were so many people who were none of the above who seemed to manage to make good relationships and have lives together. Why should he need to "prove" his lovability?

Unconditional love should be a given, a child's birthright, even though he felt it had been denied him. Perhaps there were those who were born into circumstances that precluded being loved—by addicted or distracted parents; or parents who had been abused and/or not loved themselves; or born without parents or abandoned by them, and had been left to the not-so-tender-mercies of the State. (He always thought about Nicolae Ceausescu who had banned abortion and contraception in Romania, and subsequently abandoned all of the resulting orphans to the specious ministration of the State and then stripping away all of the funding for their care). Perhaps the whole human race suffered from some form of attachment disorder, and was unable to form close intimate bonds? Maybe that's why he believed the human race *in toto* was suffering from massive addictions and a penchant for violence because of not feeling a connection with others, not having empathy with/for others?

"What are we going to talk about afterwards?"

It all really boiled down to his being loved and lovable in his own eyes. Paul had never found lower intelligence particularly attractive, no matter how beautiful the body might be. He found it boring and distracting. He really wanted the entire package of beautiful, mind and body—the Greek ideal.

Paul had always loved his intellect, as much as he disparaged the physical, especially his ever being able to approximate the cultural ideal of the twelve-pack abs. Of course, if he put as much time into the physical as he put into the emotional/mental, he would be a King Kong. The shifting of this particular ground of being might require a great deal of effort. Perhaps, just perhaps, this lifetime was actually a blessing, one in which he had been granted the many opportunities he had had in order to somehow balance out, or neutralize, his entire timeline. If so, he could conceivably approach some level of true illumination and wisdom.

CHAPTER TWENTY-SEVEN
Genius?
San Francisco November 1983

Paul felt as if he were wearing a thick, heavy cotton blanket, or jacket so sodden with moisture that he was almost unable to move, like an ungreased robot in slow motion. In spite of his best efforts, there were days when he barely managed to get through the day, dragging himself along by his fingernails, all ambition and previously anticipated joy left in the slushy sludge of his desperation for a new and different life, restraints and constraints of the past dragged behind him like a long and twisted braid of titanium wire anchoring him to his real and actual deeds. It tortured him constantly, and all the good advice in the world to simply "let go" was to no avail. It was wrapped around and through him, inescapable, penetrating like smoke through a tobacco stick, leaving a kind of sticky residua that seemed to coat his every cell, colonizing him almost, with the sorrow of decades slowing unfolding through all of eternity, and in no hurry to get there.

It felt like he'd been given an injection with a paralytic agent like succinylcholine or curare, and was unable to resist the heavy downward gravitational pull of the drug mediating his synapses. What had actually triggered this cascade of effects was a realization he'd had that morning about a book upon which he had been at work for a long time. The working title was *Tyranny of Shame*, and what he had originally hoped to share was his own process of recovering from the debilitating effects of shame, and developing an emotional antidote to his own internalized tyranny. He believed that he had managed to get a clearer perspective on his inner world, and began to make peace with himself as a result of deep introspection, expurgation and catharsis. With each new version (ten or so to this point, and still evolving), he believed that he had it in him to teach others his methods. He had envisioned, fantasized actually, an extensive and expensive book tour, fabulous book signings, and a place on the *New York Times* bestseller list. It was part of a vision that had sustained him for a very, very long time. And now the vision was seemingly gone, without a trace, disappeared, abandoning him.

The loss of his writing momentum did not seem terribly that dramatic a death. He had been editing the manuscript for the umpty-umpth time when the realization washed though him, gently it is true, that he was wasting his time working on the book, no matter how well written, no matter how heartfelt or inspiring for him personally. He had been told innumerable times—sometimes gently, sometimes scathingly—it was just never going to sell. His language was "elitist," he had been told. He needed to write for "a sixth-grade audience" in order to be a popular author. He personally believed that this book was unique—a combination of Freud's *Civilization and its Discontents*, and Wilber's *Theory of Everything.* He believed that shame undergirded all "mental illness" and addictions, with pervasive tentacles through all of "the modern world," and was comprehensive, sweeping in scope, breadth, and magnitude. Yet his personal esteem container had been so battered and beaten so many times, for so many decades, that he had internalized others' views that he was perhaps delusional, and that "they," the ubiquitous they, were correct in their evaluation of the world, especially in terms of fame and popular culture (to which he ascribed all of "them" as perhaps having a clearer view and closer touch because he despised popular culture and eschewed it as much as possible).

He wanted to use the book to pry up a small corner of the Universe, and describe the inner workings of the vast and cosmic machine (Thank you Sir Isaac!) in terms of this single fulcrum. He had described a single theory by which to better understand the ruinous depredations "the world" that seemed to keep repeating and perpetrating. But he had to question—but was it truly Universal? If the experience of infectiously toxic repeated episodes of shame led to internalizing an excoriating, irrepressible sense of the unworthiness to be loved, it also induced a vulnerability to the lowest, most base elements of the Universe—from which one must seek redemption and reclamation of the Self. It was a spiritual test, a spiritual duty, yet a given destination. What was at stake was the urgency of the quest—and he often found himself drowning in the lazy, even lackadaisical efforts of others and their projections onto him for which he was still susceptible. He felt sometimes like a modern Archimedes stating: "Give me a place to stand and a lever long enough, and I will move the world!"

Then this seemingly cosmic revelation, his answer to his huge psychological puzzle, was suddenly done, disappeared from his consciousness as if in the proverbial flash. No more editing, no more re-writes, no more endless speculation. Done. Just like that. In a small, still moment, the message floated across the vault of his skull like a banner thrown against the sky. There was nothing tentative about it, no hesitation, no quotation marks. It was just totally clear. There was just this this utter clarity, with almost a sweetness about it, proclaiming that he had done what he had to do; that his efforts had gotten him to where he was, and, as such, were absolute necessary, perfect, and important to his journey and his well-being—and that the work itself was the reward. It did not really matter whether anyone else ever read his work; whether it was ever published to great acclaim, with scholars and pundits praising him to the heavens for his brilliance and erudition. It didn't matter. It was done. That was the importance of the work. This was the mandate of heaven.

He cried then, sobbing away the decades of his desire for retribution, for acclaim, for recompense for his suffering, for desire to be seen and heard—that was what really lay at the core of his desire, listened to with thoughtfulness and care and attention; mourned and released the decades he had carried buried within himself, feeling the sweet relief like a cool breath on a hot windy day, like a zephyr blowing across the endless plains of Kansas. It struck him as odd, ironic even, that his metaphors often involved his mid-Western roots, even though he had never cared for that part of the world and certainly never wanted to ever live there again. There it was.

"Please take it away," he cried out, imploring the heavens. "Please make it stop! Please let me go! Stop torturing me!"

He cried as if his very continued existence depended upon it, releasing the accumulated affect of literarily his whole life, flushing it out of his cells, all the pain, all the toxins, all the shit and shame—snot running down his chin, tears staining his cheeks and dripping onto his belly, until at last his chest felt clear and empty, his sinuses able to draw fresh air, his heart beating strong and true. Somehow this was yet another surrender, an appeal to the mighty Universe for help, having been stripped bare of all pretension and shielding, all ornament, all fabrication. He knew it was real, as real as anything could get, or would get. And then it hit him, he really didn't care. The work had been extremely helpful and profitable to him, and to hell with being acclaimed by all of the literary aficionados, connoisseurs and literati. It suddenly just didn't matter, as immense layers of ego melted off him like candle drippings down the side of a raffia-wrapped Chianti bottle.

Whatever other considerations were involved, and by whatever convoluted manner he had arrived, all of the events of his life had exquisitely and fortuitously coalesced to produce in him the flower he was about to become, a gift, a blessing to the world forged out of his pain and shame on the great anvil of Life Itself. No matter how he had suffered, how many eons of this lifetime he had spent grieving a lost and distant past that he could only dimly see through the mists and twists, the spirals of time, and he knew, in that moment, a freedom he had not even known could possibly exist, one that was created—a relief, a release from the burdens of sorrow, and the restraining chains of memory, but not in any of the ways he had ever thought it might.

This felt more like an emptiness, an absence of turmoil, a calm he had only rarely tasted, shimmering like a wave of sparkling delight. He kept wanting to say it "filled him," when the exact opposite was true—he felt relieved and emptied, a happy emptiness, a calm, empty emptiness that was ephemeral yet seemed to spread simultaneously in all directions to the furthest horizons. It felt like home, as if he really belonged. It was the destination and the journey simultaneously—a place to be explored and savored repeatedly, and for an indeterminate, undeterminable time.

He was concerned that his acute awareness was vapid, as all such experiences were naturally ephemeral. As always, he compared it to many of his drug experienced, that he called "altered," while others claimed he was "delusional and brain damaged," even though he had believed his transcendental states were permanent and eternal—although he realized he was not "done" yet, as in completed, finish line, over, full, totally complete. There was still far too much to do, still too many things he had yet to see and do, far too many spaces both internal and external that he believed required his attention. Even in the midst of this extraordinary gift and blessing, there was an angstrom of disappointment and frustration with being on a planet, in a time and place, where he sincerely believed he was so much more intelligent and spiritually advanced than the bulk of the population. He decided to sit with the stillness and the beauty, to allow it to permeate him as a kind of template, a new opening, a starting place, from which to remember where he had been, and to which he could go again, to remember, in other, later times when his mood had shifted, or the world turned. It was enough for now. He was grateful. Very, very grateful!

CHAPTER TWENTY-EIGHT
Continuing Explorations
San Francisco December 1983

Paul felt himself being remade from the inside out, not re-manufactured with the aid of schematics and diagrams by an engineering team, but more as a participant, a full and willing partner in his own rebirthing; having had an active hand in his remaking from a severely depressed and suicidal individual into someone he was getting to know and love better than he ever had, with whom he could develop a loving relationship; could honor and respect, someone bright and intelligent with a deep and tender heart; someone sensitive to his own needs and those of others; someone, in short, with whom he could spend a great deal of time conversing and exploring, yet never grow bored or tired; someone who would be, could be, and was, endlessly fascinating, and with whom he could communicate as easily as he did with his journals or manuscripts, who always provided what was needed, even in the very toughest of times, come what may, come what might. He had, in fact, begun to really find and love himself.

He felt blessed, uplifted, changed forever, mutated in the incandescent flames of his own heart connected to the very heart beating in the atomic furnace of the Universe itself. He been heated and folded, and then repeatedly re-heated and hammered on the Grand Anvil. He felt full of love and gratitude, sobbing now even in his happiness, his joy. He felt the uncontrolled, untrammeled Presence of some power far, far greater than himself radiating vibrantly in his life, resonating through his every organ, and shimmering in the very cytoarchitecture of his flesh and bones. That he could be so filled with such radiance and sorrow simultaneously was far beyond any model he could have constructed. Wave after wave of utter helplessness that was deeply empowering, flowed through him as if the detritus of many, many lifetimes were being flushed out of him in a kind of mental and emotional diarrhea that was not depleting but enhancing of each and every, even the most miniscule, function.

He knew he would never get "out of the trenches," and excel as a clinician unless he had more paperwork and initials behind his name. If he were ever to have a private practice that would allow him to set his own hours and make great money too, he would definitely need far more academic weight.

What was at the very heart of his being, grated on him most, was the extreme contrast between how he had changed, and being back in the muck and mire of an in-patient unit. It was extremely frustrating! Paul longed to have the power and position that would allow him to unfold more completely as a professional.

In clinical gatherings, he felt denigrated and shuttled aside like an ignorant peon, as if his life experience, and he himself, were second class at best, especially when he knew he had so much more to offer.

In the depths of his dissociated emotions, he had found a clarity of light developing out of events accompanied by a rising tide of gratitude and love. He had been able to embrace a deeper gratitude for his accomplishments, and all of the superb guidance and mentoring he had had as if connecting with the eternal movement that articulates the Universe. He had become less driven, less compulsive, even less ambitious, though he knew there was still a depression underlying whatever progress he might make, perhaps always would be.

He fought against it mightily, fearful that, if he did accede to it, he would stop striving, stop using the mighty fuel within him, stop pushing to excel, to improve, to be more. He realized it was possibly delusional, his wanting to be more in the fickle, adoring eyes of others, those same eyes of others that had always betrayed him, shamed him, harmed him, drove him from exercising his native intelligence, his innate soulfulness and sensitivity, and pushed him into adopting the merest shadow of the great soul he believed himself to be; and taught him to subvert himself, disallowing his beauty and power from manifesting in the world, radiating goodness and positivity.

Paul had come to believe that all violence, whatever form it took, was the direct result of suppressing and frustrating innate joy. This unconscious and unconscionable process twisted the emotions of newborns to meet the needs of their ostensible caregivers, who themselves stand in aegis for the whole of the corrupted and corrosive society. Failing to examine and integrate one's own emotional needs—and projecting them onto others as a result of the complex inner war that created, resulted in the collective insanity mostly referred to "reality." Alice Miller had spoken eloquently about the process by which a child learns to squelch his or her screams of distress, and suppress them, becoming a "prisoner of childhood." Paul agreed that such actions mutilate the soul, and the child loses the ability to be aware of and remember the trauma, banishing it from consciousness.

Reading Alice Miller and John Bradshaw had opened doors for him about family dynamics. Inspired writers had always been his lifeblood. He was grateful for those who had explored the ancient paths of self, and documented their journeys for posterity; who had left behind them maps demarcating the paths through the puzzling mazes of consciousness they had tread, often centuries, even millennia, earlier. He always found parallels with his thoughts and his life, identified with them, and came to believe that, not only was he a channel for all he created, but that that it was his destiny to manifest something lasting, and eternally connected with, The Creator. His heart ached when he all too frequently felt angry, out of synch, and unable to muster the enormous gratitude he felt in his clearest moments when he felt completely connected to, and a part of, this enormous Love that permeated everything.

Stefan J. Malecek, Ph. D.

328

CHAPTER TWENTY-NINE
And Comes the Return
San Francisco January 1984

Remnants of ancient fears and intrinsic doubts intermittently reappeared in Paul's inner landscape soon after his most recent amazing breakthrough, like blue-white tentacles lacing across a charcoal horizon, announcing the coming of the dawn. Though not strong or virulent enough to even sway the basic foundations of his writing and character, they seemed no more than the small mini-quakes that plagued The City.

What did seem to be arising out of the ashes of this, his most recent incarnation, was the sense that there was something greater, more magnificent, more enriching, more beautiful, for him to do in this life than to be a rich and famous author—though he had followed the imperative of this vision for more than thirty five years, like an eagle tracking a fish flashing in and out of view just beneath the surface of a lake.

Paul felt as if the very fiber of his beingness had been exposed to a level of awareness that had radically altered his perspective, increased his desire to talk about his life, this extraordinary life, with all of his adventures and hard-earned insights, and to share them broadly. He laughed to himself, thinking how the irony that this might be the basis for yet another book. He laughed again, as if, having climbed a precipitous peak, he had gone to meet his guru waiting in his cave.

He considered the possibility that therapy was having a deeper effect on him than he had imagined; maybe, he reluctantly admitted, the medication was helping. He was less depressed, and seeing the world with brighter eyes, with an uplifted heart. He fervently hoped it was his own efforts, not the meds. He had begun to see the folly of his earliest motivation to be rich and famous; and had even considered abandoning the vision itself, despite a deep well of reluctance to do so.

He considered that it might be an elaborate dodge created to allow him the opportunity to avoid further work and uncovering. He hated the thought that he had not yet gone as deeply as possible, that he was still not 100% dedicated to the pursuit of his life and art, which quest allowed him to eschew responsibility for his outrageously entitled behaviors. If he was indeed in pursuit of a "higher calling" that demanded of him far more than was required by the stuff of ordinary daily life, he believed it gave him *carte blanche* to act and speak any way he wanted, as if he had a free pass signed by God; to absolve himself for his irritability, his temper, even his bad sleep habits and vast appetite for food, wine, and drugs; of his eternally discontented obsession with "something better" always being around the corner, continually damning the present to a subservient position, and being constantly discontent with everything and everyone, especially himself. It had been an awesome ride, and he sincerely wanted to believe that the inevitable change had arrived.

He sat at his typewriter contemplating the next moment, in a Zen-like meditative trance, a mental mist that penetrated his cells in an osmosis-like manner. Despite his nascent calm, he felt into the silence and realized he had a strong desire for the material signs of victory, the trappings of success. As much as he hated that goddamn puppet Ronald Reagan, who, in his opinion, was the absolutely worst president ever (completely at odds with his overinflated public persona), he understood that his opinions were just a veneer, a thin coat of glitz or gilt. Another of his many favorite lines from the Bard of Our Times, Bob Dylan, floated through his head: "On Housing Project Hill, there's only fortune and fame. You must pick one or the other, though neither of them is to be what they claim."

He sometimes wished he were jaded at age 37! Paul occasionally longed to be that world-weary, that beaten down, that wrung out and tired of the world. It seemed to him to embody the beatific/beat ethos of the Beat Generation: world weary, transcendental and ready for the final surprise. He recognized that he had been preserved, granted refuge from the depth of the extreme life-changing events he had had, or rather than wanting more because he believed he needed more in order to have gone far enough down in life to have a hard, gritty edge about which to write or sing or paint. He had always gone down the road that had opened before him, had taken many risks, and had incredible adventures. He still could not shake the aching sensation that, if he had been a combat infantryman, or a hard-core heroin user, and survived, he might be able to write the kind of nitty-gritty material from the center-of-life stuff that moved him. Conversely, the many he had known who had had these experiences had paid a very, very high price for them, and were usually unable or unwilling to express the essence of their experiences—often because they had expended so much energy on the very edges of beyond, that they had little or nothing left to document their journeys. Of course, every once in a while, there was a brilliant, resilient individual who was able to document his or her journey, to bring back the essential material and frame it artistically so that others could profit from the quintessence of his or her experiences as wayshowers.

It felt a little like death, yet also a celebration. Now he could move on without being burdened by the constant need for examination of every single life choice, of every word he selected to put on paper. There was just the slightest edge of light between the two major extremes. He was, in a sense, freed to pursue whatever was next for him, without regard to having to maintain his "artistic" status.

Going to school drew him even for venal reasons like showing all of "them" that he had triumphed, having borne and transformed all the mean taunts and the petty jealousies, the ill-spirited curses and depreciations—and now had something to show for it, a prize beyond all valuing that gave credibility and honor to his intelligence. He lived for the day when he could call his father and announce getting his doctorate and say, "Hey! I told you I would be Dr. Marzeky one day!"

He did have motivations more pure, emerging from him like the Golden Gate Bridge magically revealing itself out of the fog as the marine layer rose, burned away by the mighty Sun. He felt that he was being led to wisdom. What a wonderful word! A working knowledge of the knowledge of what is true or right, coupled with the correct judgment as to action, sagacity, discernment, insight, sapience, and erudition!

Wow! The very thought was orgasmic, a timeless vision, so much more worthy of seeking than some high level of the ordinary! He did denigrate the daily bullshit, trivial pre-digested pap the world was regularly fed to make it more accessible to the "great unwashed," as the common people used to be called by the aristocrats.

Vietnam had taught him to be aware of the hidden agendas governments used to control people, the "manufacturing of consent" of which Chomsky had spoken so eloquently. Reagan's cabinet was certainly benefitting from their ability to manipulate consent without truth. Oligarchs and plutocrats always argued that it was a matter of "national security" that led to the "necessity" of certain facts and information being kept hidden, for fear of dissemination to "enemy" groups; or because of concern that "ordinary citizens" would not understand the complexities involved, in creating the Therapeutic State, in which super-patriots ("My country right or wrong!" or the Oliver North defense) led the charge in protecting their version of "our country" (versus the actual nation based on the Constitution and the Bill of Rights). Of course, their rationale for how things should be run and controlled was always for the aggrandizement of sitting politicians and maximum profit, ultimately being willing to enslave the entire planet through violence and force of arms. Convinced of their own righteousness, and the propriety of their aims and goals, such men (mostly men) did everything to attain their nefarious goals—all perfectly in tune with the distorted misapplication to the human social sphere of Darwin's original theories about the plant and animal kingdoms.

Paul harbored a secret desire to be compared with Plato or other philosophers and seers whose wisdom had survived the ages, or even (gasp!) Shakespeare. Paul wanted to be recalled with such reverence as they who were still remembered, even in these crass and venal times—the kind of attention that was so often slavered on the spectacle politician or entertainer *du jour*.

He was always reminded of something James Baldwin had said: "Any writer, I suppose, feels that the world into which he was born is nothing less than a conspiracy against the cultivation of his talent, which attitude certainly has a great deal to support it. On the other hand, it is only because the world looks on his talent with such a frightening indifference that the artist is compelled to make his talent important."

He thought about how media coverage had changed and shifted, certainly not for the better. If things were then the way they were now, Nixon would have gotten away scot-free with the Watergate Scandal. There could hardly be a Woodward and Bernstein in modern media circles where the press has become dupes for the White House, cheerleaders for the Spin Doctors version of events modulated as per Ronnie Ray-Gun's mental vacuity and piteous needs for aggrandizement—Gergan, Baker, Meese, Regan, and Deaver were the living embodiment of double-think and double-speak, servants of the fascist technocratic state, committed "super-patriots" all who thought their shit did not stink. The worst of it was that RR had no real idea what he was doing, being controlled by his handlers, especially Nancy. He smiled and read his lines, being the good little boy that everybody praised as an economic genius, yet his spending policies had tripled the US debt in just three years ($73.8 to $207.8 billion). Unbelievable! Paul was in the wrong job! Maybe he should have trained as a B-grade actor, and gone into politics!

Politics was such a travesty! Getting wound up in all of the machinations and manipulations was such a waste of time, especially since he had become aware of something beyond the petty ordinary, something far more important. He now had a new direction for his life that had absolutely nothing to do with money or political cacophony. The key words were perception and belief, the real driving forces behind how the world operated. He was reminded of a verse from *Further On* by Jackson Browne:

> "In my early years I hid my tears,
> and passed my days alone,

adrift on an ocean of loneliness,
my dreams like nets were thrown,
to catch the love that I'd heard of,
in books and films and songs.
Now there's a world of illusion and fantasy
in the place where the real world belongs."

That piece of the song so succinctly characterized Paul's developing a more transcendent global view. It also pointed to what all of the great sages had said throughout time: What's real lies hidden behind the ordinary world of illusion. His internal curtain had been pulled aside, and he now knew he had to pursue this mystical new direction—one he had barely glimpsed, yet was so compelling, so enticing, so seductive, that he must pursue it. It no longer mattered if he disappeared; if all of his hopes and dreams were just so much smoke, created to justify less-than-sterling life choices and behaviors. Abandoning the vision and all of the attendant life choices that had haunted him like a hellhound on his trail for the last thirty years would feel like abandoning a child he had reared from birth. The hungry ambition to be acclaimed, that had been at the heart of his drivenness, that had hidden his desire to be seen and recognized as a human and an artist, had stopped clamoring quite so loudly; it had been reduced in the intensity of its pitch in such a way that, while still visible, had been reduced enough that he could see beyond into an as-yet-undefined future, seeing another branching of his timeline that had always been there, but obscured and just was now becoming visible. Even though a bit amorphous, it filled him with a sense of potency and richness of color.

From his altered perspective, everything seemed right and proper; as if he were going to use all of the artifacts of his entire life as a kind of rocket fuel to go to the stars or beyond. It was as if the entire of his astrology chart had been set up in such a way as to facilitate his getting here, in order to hit the wall with such power and force that he would be shaken to the very roots of what he always believed—as if all that had transpired previously were just a prelude for what was to come. He didn't feel driven to push toward it relentlessly, without regard to safety or comfort, but more that he was being shown a newer, better way that was related to just being, not doing, and therefore not compelled to act in any particular way. There had been some intimation of direction, but without any of the usual "do this so that you can maybe have that," but more of a gentle suggestion that he improve his life without secondary motives or desires, and allow the Universe to move through him at a different pace. It was wonderful, exhilarating and calming at the same time.

A Toltec process called "Recapitulation" embodied the idea that each of us, when coming into a new life, had to recapitulate all of the triumphs and tragedies of our entire timeline to the present, until the soul was ready to move on to the next great adventure, having completely integrated one's rich and variegated past. No matter how joyous the transition, he still had a lingering sense of loss, and a need to grieve—because something always remained undone, and was, in that sense, desirable, no matter how much richer, deeper, more satisfying, or invigorating was the new way being shown. It seemed sometimes as if he were swimming in an ocean of bright green ink, food now for leisurely digestion and absorption, as if the quality and depth of his prior life experience had been powered by the false enthusiasms and abysmal disturbances of the illusion, and was now being replaced by an endless ocean of ever-deepening peace whose reflection in daily life was a vast array of new behaviors, new horizons to explore within—no longer the purview of the world-at-large, but the ever-growing world within, with its connection to The Creator assuming even greater significance, requiring and desiring increasing amounts of attention and devotion.

CHAPTER THIRTY
Ever More Questions
San Francisco February 1984

Paul hated the thought that his incredible mood shift may have been facilitated by the bloody damn medication! He believed the experience to have been less than valid because of the artificial mediation of the chemical; tainted, and although qualitatively different than any of his other experiences with mood altering substances, it was quantitatively the same. Ultimately a drug is a drug, no matter the arbitrary "legality" of it; and fostered the idea of there being an inside-outside duality—including the chemically-mediated illusion/delusion-making mechanisms facilitated and ultimately triggered by his own brain.

As the months passed, he came more to see that taking the Imipramine was, in fact, a two-edged sword. It had provided a modicum of relief—no, far more than that, a genuine uplift, a true shift from the morose state that had pervaded his consciousness prior to taking it. On the other hand, it was like the Sword of Damocles constantly hanging above his head. He knew it was a foreign presence, a temporary respite from his own multiple views of himself as if seen in a hall of mirrors. Perhaps it was true that no one ever saw themselves as he or she actually was, but simply reflected images. It was much the same as the idea of "reality," that word so many people bandied about as if they knew what it meant, rather than defining it in terms of their own perceptions and judgments, (properly called "naïve reality"), allowing individuals to not have to spend the time and effort to delve more deeply into their more obscured interior regions. It promoted the illusion/delusion that drove the superficial view of Life that most people embraced, the vapid artificial passing of time and events that impotently masqueraded as substantial and omnipotent.

His greatest fear was that spiritual surrender might actually be capitulation, a total loss of will, of choice, that he was expected to buy into blindly without discrimination; and that could only result in turning over all of his already meager human power to the oligarchs and plutocrats, facilitating even further contemporary human slavery! Fighting against someone or something had always seemed to bring out the most aliveness and sense of purpose in him. But, he always argued, if all was the will of the Creator, then how could one not simply surrender to this greater will? He feared deeply being swept up in the kind of will-less river that had so strongly captured him in his early years. Surrender, true voluntary surrender, could only come if one were no longer fearful; if one truly felt the grace and munificence of the

Universe—and were, therefore, unneedful of self-protection and a certain distancing. If one were completely identified with everything, loving of everything, embracing of everything, forgiving of everything. Until he attained that exalted state of identification, then what ever was he to do? He remembered a saying: When all is understood, all is forgiven. When all is forgiven, all is understood.

He remembered awakening that Christmas morning two years ago, his old life in ashes, and arising, Lazarus-like, to breathe again to pursue all manner of life, to indulge in its effulgent opportunities, to fully commit to his decision to never use again. Never!

His writing had always served him well as a record of his thoughts, as an outlet for his pent-up and often twisted emotions, as artifacts of his having passed through this life, and potentially, perhaps as a monument of his life that would outlive him. In many ways though writing served the deepest therapeutic purpose of allowing him to so very well to reflect his progress through life—all the ups and downs, ins and outs, even the times stuck or traveling sideways. His writing was the extension, a direct outflow of his essence. It embodied his spiritual awakening and direction. He was so often bursting with possibilities, as if overshadowed even, with feelings and remembrances stuffed with emotional richness and beauty, as if he were a fresh whipped cream-filled éclair topped with chocolate ganache. His fingers became extensions of his brain, often generating emotional surges directly from his vibrating amygdala and pineal gland, bypassing the pre-frontal cortex altogether, creating full-spectrum thought/feeling pictures, entire gestalts that starburst into his releasing long-suppressed toxic contents stored and carried like a spoiled treasure of the ages long hidden from gods and men.

On and on he wrote, often bent over the tear-stained pages of his journal, daily filling pages with his tightly-knit thoughts, or meandering from prose to poems, enunciating his heartbreak, flushing his adrenal glands and his lachrymal ducts, giving him momentary respite from the turbulent inner seas on which he usually sailed; and finally, finally expressing his longing and loneliness, his insatiable hunger to meet the woman of his dreams, the Twin Flame to his soul; that led to ever further, deeper, wider releases of angst and tension of the seemingly endless, unrelenting seething torrent seeking balance and equanimity in the great heart of his time, in the great art of his heart.

On and on he wrote, accumulating manuscript pages and ring binders full of poetry, documenting the meandering journey of his life on Earth; filling filing cabinets with exotic, sometimes quixotic and arcane information held against the day when it might come in handy for yet another book he might write: all of his faults and foibles; all of his trials and tragedies; all his joys and exultations; all his flights of fancy and enthusiasms—written down to try to capture the details of the incandescent flow of the all-too-brief path of his life. There always seemed to be more, so much more, that he could have done, should have done, or might have done that may, or may not, have changed or improved his life, or at least the felt-expression of it, in countless ways—ways that he too often had had to mourn and release, despite an extremely deep desire never to do so sometimes; despite his desire to have a another chance, second chance, to relive it all in a different, more awakened, more aware manner than he had; to have been born into other circumstances, in other conditions than the ones into which he had been; believing he could have lived a different life, a richer, deeper, more sophisticated, more urbane life than the one he had, at least in part so that he could feel he was a better someone else than he was, someone in whom he could feel more pride, greater confidence, and the ability to love more fully and completely; someone he himself could love and cherish, with whom he would want to have passionate sex, as if he were the hot woman who lived in his own heart!

It went so far beyond personal relationships; than the simple fulfilling of his personal fantasies of salvation and redemption; than his personal boundaries and desire to embrace a loving, connected, hot, sexy, intelligent, passionate woman in a deeply interconnected relationship as a foundation to rebuilding or transforming the entire of society therefrom; to create an entirely new world of living with vibrant interconnections with others on a moment-by-moment basis, with individuals beaming joy and love for one another, for the whole of the society, for the whole of the Universe—completely shattering forever the illusionary/delusional chains of separation that operate out of the fallacy of scarcity, the delusion of efficiency, in keeping each one apart from all others in our heart of hearts, and keeping the world the jumbled chaotic mess it so often seemed, and forbidding the opening for one and all to the vibrant thriving beauty that always exists, always is, dwelling at the absolute center everywhere of all things, filling each cell and soul with massive, transcendental fullness erasing forever all tears and all fears.

CHAPTER THIRTY-ONE
And Maybe an Answer
San Francisco March 1984

Two full years clean! Unbelievable! Un-fucking-believable!

It had been such a rude awakening to emerge from the nightmarish free-base dreamscape—destitute, indebted, debilitated, hunted, haunted, scared shitless, homeless, emotionally fractured, unemployed and unemployable, shunned, derided, castigated, repudiated, unwanted and unloved, at the mercy of the merciless everywhere he went. It was truly amazing that he had survived! And he was so, so grateful!

He felt as if were akin to the awakening he had experienced when he first entered the Army—the sense of liberation from the incredible binds and constrictions of his earliest environment. He had stepped forward, and embraced the somnolent monster that had long lived in his chest, feeling called to the task of arising out of the primal ooze and summoned to great deeds and adventures. Some vagrant pulse of life that had lain feathering in him burst into flame and engulfed his beingness, awakened him from his long hibernation in the crèche of his ignorance and unawareness, led him deeper, ever deeper into contact with the accumulated contents of his heart; and to the shattering realization that he had had absolutely no idea of the magnitude of that into which he had stepped. It was clearly not going to be a relatively quick and easy task. It was to be but the launch pad for an arduous and protracted undertaking, requiring years, decades, more, to heal and equalize; to cleanse and internalize; to digest and integrate, into the larger wholeness of "Self," the very notion of which had been brought before his eyes repeatedly through the long years.

Who was he? Really? His essence was of great mystery to him.

He was questioning his origins yet again. Every time he entered a distinctly new arena of energy, his "lifetimes within this lifetime," he came up against having to examine everything afresh, and re-order his priorities in accord with yet another new direction psychologically and emotionally. It had been hard work, learning to not blame his progenitors and their hysterical, blind-groping-in-the-dark childrearing methods. Of course, they were just attempting to repopulate the planet after the ravages of the Great Depression and the loss of more than a hundred million people in WWII.

Though he hated all of the right-wing demagogues and the corporate psychopaths, he felt exquisitely attuned to the emotional bases and biases! He knew it was his personal fascism, yet could not help but sincerely wish he could eliminate two-thirds of humanity in one fell swoop—though it would ultimately make no difference because the corrupt system would just grow another Hydra head to assume the "leadership" positions just vacated. It was just the current dimension of the Universe we were currently settled in, and it would roll through its dramas and traumas before moving on. It seemed totally inescapable.

But so what? It did not change his anger and frustration a scintilla, his inability to manifest what he perceived as his power and greatness, the magnitude and beauty of his thoughts and words, the grandiloquence of his art. He acknowledged that what was usually viewed as "changing the world" was an illusion, as simple or difficult as shaping smoke into a coherent pattern of one's choosing. Conversely, he believed that it was also a mirror for the self, that it was actually one's attitudes and inner world that needed shifting in order to see the universe as perfect. As Hermann Hesse once said: "What we can and should change is ourselves: our impatience, our egotism (including intellectual egotism), our sense of injury, our lack of love and forbearance."

After Paul's "cosmic download," he felt he had the clearest sense of cohesion with the Universe that he'd ever had. For one moment he was filled with an entirely new understanding of the world, one previously hidden from his sight. It felt akin to William Blake's' vision: "To see a world in a grain of sand, and a heaven in a wild flower; to hold infinity in the palm of your hand, and eternity in an hour." Though fleeting, he had had the strongest awareness that there is a world of contrasts, or polarities that exists everywhere, opposites existing simultaneously, interactively, blending smoothly one into the other eternally. It was only when an individual applied his or her focused attention to any object, that it became visible, took form, seemed tangible, but only due to the attention of the observer. Thus, in this sense each of us was creating his or her own "reality" constantly; and, only by choosing not to resist what might initially appear to be negative or harmful, could one allow that portion of the duality to pass through, and therefore permit the positive or healthful aspect to come fully into beingness, and be of benefit. It is resistance that enriches the undesired portion of the paradox. If it is not resisted, it will diminish, even disappear, of its own accord.

In his heart of hearts, he knew he resisted because he believed that he had something to protect—image, reputation—based upon the constructions of the false self, and pretending that no one else could see his pain and shame if he ignored or denied it. That, in turn, allowed the illusion to persist. As time went on, the carried emotional weight simply metastasized, attracting more similar energy, requiring that yet more energy be diverted to defense, mustered against his own fears and ideas taken as real. In that exquisite moment of awareness, it became very clear to Paul that he had been creating all of his own problems. But why could he, why would he wish such pain on himself? It fit perfectly with what Freud had called "the sadistic superego," created to punish oneself for reasons accumulated and stored in deep memory, and resonating down through the hallways of time to manifest in the present as illness and injury, attempting vainly to expiate the old injury through exacting extremely harsh and punitive measures on oneself.

He felt he had been shown a new and better way to enrich his consciousness and be of benefit to his work with, and connections to, all of humanity—though this seemed far-blown, perhaps grandiose.

He wanted to hold on to that sparkling awareness, although, of course, doing that was its very antithesis. It was ephemeral, one of an infinite number that filled the Universe with richness and constant meaning, yet went unnoticed by almost everyone in search of their own hermeneutics, too preoccupied to see and feel what was right in front of them, available for no more length than a deep breath to steady mind and heart.

He had lived most of his adult life by himself, no pets, and certainly no children. Except for loving forays with women, this had been his standard bulwark in order to avoid the major bulk of complications arising from the presence of others. He felt both incapable of sustaining a solid relationship, and, quite honestly, did not want to put up with restrictions of any sort—especially when it came to what often felt like the intrusive "suggestions" women so often seemed to make ostensibly to improve men's lives that frequently felt invasive and pushy.

As he ruminated about changes in his situation, he was automatically reminded of the new neighbors who had moved into the apartment above him. Oh well, more new neighbors. Big deal, he had thought initially. The apartment above his had been alternately filled and emptied with some regularity for the last two years. He kept up the regular pace of his life, doing all of the regular things he had been doing—which for him often included watching television all night long and writing, either on the manuscript or journaling; and doing his laundry naked at 0400. Essentially living inside of himself, and following his own pursuits seemed perfectly normal and rational to him—living his life in accord with his own principles and choices.

Then, of course, as if it were a test for his newly initiated mind, something or someone had to come along to disrupt his calm, to intrude upon his quietude and privacy, to interfere and throw a giant wrench directly into the gears of his own particular order of the Universe!

When his landlady called at 0213, and asked him to come to the front door, he was completely thrown. The two of them had always been on excellent terms. She was a former actress, probably fifteen years his senior, and still quite hot. He'd been attracted to her immediately, but she'd made it very clear that she was not interested. When he opened the door to her, unslept, hair down, and a little raggedy looking, he was not quite prepared to be ambushed—although he had an intuition that was quickly proved right.

"The neighbor upstairs called me!"

"WHAT?!!"

"He complained that your television was too loud! He was worried that you had fallen asleep!"

"WHAT?!!"

Paul was so enraged with the intrusion that he could only sputter, aphasic, unable to find words to express himself. His skin flushed and prickled as if burned with scalding water; and his neural system unraveled at the rate of a thousand miles per second, attempting to find something upon which to anchor. He started shouting, and just didn't care. He started sputtering and raised his hand in the air, pointing at the ceiling above his head.

"HOW IS IT ANY OF HIS FUCKING BUSINESS?"

"He has a right to a certain amount of quiet!"

"I HAVE A RIGHT TO A CERTAIN AMOUNT OF PRIVACY!"

"Please don't shout at me!

"WHY IS HE SPYING ON ME LIKE THE FUCKING GESTAPO? I BEEN HERE ALMOST TWO YEARS! HE'S ONLY BEEN HERE TWO DAYS!"

"This is my property, and I'm asking you to not yell at me!"

"WHO IN THE FUCK DOES HE THINK HE IS, TELLING ME HOW TO LIVE?"

He shouted again and again, alternately pointing his finger or his fist at the ceiling. He could only repeatedly enunciate his negative feelings about the new neighbor's intrusiveness, as his body roiled, shaking with spasms like *grand mal* seizures.

"I'm asking you to calm down! Please!"

"TELL THAT FUCKING NAZI TO COME DOWN HERE, AND FACE ME LIKE A FUCKING MAN!"

"He was concerned that you had fallen asleep with the TV on."

"SO FUCKING WHAT IF I DID?"

She adopted a very stern tone, and attempted to divert his attention.

"Remember when you called me about the kids running across the floor above your head? That's why he called me!"

Paul was still seething, filled with rage, at the intrusion.

"WHO DOES HE THINK HE IS, THE FUCKING GESTAPO?"

Again, she adopted a stern tone.

"You need to take a 'chill pill!' Right now!"

"I PAY MY RENT, ON TIME, EVERY TIME! WHY DOES HE SUDDENLY GET PREFERENCE?"

"He's paying rent too! He has rights"

"ALL OF A SUDDEN I DON'T FUCKING COUNT?! AFTER TWO FUCKING YEARS?!"

"Please don't yell!"

"THIS IS TOTAL BULLSHIT!"

She walked to the door, opened it, and made to go upstairs.

"AFTER ALL THE BULLSHIT I'VE PUT UP WITH? ALL THE CHILDREN AND ALL THE DOGS—AFTER YOU PROMISED ME! AND THE FUCKING RATS!"

With that he slammed the front door so hard he could not turn the lock. After three tries, he finally managed it—and immediately sat at his typewriter to document the events that had just transpired, knowing he would be unable to settle until he did something creative with the energy. Feeling that he had made a fool of himself, yet knowing he had honored his own feelings, it was not until several hours later that he finally managed to feel quiet; before his hands stopped trembling; and before the continuing ripples of ire and irritation stopped washing through him, like an endless, relentless wave from the very heart of the Universe.

CHAPTER THIRTY-TWO
A Zephyr from the Heart of Darkness
San Francisco April 1984

As the months sped by, Paul continued to have "bursts of rage," a term he had found in the literature on PTSD, even though the "Bible" of psychiatry, the Diagnostic and Statistics Manual (DSM) took until the Third Edition (DSM-III) in 1980 to confirm the diagnosis as carrying official weight. Psychiatry had previously used the term "gross stress reaction" to describe combat related symptoms in the first DSM from 1952. Such thinking completely failed to acknowledge Homer describing PTSD in 800 BCE in *The Iliad*; and Herodotus' work some 300 years later.

Unfortunately, according to the psychiatric authorities (many with ties to the drug companies), biological factors were the prime consideration in determining etiology, which was extremely stigmatizing because the diagnosis was used to call those who suffered "physiologically weak" or "constitutionally disordered." And, they claimed, could only be treated with brain-damaging neuroleptic chemicals. It was insulting! Yet this was supposed to be the most enlightened position possible offered by the guardians of society's mental health! Total bosh!

Paul considered the possibility that his bursts of rage and his huge gouts of crying might be two sides of the same coin—related to releasing previously suppressed emotional materials, both avenues leading to ever greater freedom of self-expression; generating greater health and integration in the expurgation of them.

He remembered watching a John Bradshaw series on PBS called *On the Family* during which Bradshaw had said that to heal the ravages of the past, one must "Hear what one actually heard, and see what one actually saw," thereby giving oneself permission to completely acknowledge exactly what happened at the time of the original injury—not the lies and misrepresentations created to appease adult authorities, and therefore choosing to not pass along the cultural insanity to the next generation.

Somewhere in this profusion of confusion, he had stumbled across Dionysian and Apollonian philosophical approaches to both literature and life. They were both sons of Zeus in Greek mythology. Apollo was the god of reason and the rational, while Dionysus was the god of the irrational and chaos. The Greeks did not consider the two gods to be polar opposites or rivals. The Apollonian expression was based on reason and logical thinking, while the Dionysian was based on the emotions and instincts. The content of all great tragedy (and indeed, Life itself), is based on the tension created by the dynamic interplay between them. He saw this in his own life as intersecting forces constantly engaging in continually flashing crescendos and diminuendos, producing in him the reflected chaos and glories of their higher powers. He continued to experience the extremes of his own emotional spectrum, giving himself full permission of expression without judgment. He felt stronger, clearer, and less depressed every day. Through it all burned the essence of his mission: to get off the medications forever, and be truly drug-free! He believed it was the only way he would ever find out who he truly was, cleansed of all mood-altering substances before assessing the contents of his consciousness.

When he first started working in psychiatry, all new in-patients were taken off meds for a week, in order to get a really clear picture of what the person looked like without chemical distortion. He still thought it was the best approach for good patient care. The new "corporate business" of psychiatry considered it not to be "cost effective," and eliminated it, instead generally adding more new meds! Of course, this was totally in keeping with the directives of economic parasitism that mandated that even compassion have a price tag.

Corporate mandates had infected American business practices, politics, and economics. The collective impact of this had, of course, affected Paul's choices by default by limiting the arena of the possible. Paul felt so ineluctably sad to think of all the opportunities he had squandered. That he sometimes broke down in tears thinking about the many chances for advancement, or self-sabotaged a golden moment, especially with women! There was a certain beauty to the process, as if everything he had experienced were a part of a very large and intricate script that had been written by the hidden hand of a great playwright who wished to remain anonymous whilst influencing the movements and dialogue of all of the players upon his/her vast stage. In moments of greatest clarity, it seemed that there was both perfection and necessity to everything that had ever happened; and even if it didn't make sense, or even caused tremendous pain, that eventually, in the fullness of time, there was created a confluence of events and experiences that were suited to his furtherment in ways that he could not have imagined previously. The older he got, the more of his baggage he shed; and the more available he became, opening himself to what he described as "a larger level of the Grand Plan." He had always felt that he was destined for greatness, though as things unfolded, he became more and more aware of the fact that nothing ever happened exactly the way he envisioned it. Even the keenest sight could only approximate the glory and magnificence of what actually lay in store, waiting to unfold, in the grand and sacred vaults of the future. He saw himself more and more to be the servant of the Universe, rather than a directing agent imbued with responsibility for creating focus and fundament on his own. All he had to do was allow himself to be led by the enriching and fructifying forces of the Divine. It was only then could he be guaranteed fulfillment from the very heart of All That Is.

CHAPTER THIRTY-THREE
Alchemy's Angel
San Francisco May 1984

He had met many sensitive, psychic people during the course of his life. Johann Augustus Frederich, M. D., had shown himself to be extremely perceptive, even prescient, in acknowledging Paul's potential, and seeing something in him of his spiritual aspirations beyond treating his combat trauma. Since Paul was still taking the meds, the good doctor had agreed to extend his disability for another six months. Even that extended time was now nearing its end.

Paul had developed a positive relationship with Dr. Frederich. Of course, that was the nature of the therapeutic alliance that allowed for the psychological transference of emotion to take place. The biggest difference was that Paul had revealed many of the intimate working details and architecture of his psyche; had cried and wailed and despaired; had shared his deepest fears, pains, hurts, and shame; had openly displayed his rage and the severity of his depression, even his suicidal tendencies and ideation; had turned himself inside out in search of comfort, and healing; had revealed all (well, almost all) of his most secret thoughts, dreams, and desires; had thrown himself abjectly on the floor of his doctor's office, seeking relief from a lifetime of pain.

Dr. Frederich had done none of the foregoing. He had maintained pristine boundaries, whilst being steadfast, a rock against which Paul had bashed himself repeatedly like a roiling ocean testing the limits of its boundaries and containers; that refused to yield any but the slightest bit of substance from its massive might to the relentless sea that might take millions, even billions of years, to erode, to reduce it to dirt and grit and sand. He was, in some ways, indomitable. Paul knew he had a far more tender side than that which he presented professionally, but he had rarely exposed it. Not that he had been traditionally psychoanalytic in a stone-faced and brusque manner—and he certainly did not sit at the head of a couch making no eye contact with Paul—but he had always given the impression (if not the actuality) of being "there" for Paul in his meanderings through the laden minefields of his mind, providing presence and persona (both were, after all, absolutely necessary) as well as the often perfect response either verbally or otherwise.

They had worked together to carefully design a titration for his medication such that he could taper off of it with the least difficulty. He had done so, hardly noticing the slight changes in his physiology, and only the smallest ripples in his emotions, managing to work through what upsets that arose over the course of next several weeks, with each succeeding increment bringing greater freedom and inner release, while at the same time not diminishing the enormous import of the months of therapy, that were for Paul the most rewarding and transforming interactions he had ever experienced with anyone.

During the course of their many explorations of his consciousness, his wide-ranging contents and interests, Paul had rejuvenated his intellect. The good doctor's gentle, and often not-so-gentle prodding and excavations had fertilized and encouraged his gifts. He was convinced that Paul had the makings of a good clinician.

"But I don't have the patience to go back to school for four years!"

"You have some credits, don't you?"

"But I would still have to...endure sitting in classrooms for years! And I have to go back to work eventually—unless you're ready to certify me as permanently disabled!"

"Then you'd have to go through the whole SSDI (Social Security Disability Insurance) process. That usually takes two years at the least!"

"I just don't have time! Or patience!"

"Your impatience is, and has always been, a symptom of your depression."

"But I'm a lot better now!"

"Yes, but still not complete!"

"What does that mean?"

"You've made a great deal of progress, and you still have a way to go!"

"Meaning what exactly?"

The doctor took a deep breath, and sighed before continuing.

"You're feeling a rush of exhilaration right now, greatly relieved of your depression. But the medications are still in your system, and you are still getting some relief, whether you like it or not."

He held up his right hand, palm out, to forestall Paul's anticipated interjection.

"And," he said as he continued, "You will continue to get better, though you may experience some, let's call it 'regression,' from your current heightened state."

"And?"

"My final recommendations for you include once a month follow up visits for three months," again holding up his right hand, "that I will bill you at the cash rate. And, I am going to strongly recommend that you enroll in a special program at New College of California."

"What's that?"

"New College has a program for working adults called the Weekend College."

"I told you—I just don't have the patience, or the time!"

"I'm acquainted with some of the faculty, and I have been told that there is a program where you can attend on weekends and still keep working."

Paul started to bluster, but couldn't find the words.

"I'm told you can get credit for the military and past work experience, so you will likely have to be enrolled for less than two years."

"But..."

"I believe you will make a really good psychologist one of these days."

"Me?"

"You've been working psych units for what, twelve, thirteen years?"

"Yeah, but I'm burned out!"

"Maybe because you're 'stuck in the trenches.'"

"Well I am!"

"The best way out, especially with your skill set, is to go up, not down!"

"What's that mean?"

"Going down means quitting! Or permanent disability! Going up means going deeper into who you are."

"Wait a minute! Wait a minute!"

"Just a suggestion."

"You mean getting a Master's?"

"Certainly!"

"No! Not me!"

"Just a suggestion."

CHAPTER THIRTY-FOUR
The Doorway of Friendship Opens
San Francisco mid-May 1984

It was around this time that Paul met someone who instantly became an old friend, despite the eleven years difference in their ages. They had an immediate recognition experience, perhaps from other lifetimes, or maybe they were brothers from different mothers—though, for the life of him, Paul couldn't figure out how his father could possibly have had sex with Dore's mother! It was one of those universal imponderables, doomed never to be answered.

His name was "Dore," pronounced "door." His earliest childhood friend from first grade had also been a Theodore, so one became "Theo," and he "Dore." The two had stayed friends through countless adventures, even married cousins.

Paul had briefly taken a position as Assistant Manager at a small residence hotel and there had met Dore's girlfriend, Mindy. She was gorgeous! Paul had befriended the luscious and leggy woman when she arrived, making an oblique attempt to hit on her—though she was dressed far too stylishly and was far too beautiful for the likes of a lowly service employee. Nonetheless, delusion dies hard. He had kept "chatting her up," and had gotten to know her relatively well. In the course of this, he heard numerous tales of her boyfriend who would soon be arriving from Big Sur.

They had taken a co-management position at a soon-to-be-reopened venerable Pacific Heights watering hole and eatery that had been in the same location since the 1920's. They would only be staying there only long enough to find an apartment in the neighborhood. She liked Pacific Heights, but she and Dore were more concerned about the quality of life than they were about money. Paul figured one or both of them had plenty of the latter, and could afford to look until they had found exactly what they sought.

He listened to daily tales of love and adventure from Mindy, so it was without hesitation that he walked up to the tall, good looking young man who parked his Porsche in the hotel's loading zone one bright afternoon, held out his hand, and said, "You must be Dore."

Puzzled, even nonplussed, he shook hands with Paul, and asked, "Do I know you?"

"No, but I've been talking to Mindy about you for the last twelve days, and I feel like we're old friends already."

They both had that immediate connection, that encouraged Paul to extend himself beyond the normal call of duty, making sure the young couple had enough pillows and blankets; giving them brochures for galleries, parks, and museums. He made a point to sit and sip a cup of tea with them occasionally, and gave them directions to places like Mount Tamilpais; The Matrix or Freight and Salvage in Berkeley, or Yoshi's in Oakland for jazz; or sensational spots in Golden Gate Park where they could walk and unwind while in the heart of beauteous Nature. He recommended good eating spots, such as Asimakopoulos Café, his favorite Greek restaurant. He regaled them about the Dancer sisters who ran the place at 17th and Connecticut—all blue and white tile with the kind of authentic Greek food he loved—thick, rich lamb stew, spanakopita, and wonderful though oh-too-sweet baklava.

They stayed at the Monroe (referred to by local wits as "The Moron"), It was on Sacramento near Franklin. They stayed for almost three weeks in the best room in the house—a really nice one bedroom with a private bath. Paul had helped accommodate their wishes and desires for things like a small refrigerator; extra towels; extra sheets and pillows; and a copy of the weekly menu, so they could better plan when to go to one of the many excellent restaurants in The City (versus eating what pretty damn good institutional offerings at the hotel—two meals a day, six days a week, and a brunch on Sunday, for which planning Paul was responsible). Dore and Paul stayed in touch after the couple moved into a large flat in a subdivided Victorian mansion on upper Pine Street within walking distance of the restaurant. Though they were vastly different in age, and grew up 1500 miles apart from each other, both spoke what they had learned in grade school as "Cow Spanish," or in that vernacular, "Spow Canish." Most people called them "wacky," and they both had definitely twisted views of life and the Universe that often left them breathless and spilling tears from laughing so hard.

When Paul went back to work in psych, their friendship survived. It also transcended Mindy, and countless other girlfriends; as well as multiple moves on both of their parts (he mostly within the City and County of San Francisco; Dore's back to Big Sur; Carmel, Pacific Grove, even once to Fresno, for love and marriage, and a subsequent divorce).

It was Dore to whom Paul turned when he found himself increasingly dragging, begrudgingly having to go to work—and yet, conversely, feeling as if he couldn't stop or quit or even take excessive days off, though he felt incompetent and burned out—what he later learned was called "compassion fatigue."

"Hey Dore, it's me, Paul."

"How you doing, man?"

"Not too good, actually."

"What's up?"

"Just feeling really burned out and depressed."

"The job or life or both?"

"All of the above."

"Ah!"

"'Ah?'"

"I don't know what to say to you."

"It's OK. I just want somebody to listen."

"OK. So, what's up?"

"Just the usual bullshit of my life. No matter what I do, it just never seems to be enough to satisfy me. I'm always hungry for more."

"I don't know if anyone ever is...satisfied I mean."

"You've always seem pretty squared away to me."

"But you know better."

"I do. But I still can't help but wish sometimes that I could be somebody else. Somebody rich, thin, and good-looking."

"Then you'd have a whole other set of problems to deal with."

"Yeah, like The Doors said, 'No one here gets out alive.'"

"I'm not talking about that!"

"I am!"

"You're suicidal again, huh?"

"Brother, there's some days when I can't get out of bed. Sometimes it's not worth the bother!"

"You sound angry!"

"I am! I'm sick of being sick! It just pisses me off!"

"I know you are. I wish there was something I could do to help you!"

"Sometimes just knowing I can reach out to you that you'll really listen, is the only thing that keeps me from jumping in front of a BART (Bay Area Rapid Transit) train!"

It was at that point in the conversation that Paul broke down sobbing for some indeterminate amount of time, slobbering and moaning, occasionally punctuating the silence with "Fuck!", or "Shit!", or "Goddamn it!"

Dore just sat and listened to this dear friend who knew more about psychology and psychiatry than he did, though in this instance, it seemed like the roles had been reversed—and he was called upon to be the therapeutic agent. It was that thought that eventually led him to the best suggestion he could muster, once Paul started using words again.

"I'm sorry, man. I didn't mean to do that to you!"

"No big. But listen. I've got an idea."

"Oh really?!"

"No seriously!"

"OK. What?"

"You've worked with all kinds of shrinks, right?"

"Yeah. So?"

"Any of them make a good therapist for you?"

Paul grimaced, and said "Not really. That might be kind of sticky, especially having seen them on the units too."

"How about asking for a recommendation? Or from your insurance company? Don't they have an approved list you could check out? See if there's anybody you might know, or have heard of, who might be good?"

"Brother, I am electing you to the BMF Club!"

"'BMF Club?'"

"Yeah, man! I am the President, and I'm now officially recognizing you as a Brilliant Mother Fucker! With all of the rights and privileges thereof!"

———

Paul dragged himself out of bed at 1100, having found inspiration in, and drawn courage from, the conversation he had had with Dore; Dore who persistently called him until he answered; Dore who kept pushing him to come "do some errands" with him; Dore who would not take "No" for an answer; Dore who dismissed Paul's being "too tired," needing to "rest in bed," and every other passive-aggressive ploy Paul concocted, as not OK That day's major exemption came from a telephone booth that had not only failed to connect his call, but kept his quarter as well—which was unconscionable!

Paul felt totally persecuted, completed humiliated—as if he were the sole object of the Universe's scorched-earth shame policy! Paul reacted as if the beast within him had sniffed the door to his prison cell for the thousandth time, and found it open for the first time, reacting with wild joy, a total abandon from deep in his bones, but rarely allowed to surface. When the red-hot river of molten lava erupted in him, his rage exploded. It erupted unabated, untouchable by any human intervention! Gallons of superheated adrenaline and cortisol flashed out of control into his tissues as his blood pressure skyrocketed, and he gave vent to one deep and atavistic roar as he started kicking the telephone receiver and housing with his heavy-duty Frye Americana square-toed boots with the waffle-stomper bottoms.

"RAAAAAAAAAAAAAAAAHHHHHHHHHHHH!!!!!!"

Over and over, he side-kicked, and then front-kicked, even back-kicked the goddamn phone booth apparatus—the object that, in that moment, represented everything he hated about himself, his circumstances, and the world. Over and over he released the tremendous pent-up rage and all of the vituperativity that overshadowed what he knew to be a great and mighty healing force within him, that only appeared following the wrathful, fulminous, lava-expectorating power and released the purest of his negative emotions because it was now "safe" to feel them; "safe" to not be exposed to the tenderness and softness, his vulnerability, not be exposed to any wounding he might otherwise experience, that he had seen countless times lead individuals to becoming psychopathic killers for whom only extracting the ultimate in human penalties was ever enough to even temporarily stanch the flow of violence and power. This all came in a hot-blooded moment, feeling it all flow through him, and he completely empathized with every single man throughout time who had gone berserk "for no apparent reason," randomly" killing and or injuring many others. There were just times when social restraints were exposed as superficial and ludicrous, artificial and transparently puny artifices. The reason that vets met with such negative stereotyping was a direct result having been exposed to situations wherein they took the primordial lid off, given full access to all of the energies normally suppressed by the most odious of civilizations, those who hid behind what was "right" and "proper." Such behavior was generally reinforced in order that the cultural elites could ultimately control entire populations by never allowing individuals to go "too far" and actually feel their own deepest feelings, needs and desires—and channel that vast energy into war-like pursuits and other violence from which they could make tremendous profits. Yet not a scintilla of benefit ever went to those who suffered the pain and shame, who endured the hardships and deprivations.

All of this denied and obviated the view that every individual had inborn autonomy, and was therefore free to seek his or her own level of self-expression and soul growth—whether or not governments agreed or acquiesced, and continued to attempt to impose authoritarian mandates and laws.

Personally, Paul saw no value in not expressing one's deepest needs and hungers. He branded the dictates of governments and institutions as fascist and totalitarian, benefitting only those who had amassed large fortunes, and used the laws against those who had not. He felt the import of these splits within himself as he mercilessly kicked the innocent phone booth, uttering curses and invective at the top of his voice as if it were a Primal Therapy session, until he fell limpidly in a sodden heap on the sidewalk, unable to stand. Dore helped him to his feet, and into the passenger seat, as they made their way to North Beach to get something cold, and alcoholic, to drink. Paul groaned as they drove away, "Now I see how not releasing sexual energy in a positive way contributes to violence! Fucking Catholic Church!"

CHAPTER THIRTY-FIVE
And so, It Came to Pass
San Francisco June 1984

Paul had applied for admission to New College, and then had been vetted, not once, but twice, by different sets of instructors, mentors, and administrators. It was not a new circumstance for him. All of his life he had been questioned about the sources of his knowledge and experience that were so much larger than his "credentials." It didn't help that he always appeared to be impatient, perhaps even impudent or impertinent, in some peoples' eyes. He only wanted educational credentials to validate what he already knew that he knew, while most people sought academic accreditation in order to become an "expert" in some chosen field.

"Why do you think you'll do well in our Weekend College?"

This was addressed to him by a rather prim, bookish-looking fellow who Paul had heard was a brilliant poet as well as an attorney.

"Because I'm smart and articulate. I'm a voracious reader, and a really good writer. You must have checked out my writing samples!"

"Yes. Yes, we have. But that does not guarantee you will succeed in a rigorous, demanding academic program!"

"I have a huge knowledge base! I'm really good at synthesizing a variety of topics!"

"How well acquainted are you with the classics?" came the question from a vivacious, long, dark-haired, middle-aged woman who was head of the Social Sciences Department, and taught both sociology and psychology with a definite Left-leaning political bent that seemed typical of most of the faculty.

"Not as well as I would like." It seemed to be an answer she liked. "More perhaps with classic mythology and philosophy than with the classics of literature."

"Why is that?"

"My uncle had a Ph. D. in Philosophy. He was also a Jesuit priest. He was my earliest mentor. I taught myself to read when I was four, and he started giving me books to read. By the time I was eleven, I'd read Thomas Aquinas, Augustine of Hippo, and Thomas More, even some of the more modern Catholic writers like Thomas Merton. I read Camus and Sartre when I was twelve, and Simone de Beauvoir at thirteen."

Some of the members of both committees were hesitant to wholeheartedly recommend him. He was told he would be an "experiment," because he had less than two year's academic credit. One of the Senior Faculty members seemed to recognize something in him, and volunteered to be his

Academic Advisor. He was admitted as a "test case." He immersed himself in the kind of academic atmosphere of which he had always dreamed. One weekend a month he was surrounded by bright, excited people hungry for intellectual and emotional enrichment, who really craved to share knowledge and information. Most of the students were pursuing a degree to further pre-existing desires and interests, rather than to fill a slot in the mega-bureaucracy. They were not universally left-leaning or liberal, but they were really up-front for the most part.

The format for the classes was perfect for him, as if he had been waiting to be there his whole life. Attending classes all day Saturday and Sunday once a month, and then incorporating the learning experience—social science, art, political science, philosophy, psychology—of the entire experience into a 35-page comprehensive paper due the following month. It was exactly the kind of situation in which he excelled. He thought globally, and was easily able to connect and blend the themes of each weekend.

At New College, he came to realize the vast extent of the gay and lesbian underground for which San Francisco always got so much press. Here the faculty and students were often openly gay and lesbian. Although he had worked for years with many men and women who did not conform to the expected (and very questionable) cultural "norms," and here he was forced to confront old fears and prejudices—and encounter at least an occasional blast of hostility, especially from the separatist lesbians who would have preferred that there be no men, gay or straight, in attendance at all. It somehow added to the richness of the brightest and most uplifting learning atmosphere that he had ever experienced! There were bright and hungry-to-learn people from at least twenty countries attending. Paul could almost smell the lush academic freedom in the air! It was as exhilarating as the rarified air of the Himalayas! The shared atmosphere was communal, as if everyone were aware of how much difference this education could make in actively changing their lives and the world.

Jekker DuBois was one of the most refined and sophisticated man Paul had ever met. The wore gay pride in a natural and open radiance. He was intensely intellectual, and extremely passionate about the entire panoply of his interests in art, literature, ecopsychology and a deep immersion in Buddhism. He was also fluent in at least twelve languages—probably an innate talent—enriched by having lived and worked around the world, and embedding himself in a variety of cultures. He always managed to draw far-ranging, often abstruse connections between topics upon which he chose to expatiate. From Kant and Heidegger, Kandinsky to The Grateful Dead, he never failed to make some kind of relevant connection. He was the most brilliant man Paul had ever met. Paul was attracted to him despite the fact that he was gay.

Going to school led Paul to buy his first computer. It was such a revelation for him to be able to organize, store, and revise all of his papers and poems, even just random passages of thoughts, ideas, and narrative, little slices of dialogue, sometimes gleaned from conversations overheard on the streets, or fragments of his dreams. His re-writes of *Brotherhood* now jumped from version to version, each new iteration becoming stronger, bolder, and richer. He had lost track of what version upon which he was working, though the machine told him "version twelve." He ached to produce ever newer drafts, especially since the work was more about his emotional expurgation and expiation than it was *per se* about literature.

In a later class, he was able to use it when he created Prior Learning credit-for-life-experience classes entitled *Novel Writing I & II,* authenticated and approved by an academic mentor who had the appropriate expertise in the same arena. He felt so inspired and uplifted, exercising his brain in ways that he never had, and never would, working on a psych unit.

He strove constantly toward the goal that shimmered like a lodestar on his horizon. He was infused with the belief that he could make a difference both personally and professionally; be acknowledged and acclaimed for his own sake; become an inspiration to others, like his Uncle Francis and Professor DuBois had been for him, simply by living their own lives in the very best way they could. They had clearly assisted him in upgrading his world.

As graduation approached, he began to feel the academic equal to his father, an intellectual peer at last, and began believe he was building a more solid and tangible future, toward being; proud and strong and worthwhile, feeling he had earned something tangibly valuable that he had always craved; and that he had created the basis for his moving up in the world. He also believed that the entire world would change—that he would soon be recognized, even lionized, his brilliance and talents regaled; and his adoring public championing his previously obscured greatness, and heap praise upon him.

He had proved the faculty and administration right in approving him as a "test case," and had opened the doors for dozens of others with more life experience and expertise than academic standing to enter college and succeed. What's more, he had proved himself right, graduating Summa Cum Laude with a 3.974 grade point average (the result of a single "A-minus" during his sixteen months matriculation).

As much as he wanted a respite from the intensity of the work, his inner restlessness and ennui returned with a force as soon as he went back to work on the Tuesday afternoon following graduation. He was struck by how utterly banal and vacuous it all seemed. It struck him that absolutely nothing had changed, except for himself. Everything at work was exactly the same-same, maybe even worse. He felt acutely aware of the difference in himself, and severely disappointed that "the world" out there had not shifted a nonce. It totally freaked him out to admit that his newly minted BA was totally insignificant on the unit! He was still a Psych Tech, just a Psych Tech, despite having more education. He vowed that he would further close the immense gulf that stretched between where he was and where he wanted to be, no matter that it was fraught with obstacles and opportunities.

This thread of thought led him to again consider changing employment, maybe working with vets in some capacity, giving back some of what he'd been given in his recovery from both war and cocaine, at least a tiny taste of what he had reclaimed for himself. In his heart of hearts, he was convinced that his life had not been, and could not ever be, in vain. He just <u>knew</u> there had yet to be something more!

CHAPTER THIRTY-SIX
The Beat Goes On!
San Francisco September 1986

After graduation, Paul had quickly reached the apex of his frustration, and he returned to working in-patient psychiatry, finding it the lesser of two evils. He had found the "hospitality industry," even as Assistant Manager, rote and boring, and the fact that it did not stimulate him intellectually turned the entire experience rancid.

Returning to in-patient work had led him to being increasingly dissociated, acutely feeling the loss of the expectations he had envisioned when his degree was conferred. It seemed the inevitable rebound from his heights of exuberance. Day after day, he continued to show up, as valiantly as possible, in spite of wanting to give more, both personally and professionally.

He had done vital signs and handed out medications to recalcitrant patients thousands of times. The usual bright spot in his routine, the one-on-one contact required with his assigned patients every shift, seemed more routine, even pointless—especially since most of the patients would, when discharged, stop taking their meds, and come back through the system yet another time. He hated the fact that the brain-damaging chemicals he "pushed" as a part of his job description were made from petroleum! No wonder there was an oil crisis! That too seemed totally anathema to him in terms of his search for a higher way to live.

After laboring in the rather cloistered environs of in-patient psychiatric units, and weeding the fields of hallucinations and delusions for so many decades, it was both agonizing and disconcerting to think he might have to leave his beloved San Francisco for some unnamed location and occupation, just to escape his ennui. He prayed, fantasized, hoped, wished, and dreamed of a new job. He envisioned working in a clinic with friendly staff in a good neighborhood.

It was an ancient pattern of initial excitement and promise that led to frustration and disappointment, that led to abject despair and the desire to abandon the pursuit, that then led to fulfillment of the desire. It seemed as if insisting on creating his vision actually kept it from manifesting.

CHAPTER THIRTY-SEVEN
Pass it on, Brother!
San Francisco November 1987

He went to a pre-Thanksgiving party on Belvedere Street in Ashbury Heights. As he walked in, he scanned the gathering, and his eyes lit upon another stoned out looking fellow. They traded names—he was Daniel—and quickly identified each other as fellow vets.

"Marine Corps! '68-'69!"

"Where were you?"

"I was on the South Wall in Hue during Tet, Rockpile, Khe Sahn after the siege, all over Quảng Trị, and Thừa Thiên Provinces."

"Jesus, brother! Welcome home!"

"Thanks, you too!"

They talked more about the 'Nam, about the idiocy of the government and the shitty politics—and, in short order, decided to share a joint of some his primo lime-green weed. During the course of getting more loaded, their raucous laughter attracted two women who insisted on sharing the last of the joint with them. That then led to going for "a few drinks." Alcohol further loosened them up. Tiara and Janice ended up pairing with them, and going home with them.

Paul handed him a card before they parted, printed with just his name and number.

"Hey! Call me!"

When he called a few days later, they decided to get together to get blasted. They were both fans of '60's music, and smoked an entire joint of one-hit weed listening to Country Joe, Jimi Hendrix, CSN&Y, Bob Dylan, The Doors, and The Incredible String Band. Somewhere during the loose and rather disjointed conversation, Daniel mentioned that he had been getting counseling and logistical support for his PTSD claim from an agency in The City called Stand Down. It represented vets and was devoted to providing a wide range of services for them—from getting service records to discharge reclamation; from housing to Disability and Agent Orange claims. Daniel told him about a two Purple Heart, three tour vet who had finally gotten his 100% Service Connected Disability rating, and then $176,000 in back pay! Paul was impressed! It sounded like the kind of place he might like to work. He decided to investigate the agency further, hoping it might be a new career direction.

He went home nicely toasted, looking forward to the next day off—maybe even giving himself a day off in bed! He decided he would sleep until he awoke naturally, have a little food, maybe watch a film, and then read until he was sleepy—and then take a nap! He was going to give himself the entire day without allowing the world to intrude on him. Nothing! And later in the day, take a walk in Golden Gate Park, or maybe go to North Beach and have a late meal at one of his favorite spots, Viva—Italian cuisine, owned by Japanese, and run by Greeks! How very San Francisco!

There he had *pasta Rustica* with olive oil, green olives, garlic, and sun-dried tomatoes: and a side order of Italian sausage with marinara—accompanied by hot, fresh sour-dough bread dipped in olive oil and salt. Oh my God! He wanted to float home, but elected to take the bus instead, the #41 all the way up Union to Divisadero, and then made the short walk down to Jackson, where he lived in a large one-bedroom. He had thought he might have a coffee and write, to milk the absolutely last drop out of the day, but by the time he had his clothes off, he simply dropped into bed, and dreamed. Boy, did he dream!

Technicolor, brightly-lit, even psychedelic colors, filled his night with images of him at work with vets, and long lines of people flowing out the door of Stand Down, asking to work with him because he was a vet, and therefore had maximum credibility. He heard himself being praised by his bosses and co-workers. He became a kind of a Geiger counter for determining whether anyone was loaded or not. Agency policy was not to serve stoned clients, especially those using hard drugs. He saw too that he would become a bullshit detector for the agency, helping determine whether a man was a vet or not—especially since they'd had a record of spending and losing money on non-vets who lied about their status. He decided he could just ask three simple questions: "When were you in? What did you do? Where did you serve?" The dream told him he would sort out 95% of the cheats and liars that way.

What the dream did not tell him was how incredibly boring it would quickly become. After a very short time, dealing with the same vets over and over and over, seeking services because: "I guess I fell off the wagon again;" or "I spent my whole SSI check on a coke run! I'm broke and homeless again!" Paul started encountering the same compassion burn out he had on the units, and he'd taken a pay cut to follow his dream! Jesus! There was no mercy!

In retrospect, it seemed ludicrous that he had pushed so hard to get a BA, when the net result of all of his dreams and schemes was to return to the trenches in another format. At least on the units, he was afforded some measure of status, being licensed and working in a medical center. Stand Down was far more casual. He came to work wearing jeans and chambray shirts, or a mock turtleneck, with his favorite Frye boots. It was a lot more fun than working in a hospital, with no intrusive supervisors attempting to enforce absurd rules and regulations.

The only boundaries for which he cared were the ones that allowed his flow in producing prose and poems; and the illumination he felt in quiet moments, the delight he experienced when he was visited by the gods and muses; that permitted the transcendental movement down through his fingers onto paper. Now he had indisputable proof—black-pebbled journals, and stacks of files containing numerous manuscripts. He often said, "I don't write books. They write me!" And then quoted the brilliant Henry Miller: "What need have I for money? I am a writing machine. The last screw has been added. The thing flows. Between me and the machine there is no separation. I am the machine."

Being a healing presence for others depended on his giving freely from his own healed space, and extending this vibration to others. His writing had also enabled him to utilize it as a medium of expression to approach divine emptiness, the foundation for his wanting to be seen and heard and validated. It helped him manage his molten rage as if it were a malleable bar of molten metal; and harness the wild, volatile, intractable quicksilver of his heart, directing it back within himself, recycle it, and transform it into a more magnificent, accessible form.

The people who came through Stand Down were usually too immersed in their own traumatic excreta for him to reach, almost as if they were committed to being ill. He was reminded him of a joke, one that non-vets just didn't understand.

There's a WWII vet, a Korean vet, and a Vietnam vet sitting in a bar when Jesus walks in. The WWII vet tells the bartender to buy him a beer. Jesus raises his beer in the air, and says, "For your service, may all your wounds be healed." The old man immediately stands up straight, the metal plate falls out of his hip, his toes grow back, and he says "Thank you, Jesus!"

Then the Korean vet buys Jesus a beer and is immediately healed—his arm grows back and all of his teeth too. "Thank you, Jesus!"

The Vietnam vet buys Jesus a beer, who then starts to offer a healing.

The young vet jumps up, and grabs Jesus by the throat and says, "Fuck you, motherfucker! I'm 100%!"

After often decades of pain and suffering, no vet wanted to have his disability pension taken from him, not even by Jesus! Paul reflected on what Caroline Myss had called a "wounded identity," in which an individual became so identified with his or her wounds that the individual incorporates them as a core identity.

He encouraged people to release their old, stuck energies; to change, sharing the power of his healing suasion and the triple-canopy jungle of his heart. It was the most gratifying thing he could imagine, being an inspiration to others—including sharing examples of his own life, which was so often *verboten* on psych units.

His dreams did not prepare him for the ambush awaiting him one otherwise ordinary day. He'd not slept well the night before, and even three cups of his favorite freshly brewed coffee had barely banished the always somnolent specters from his head. He was drowsily plowing through a rather large stack of paperwork to be reviewed and signed, when he was summoned to the front desk to evaluate a potential client who might be intoxicated and therefore to be denied services. He was in the lobby. Paul took two deep breaths, shook his head, and descended the stairs.

Paul immediately spotted the man, who seemed highlighted by a powerful pin spotlight, even though he was surrounded by at least a dozen other people filling out paperwork on clipboards, or standing around drinking coffee and eating donuts. Paul recognized him. He was a short, wiry Latino man with a bushy moustache, someone with whom they had had trouble before. He was leaning against the far end of the reception counter, looking a little like one of the melted pocket watches painted by Dali. He was holding a cup of steaming hot coffee. He scowled as Paul came down the stairs, and met his eyes.

Paul's blood pressure shot up, and immediately spiked through the roof of his skull. Paul thought the guy was an inveterate asshole, always coming in and asking for services; chronically without any kinds of funds; and always demanding maximum attention, and blaming the staff when he didn't get it immediately. Paul's skin cracked as if he had been immersed in superheated water and scalded. His rage rose like a gorge in his throat, belly roiling, and he just barely managed to keep from clenching his hands into fists. As he approached the man, he could smell ozone in the air, as if he were in the face of an approaching thunderstorm.

As he got closer, he smelled the alcohol pouring out of the man's pores. Then he noticed the man's eyeballs rolling around in their sockets like pinballs. His gut sense was indisputable.

Despite making a momentary effort to stanch them, the words blurted out in a burst of disgust.

"Barbiturates!"

No sooner had the words left his mouth than the man threw the scalding contents of his cup directly into Paul's face!

Paul heard an agonizing scream, and it was only much later that Paul found out it been him.

A gigantic red cloud with lightning bolts streaked through his brain. He reached out his clawed hands to strangle the man, as the pixelated image of an empty Styrofoam cup melting stored in the nether regions of his brain.

When the staff later gathered (with his supervisor, of course) to re-hash events, the only thing Paul could remember was one moment lunging at the man—eyes filmed red, heart full of malice—and next, opening his eyes, a timeless time later, lying on the floor, surrounded by six staff members loosely arrayed around him.

"What happened? Where am I?"

As he spoke, the men collectively loosened their grip. Troy, originally from the Dominican Republic, looked him directly in the eyes, and smiled.

"I knew exactly what you were going to do!"

"I...I was gonna' kill him!"

"I know. I saw your eyes!"

As events later transpired, no blame ever fell upon the intoxicated man, while Paul was dunned verbally, and later in an official write-up for his actions, though nothing had actually occurred. This was yet another in an endless seeming series. He viewed it as an indication from the Fates that he had failed to listen to the voice echoing through the caverns of his brain. He had to go back to school, and get a Master's degree to ever escape the trenches.

CHAPTER THIRTY-EIGHT
Is it Live, or is it Memorex?
San Francisco August 1, 1970

Originally called "Mooneysville-by-the-Sea," what was to become Playland-by-the-Sea began life as a 19th -century squatter's settlement. The original Cliff House opened in 1858, and was rebuilt in 1863, following fires. By 1884, a steam railroad arrived, bringing people to the "Gravity Railroad" roller coaster, and to the Ocean Beach Pavilion for concerts and dancing. By 1890, the Ferries and Cliff House Railroad, the Park & Ocean Railroad, and the Sutro Railroad all brought thousands of visitors. The Cliff House was rebuilt yet again yet after another fire in 1896, and the Sutro Baths and the Natatorium became instant attractions.

The hall that housed The Family Dog at 660 Great Highway felt vast. It seemed miles from the entrance through mixed shadows to the brightly lit stage. The din of excited conversation rose and fell, reverberated off the walls, and swelled in counterpoint to the rhythmic tempos of the mighty Pacific meeting Ocean Beach in the near distance.

Tonight was a most hip historical event. The final weekend of Family Dog Productions at Playland-by-the-Sea, it would be echoing with the monster rhythms of some of the finest psychedelic music ever made. The doors were closing forever to make way for specious "progress" in the form of a condominium project by yet another greedy developer!

It hardly seemed possible that Chet Helms had lost the last of a long and protracted series of battles with Bill Graham for superiority in producing rock shows in San Francisco. Graham had won, forcing Chet Helms out of business! Helms and the Diggers had produced a free concert in Golden Gate Park, and had invited Graham to attend after he had moved there from New York in the early '60s, and it was there that he initially met, and later became the manager for the San Francisco Mime Troupe.

He and Helms began promoting concerts together that created a social mecca where all the differing ideologies were welcome—peace/anti-war folks, civil rights, and Caesar Chavez and the United Farm Workers and many, many others.

Then, Graham garnered exclusive rights to promote the Paul Butterfield Blues Band on both coasts after promoting a successful concert with them. This was the beginning of the feud between he and Chet that initially led them to alternating weekends at the Avalon Ballroom. Graham became a "rock impresario," and brought the Jefferson Airplane, Big Brother & the Holding Company, Country Joe and the Fish, Lawrence Ferlinghetti, The Fugs, and the Grateful Dead to concert stages on both coasts.

Paul's every nerve was screaming for him to join the raucous crowd gathering underneath the speaker systems. He wanted every note, every chord, every word, of every lyric to osmotically pass through him! He so often wished he'd come to San Francisco in 1966 instead of joining the fucking Army! Still he could not help but fantasize about being there in '66, before the Summer of Love, before the Death of the Hippie funeral procession down Haight Street in October '67; when Stephen Gaskin was still doing Monday Night Class at the Straight Theater, and the Diggers were providing food for the hungry, and concerts in Golden Gate Park were still a very insider thing—like one Airplane concert he had attended that had only been advertised by word-of-mouth that very morning, and three thousand people showed up at Speedway Meadows!

He still severely regretted his father not taking the job offered to him in San Francisco! He would have been born there! He might have even ended up hanging out in North Beach with the Beatniks as a teenager! In the words of Marlon Brando "I coulda' been a contendah!" Coulda, woulda, shoulda—the eternal refrain of his life! If only this, or if not for that—when would he ever feel that he was enough?

Paul's was only one of the many psychedelically-stoned beautiful faces, all the exotic-looking people, and so, so many extraordinary women! He was always amazed and in awe when beautiful women trusted enough to take off their blouses and dance topless at the new/ancient tribal stomps. Generally, a protective, respectful circle would gather around a woman when she felt safe and comfortable to do so. He had never seen any woman get topless and be hassled or harassed.

Paul drifted more deeply into the gathering crowd, as the whole collective mood became increasingly more stoned. This was historic! One day he would say he had been there, thought Paul, always working on his personal mythology; always seeing himself as a famous writer who would be regaling crowds of adoring fans with stories of his adventures; and always looking for opportunities to do so, a true believer in what might end up being a delusional mythology he was concocting for himself!

Many people handed him joints that he hit and passed on. Jugs of wine (often spiked with LSD), apples, and loaves of bread were passed amongst those gathered. The electricity was already crackling as strains of ethereal music floated through his head. He wasn't sure if it was simply memories of great tunes, or his receptivity to the musical energies impregnating the walls of the great hall that had seen so many amazing events.

As a thrilling wave swept through him, he twisted on to the tips of his toes and started dancing, twirling, stomping, kicking as the scintillating power blasted him with flowing power. He wondered, not for the first time—did LSD imitate kundalini energy or did it actually liberate it? He didn't really know, or care. As the rush of sensations in his body rippled from the bottoms of his feet through the top of his head, radiating out into infinite space, he gave thanks for the great grace that had brought him here, and lifted him to a totally new and unknown level of awareness.

Paul spaced, soaking in the intensity of the power and energy flowing, flowering in the air. Then suddenly he incomprehensively flashed on the whole realm of need-mediated use, the brain's ability to repair damaged organs, even itself in certain instances (as following a stroke), routing new neurons around a damaged area. And he wondered yet again: How was LSD affecting his brain? Was it really the evolutionary tool so many touted? Or was it perhaps an evil tool of the CIA to damage the thinking organs of an entire generation in order to subvert them more easily to fascist goals?

He felt the music pumping from the PA system, his every cell indulging in the brain-enriching sounds, drinking them in, drawing nutrients and soul-inspiring nutrients pouring through him, as he started swirling, twisting, jumping, kicking, shaking, swerving, whirling. He felt completely alive as he spun and twisted, feeling the enormous energy funneling through him.

The room swam back into sharp focus as an extremely beautiful young woman caught his eye and raised an eyebrow in as an invitation to dance. She had long brown hair, and was wearing a peasant blouse embroidered with flowers. Her long multi-colored skirt shimmied when she sinuously gyrated. He quickly joined her moving to the rhythmic magic of the music blasting through the loudspeakers. He was mesmerized by the sway of her unbound breasts and the lascivious rocking of her hips; felt his dick stiffening in his pants, despite the fact that it seemed most of his blood flow was being diverted to other, higher realms, as much as he attempted to keep his conscious attention focused on the beauty and wonder of this delightful woman.

In just the winkiest of winks of an eye, a tall, long-haired man in a flower-printed shirt grabbed the young woman around the waist unresistingly and twirled her off into the near distance. Paul was stunned for a second, trying to sort the flood of emotions that immediately surged through his body. His initial surge of rage was quickly displaced by the arrival of an ancient monster that lived in his heart that began berating him for not being quick enough, not paying better attention, for being too spaced out, or for not being spaced out enough. He felt tingling fingers of a familiar depression threaten to take him down into the darkest depths. He saw himself standing on the edge of a huge lake as a massive shadow appeared beneath him—a gigantic carp or a goldfish, one so attenuated from its normal size as to defy all but the most altered imagination—and rose to the surface with its jaws spread wide to swallow him.

He then felt a great empathy with Jonah—perhaps it had been a whale—as he staggered, then stumbled, into a happy group standing nearby, two of whom held out hands to steady him, and then went back to laughter-punctuated conversation. Paul blinked hard, once, twice, fighting vertigo, ears ringing, lips suddenly dry, fearing the worst. He immediately started freaking on having a giant bummer here in the midst of all these people, exposed, vulnerable—as a startling idea flashed across the vault of his skull like a comet through the heavens.

He did not have to get sucked down into the old shit! He did not have to cave in, no matter how vibrant his memories! Fuck that! He the Creator of his Universe!

He was too stoned for intimate sexual play anyway. The "window pane" was very clean. It was just agar-agar with tiny crystals of d-lysergic sprinkled on like cinnamon on buttered toast!

As he became progressively more stoned, wave after wave of scintillating rushes left him shaking, even anticipating now that he might be settling into a stoned groove, but he knew there was at least another blast coming.

Jesse Colin Young and The Youngbloods really raised the energy in the room, especially when they sang "Get Together" for what seemed like thirty minutes—and left the crowd totally amped and buzzing. They were all in a huge cauldron filled with savory broth and the Cosmic Cook had just turned up the heat.

As one set of roadies shuffled equipment and instruments off the stage, another set started setting up opposite them. The anticipation grew even more palpable and the crowd thickened near the bandstand like fresh cream. It felt like there were two thousand people there, all tripping their brains out. It was the hippest, most stoned crowd he'd ever experienced. Hundreds of beautiful women all gazing starry-eyed and stoned-to-the-bones crowded the stage in anticipation of Quicksilver's arrival. A deep, reverent hush overrode the din as if a single mind were coalescing whose only intent was to absorb and amplify what they were all eagerly anticipating. It was the loudest stillness he had ever experienced.

And then, the opening chords of "Pride of Man" split the air and blasted through the auditorium. It felt as if the entire building were instantly filled with flash images of Egypt, Babylon, and the mighty Empire of America—recurring images of that night so long ago when he had first heard Quicksilver on vinyl, totally focused on John Cipollina, the long neck of his Gibson guitar, and the exotic passages he'd gleaned from his early love of Chet Atkin's fingerpicking style.

The music enveloped him more and more deeply, and when the band went into "Light up Your Windows," he felt his eyes become windows into the infinite as yet another rush of LSD pulled him into the wafting waves of eternity and infinite space, his body following, spinning, kicking, shuffling, swirling like a demented dervish to the throbbing core of the music, maybe even The Music, the tonality and rhythm at the heart of everything that existed pulsed in him. He was no longer separate from it, completely immersed, going ever deeper into the very core of himself. He shrank to the tiniest of miniscule dots, down through multiple dimensions until he disappeared from the scale of spectrum—and was sucked, as if by the most powerful vacuum, through a funnel-like tube tunnel, and burst out the other side in an irradiating, eternally spreading flare of color and light and texture, each scintilla of energy developing through its own evolution, achieving fullness, and disintegrating back into the enfolding massive mother molecule to be absorbed and born again, over and over, ever-shifting in range and intensity, but always vibrant and full-of-life; always welcoming and beckoning; always filled with the joy of existence, and somehow aware that there was some larger sphere to which it joyfully belonged, even if it could not quite cognize or recognize it in whatever form it happened to be at the moment. Numinous light flashed through multiple spectrums all around him, coming from inside and outside simultaneously in such a way that he could not even tell where he or it or they began or ended—or if he or it or they even did. And it didn't matter!

The "he" that he thought of as "he" knew he was part of this extraordinary process, no matter how otherwise sullied his life might have been, an energy remnant he would carry for decades that would remind him of this moment of cosmic grace and understanding when he felt affirmed in the very essence of his existence.

It seemed eons later when Paul opened his eyes. He realized that he had managed to work his way very close to the front of the stage, still focused on the guitar god from whose instrument was issuing a veritable barrage of bent, warped, and twisting tones and notes, compliments of a huge array of wah-wah pedals, phase shifters, and other exotic equipment, furthered by the unrelenting use of his vibrato bar and a Bigsby Tailpiece. He was achieving absolutely otherworldly effects by bending and stretching the strings. Paul pulled out his triangle-shaped hash pipe, and did a small hit, then turned to the couple next to him and offered them one. Soon he had half a dozen people surrounding him, and indulging in the black Afghan hash with the blue mold. The potent, resinous smoke sent pulsing railroad trains barreling down the rails in his veins. He disengaged himself from the little mini-gathering he had created, and drifted slightly toward the back of the hall to gain some perspective.

"Let the sunshine that's in you, light up your windows!"

The lyric struck him hard, and he started really tripping on his inner sunshine, that which had often been obscured by his inner fog and rain—and wondered, not for the first time, when and how he might ever manage to get clear of the impediments in his life, the greatest and most powerful being his periodic depressions, that sometimes overshadowed even his brightest days. He wanted to blame the 'Nam and its aftereffects, but had to acknowledge that he had carried the malignant seeds of total dysfunction with him long before the Army. The type of exposure he had had in Southeast Asia really fertilized and gave birth to a whole side of him that had not previously existed—for which he felt an immense gratitude, though it still kicked his ass with regularity, and sent him plummeting him like Icarus from the heights into the utter depths of human experience. Though it might be at least slightly grandiose, he nonetheless believed his emotional experiences mirrored the entire of the human experience in miniature—part of what he felt made him an excellent writer, reflecting humanity's core, Universal experience, as if his life had been (and maybe would always be) a college survey course in "The Human Experience" taught to alien visitors to Earth. He certainly felt alien, enough to qualify.

"Hey! Hey! Hey! Mona!" poured out of a huge array of speakers and thumped through his chest as if the heavy bass line were originating inside of him. Together with the rhythms of the guitars and the pounding of the drums carried him like an ancient tribal celebration, like the birth of a new year, or even of Time itself. Some called his dancing "spastic," though he felt that the intricate series of kicks and spins corresponded directly to the joyous and extraordinary rhythms of his heart, intimately wrapped in the extraordinary precision Quicksilver brought to the spirit of their music. It was the very power of the Universe itself.

He was struck again and again by the incredible sense of communion, rapturous even, on all the beautiful faces, everyone attuned to the same joy. He spun and twisted, gyrating all over the room, mostly with his eyes closed, listening to the primal soul drive—the primal entity that lived in him, or in which he lived, he wasn't sure which and didn't care! He was as alive, as pumped, as he was in the 'Nam, but with no fear of incoming!

The chord changes ran through him like a second spinal cord as Paul swayed and rocked, small trills and thrills coursing up and down his back like a busy subway station at rush hour, impacting his brain and splintering out into space—but a space in which he was no longer utterly and existentially alone, but one that was filled with the vastness of the souls gathered here celebrating, without restraint, without fear or recalcitrance. It was the most powerful opening since his virgin psychedelic flight, little more than a year ago, when he had first tripped on five tabs—and had blown himself into a new Universe.

Quicksilver worked their way into their cover version of the Bo Diddley's extraordinary original "Who do you Love?"

"Just twenty-two and I don't mind dying..." just as he had been when he got home!

Pure unadorned pleasure lit up all his cranial centers, and sent rushes like electrical strikes deep into his brain, as he shook again and again, transported as if by the tractor beam of a mother ship. He felt simultaneously helpless and completely empowered as he danced entranced, closer and yet closer to the band stand, drawn by powerful magnetic forces. The bright white light flashed and slashed with golds and ochers, greens and purples, shooting off the players and shifted in tune with the music. He worked his way to directly underneath the stage where John Cipollina was intently fingering his guitar strings, deeply immersed in the incredible rhythms and melodious, primal harmonic leads he was creating. Paul watched the waves of energy generating and receding as the song went through all the idiosyncratic changes they were crafting. As the guitar master glanced up from a deftly executed arrangement of finger-picked notes, he stepped to the edge of the stage awash in waves of psychedelic colors, and bent forward toward Paul, and looked directly into Paul's eyes.

"I remember you! Stick around afterward!" he said, then stood and completed the tune.

The band brought the crowd to a peak of collective orgasm, and left the audience collectively spent. By the time even the most reluctant fans had become convinced that the band had definitely left the stage—no matter how much clapping, shouting, screaming, praying, pleading, lighting lighters, crying, dreaming, or scheming they might do—and were being ushered out by the security people, he only had to say once that he had been invited to stay. Apparently Cipollina had given them the word.

In very short order, John reappeared wearing a fresh shirt and his leather jacket. Some of the doors had been opened, and the ocean breezes were ventilating the variety of smoke and other odors. John was accompanied by a beautiful, slim-hipped, long-haired woman, while on stage, the roadies were packing up equipment, and casting glances at one of the stars standing in the open, smoking hash and chatting with one of the crowd, who they decided must be a "somebody," although he was dressed fairly typically in a chambray shirt with a dark green T-shirt underneath, and a pair of brown corduroy jeans with a paisley insert sewn-in at the bottoms of the legs.

Paul stood there goggle-eyed and flabbergasted, at least until Cipollina reached out to shake his hand and said "I do remember you!"

Paul reached out as if in a daze, a mini-fugue, as time telescoped back and forth in rippling tunnels and they shook hands.

"Wow! I'm not crazy after all! Nobody I've ever told about how we met has ever believed me!"

"It was a little freaky!"

"Completely! The night of my first multiple-dose!"

"Wow! Totally makes sense. But I do know you."

"Déjà vu!"

"Exactly. We're old friends from another life."

"I believe it! You completely blew my mind when you stepped off the cover! It started with the drum beat. Then all of a sudden you were there!"

"Do you remember what we talked about?"

"Mostly whether you were really real or not!"

"And I told you we would meet again!"

"You did! And it wasn't totally real until you locked eyes with me tonight!"

Paul produced his hash pipe and raised an eyebrow. John looked at his lady friend, who had not yet spoken, and simply nodded.

He loaded the pipe and offered it to Lily. She took a healthy hit the pipe and had a healthy hit before she turned aside to keep from coughing and losing the hit.

"Good shit, huh?"

She handed the pipe to John who took a light hit, and said "Asthma. I can't inhale too deeply or it will set off an attack."

"Damn! That's too bad. This is real Afghani!"

"Yeah, I see the blue mold. It's been around in Mill Valley too."

"I really like Mill Valley. Pretty little town."

"Yeah I been in Marin for a while now. Just got too intense living in The City."

"I'm living in north Oakland right now."

"I have some friends who live there—the neighborhood around Telegraph and MacArthur."

"I live at Thirty Seventh and Webster!"

"Same neighborhood. I hear there's a lot of hip people there."

"There are, but I still prefer The City."

"So, what do you do? Who are you?"

Paul took another hit, and talked about his dreams of being a novelist, Vietnam, and then briefly spoke of the Oakland PO, and the paranoia-inducing insanity there, with hidden cat-walks and peeping Postal Inspectors.

"But shitloads of stuff just walks out of there! One guy lifted the entire twenty-six volume set of the Encyclopedia Britannica!"

"Jesus! Pretty bizarre."

Summoning up his courage, Paul swallowed and said "I love your music, man! Ever since the first time I heard you guys play, I been hooked!"

"Thanks, man!"

"It's your playing that makes the band really cook for me. I would love to hear some of your old stuff, like from '64!"

"I have all of that stuff on tape at my house in Mill Valley. You should stop by some time and I'll copy it for you."

"Wow, man, that's really righteous of you!"

Paul shook hands with the man again, and was so stunned, so overwhelmed and honored, that it was actually several minutes before he realized he had failed to get a phone number! He melted into an ancient form of cosmic ooze—speechless, thoughtless, invisible—when the roadies told him John had left the building. He suddenly realized that all the swirling, lurid psychedelic colors around him had coalesced and melted into a dull liquid brown mud.

CHAPTER THIRTY-NINE
Interlude
San Francisco December 1987

Such grace to be five years clean! It had been both easier and harder than he could have, or would have, imagined! That first few months had been like living with a massive, green, scaly monster that was him, but he had had to befriend the beast, own it, bless it—and fortunately had not had to deconstruct it all at once. The Universe had been relatively gentle, allowing him to do so in more graduated stages.

In his clearest moments, he could see that what Sanskrit called "divine play" (*lila*) was simply the acting out of Creation through every human and other interaction as a form of playfulness, rather than some kind of heavy-duty drama. Joy informed all things, and allowed Love to permeate the darkest corners of the human psyche, especially when *in extremis* of the earliest stages of his recovery.

Divine play and sacred theater were so inextricably related. On so many levels, Paul always felt that he had been on stage his whole life— (upon which each must play their part, said Willie Shakes!). Quite simply, we all act out in a less-than-conscious manner, triggered by old stored emotions and memories—out of regression, re-enact them, believing them to be original, or at least socially acceptable and "normal" (another totally misused word). It seemed to him that the entire of humanity was involved in a massive form of psychodrama—acting out all the roles and feelings seeking therapeutic relief—but a gestalt that has lost, or ignored the director's instructions, and left the actors ambling about willy-nilly in pursuit of the lost chord, without awareness of their true purpose. It was as if humanity had donned a *dramatis persona*, and then promptly forgotten that they had done so—and hence humanity had been condemned to wander blindly waiting for an accumulation of experience to tilt over into a critical level of awareness to be able to start acting purposefully and consciously.

Paul considered that perhaps Freud was right in his theories of emotional release, though he had almost certainly them from the work of the early Greeks. Aristotle had originally used the term catharsis in relation to literary or dramatic work as purification of the emotions, especially related to the effects of watching a tragic play, though he always implied there was some kind of control involved. Socrates on the other hand referred to it in a more abandoned, Dionysian fashion. Freud had loosely expanded the concept (initiated by his mentor Breuer) and called it abreaction, indicating that the release of emotion related to trauma was curative, much as Aristotle had originally noted, was healing for the human soul.

So often therapy allowed individuals to simply assume different masks, or *personae,* each of which quantifies different states of emotion or consciousness that make them demonstrable in a scripted manner in the presence of the audience—much like the methods of sacred theater predicated to allow release of obscure emotions.

His lack of critical thinking had helped create the muddied muddle in which he had so frequently operated. He knew he was often impatient (fascist that he was) with how most people seemed to be unaware of their dysfunctions. It was the same old mantra: collectively we are coerced into supporting a martial culture masquerading as benevolent, one that constantly justifies excuses for war, as addicting a process as a junkie and his or her drug.

In that context, recovery from substance dependence was, for Paul, another step toward his recovery from Western Civilization. Chellis Glendenning had pioneered this concept, about which Herlong and Herlong had noted: "Working back to the causes of addiction and removing them [as] a manifestation of unconscious patterns...enable[s] one to live a whole and full life on this planet...transcending compulsive behaviors." It seemed inevitable that one had to truly "hit bottom," immersing oneself in the grace and beauty that may only come as a result of no longer struggling vaingloriously to prove how great and important one is!

Paul had calumnified himself as the single source of his own crucifixion, upon which to heap the faggots of agony, even though it had always provided fuel for his literary ambitions, dancing in the flames of his own immolation. Theoretically he owned accountability for all of his actions (even without any empirical proof) that led him to be the channel for invisible but omnipotent divine forces. They were both probably simultaneously true—and false! The question always came down to how "he" could possibly have been responsible for the conditions of "his" birth—before he was born!?

He believed that anyone might become more empowered to step forward as a more fully conscious human being, a standard bearer for humanity, and a steward of the planet. But to cultivate a voluntary dependence on the Earth and her fruits required continually asking for divine grace and giving thanks for the bounty of an equanimous Creator. One of Argüelles' timeless citations spoke to this: "We may approach a mode of behavior in which the expressive function of the human organism is so indissolubly wedded to an intuitive knowledge of the laws governing the creation and maintenance of the world that our least response is pregnant with a vitality and a meaning of which mechanized existence has long deprived us."

Paul believed that the same was true of cultures and societies. Hitting bottom was something he believed might be necessary in that framework. Just as when an individual is releases him- or herself of all artifice, and manifested their own innate glory, so could any society share their gifts freely. Paul prayed daily that this time would come soon for the planet, during the course of his lifetime (even if he didn't really believe it). He believed that it was his personal work to find a semblance of peace within himself so that he could then contribute more actively to the great peace of which Ghandi spoke.

Yet dance on he did, one grande jeté after another across the wooden floor that underlay his footing, no matter how tenuous, in stages and phases that demarcated the four quadrants of his life unfolding.

Yet dance on he would, even as regimes rose and fell; as idiot bastards were elected to prominent positions based on family wealth and heritage; as people were born and soon lost their memory of whence they came, "trailing clouds of glory," as Wordsworth had said; as wars were fought and won or lost (in the perspective of history there was really little difference); as people met and mated, relationships were consummated and inevitably disintegrated; as people used drugs and alcohol and sex and overwork, even worry, to erect barriers against the constant erosion of their false belief systems that embraced the idea there was something to protect—his life rolled on, seemingly, perhaps actually, forever, grinding into dust the large particles that had been his life, his awareness, his presence—all grist for the mill, as Ram Das had said.

Another of his literary and cultural heroes, Theodore Roszak spoke about using one's gifts, expending all of one's most vital energies in pursuit of what he called "high delight," reaching out to create a genuine place to land in the world. "What a power would be released into the world! A force more richly transformative than all of industrial technology."

Only by fully embracing every aspect of his faults and foibles, could he walk free and wild in the world, embodying all of his highest spiritual and cultural ideals; holding a vision of a united humanity; and assisting in the transformation of society as a whole, wherein each and every individual is encouraged to become the deepest expression of his or her own joy, fully expressing the inner worlds. It would, eventually and inevitably, lead to what Bradshaw had called "soulful work, behavior that has a healthy narcissistic quality to it, in which we see ourselves reflected in our work, and grow in self-love as we see ourselves and our work accepted by others."

He remembered that Buddha considered right livelihood to involve self-actualization, self-valuing, and self-transcendence—all necessary to make work soulful, and all contributing to the formation of character, wherein the soul value of work depends on whether or not it contributed to the purification of human character." This spoke so strongly to him of spiritual or psychotherapeutic integration, to the true ecstasy about which Gottner-Abendoth wrote when she said "True ecstasy unites the intellect, emotions, and action in a climax where no one power is limited by another. They are not expressed consecutively but simultaneously, and each to its utmost capacity. Ecstasy is their transitory, inimitable collision at the moment of their fullest unfoldment, only by entering the process."

In 1970, there was still immense hope for the future and the revolution was palpable in just walking down the streets of San Francisco, Peter Chang had enunciated his opinion that it is always individuals who empower institutions, with "Deliberate choice to work to reconstruct the collective structures of power which determine our lives." Paul believed that only by becoming a living embodiment of all that one holds to be true and beautiful, will one be able to model continuous transformation within one's self. In this way, one's every breath becomes a revolutionary act.

Paul looked back over the course of his life as if from a high mesa, across a vast and rugged plain he had traversed, populated with dangerous creatures and geological pitfalls—all of which had ultimately assisted him to further open his heart, to make himself more available to listen to the synchronicity of the heart beating rhythmically at center of the Universe.

He sighed deeply, and raised his hands, palms open to the sky, in a gesture of surrender and gratitude.

And smiled.

www.ingramcontent.com/pod-product-compliance
Lightning Source LLC
Chambersburg PA
CBHW022241020726
47496CB00004B/1004